T0285944

I Am My Country

I Am My Country

AND OTHER STORIES

Kenan Orhan

RANDOM HOUSE

NEW YORK

Published in the United States by Random House, an imprint and division of Penguin Random House LLC, New York.

RANDOM HOUSE and the HOUSE colophon are registered trademarks of Penguin Random House LLC.

LIBRARY OF CONGRESS CATALOGING-IN-PUBLICATION DATA
Names: Orhan, Kenan, author.
Title: I am my country: and other stories / Kenan Orhan.
Description: New York: Random House, [2023]
Identifiers: LCCN 2022008253 (print) | LCCN 2022008254 (ebook) |
ISBN 9780593449462 (hardcover; acid-free paper) | ISBN 9780593449486 (ebook)
Subjects: LCGFT: Short stories.
Classification: LCC PS3615.R494 I25 2023 (print) | LCC PS3615.R494 (ebook) |
DDC 813/.6—dc23/eng/20220321
LC record available at https://lccn.loc.gov/2022008253
LC ebook record available at https://lccn.loc.gov/2022008254

Printed in Canada on acid-free paper

randomhousebooks.com

2 4 6 8 9 7 5 3 1

First Edition

Book design by Diane Hobbing

For Ashton and for my family

CONTENTS

I Am My Country

The Beyoğlu Municipality
Waste Management Orchestra

SELIM THE HALFWIT hoarded everything from the trash—that was
the story they told me my first day on the job at the waste manage-
ment office. Selim had lost his wife, and I guess everyone figured he'd
taken up hoarding as a way to fill the hole. It started out with stuff
his wife might have liked—small earrings, a tea set, owl statuettes—
picked out of the top of garbage bins. But the way it goes, everyone
said, it's not long until you're taking home half the bin, raking
through it for treasure and convincing yourself of the value of each
thing. How stupid, you say, how stupid of people to discard such
beautiful and useful things. Well, Selim ended up with a house
packed to the rafters with trash he'd thought was gold. He tucked it
onto shelves and into stacks, put it in cupboards, under floorboards,
couch cushions, and the mattress, until there was no space left but
overhead. Then he installed a system of boards and beams into the
frame of the house, with maybe two or three inches of clearance from
his head, in order to pile trash above him. More and more he took
from the waste bins: old tattered books, bicycle bits, apple cores,
orange peels, broken printers, smashed-up furniture, crumpled car-
tons and boxes, hundreds of kilograms of paper, pens, eyeglasses,
eggshells, water bottles, shoes with holes, sleeping bags with urine

stains, jackets too small, jackets too large, bedframes, filing cabinets, coffee mugs, coffee grounds—on and on, an impossible list of trash weighed down on those boards and beams until at last, while his dreams of finding his wife in all this waste were licking the night sky, the house's framing broke and the collected works of the city's refuse crashed down upon Selim the halfwit, killing him not instantaneously, but swiftly enough to confuse Selim into believing in his deliverance.

The garbagemen laughed at the end of the story, and then the oldest one, without a hint of jest, indeed with genuine concern, said to me: "And you are doubly at risk, because a woman hoards more than a man."

And the other garbagemen stopped their laughing and nodded solemnly. The nearest to me said: "We make light of a truth; it is easy to find the merits in another's garbage if only because we hope someone will treat our own legacies with such care."

I smiled and laughed and so did they, and they all went out to their tasks. I found my assignment: a truck helmed by two men named Hamit and Mehmet. I hopped into the cab. The older man, Hamit, drove us off to our route, and as he did Mehmet said that I shouldn't take anything the others said seriously. "Garbagemen, for who knows why, make up myths and tales more readily than any other profession. Still, it is not good to take from the trash. Once you start, there's no stopping. Eventually you'll find yourself buried under it."

A DAY BECAME a week, became a month, became a year as it happens. Mehmet and Hamit made me go down the thinnest alleys of Beyoğlu because they had round bellies they couldn't squeeze between the buildings, and they laughed at themselves so that their laughter accentuated their jiggling, round bellies. They gave me a slender handcart to navigate and said, "So long, we'll see you at the end of the maze."

I went down the thin alleys because I was the thinnest, but it's not hard to be the thinnest garbageman when you're a woman. My small handcart scraped its sides against brick and stucco and stone— sometimes, too, my shoulders would scrape the walls, and I worried that over time I might erode a small Elif-shaped tunnel into the alley, or worse, the alley would grind me down into a rectangle.

I stopped at the small back doors and loading zones, the garbage bins always stuffed to overflowing, but really only half full because people are very bad at the economy of space. I emptied the bins into my handcart and continued on to the next little station, on and on all afternoon until I came out the other end of the byzantine alley-ways soiled and sweating. Then I waited for Mehmet and Hamit to finish their route in the truck and pick me up. They didn't make me squeeze between them in the cab. Whoever was in the passenger seat always moved over to let me sit by the rolled-down window.

YOU CAN TELL a lot about someone from the way their trash comes to occupy a trash bin. Take, for example, the bin I pull from this sunny corner—crooked between a barbershop and a pizza place: every day it's full of sheets of music, not the kind printed in a book and tossed out by someone quitting the piano, but handwritten compositions, sometimes crumpled in disappointment, sometimes scribbled over with one, two, three layers of corrections. The man who lives on the second floor is a composer, that explains it. I don't know the first thing about reading music, and even less about listening to it. From the state in which I find the pages, I can tell the man is tortured by the impossibility of translating what swirls around in his soul into a symphony that would render the same swirlings in the soul of a listener, and that is enough for me to know that his music is beautiful. I told Mehmet about the composer, even showed him a few sheets of music, and Mehmet shrugged. "Or else a piano teacher, or else a student, or else a lunatic. How can you know if you don't read music?" He went back to arguing with Hamit over national policy.

Without any reason, I promised myself I'd find something to convince Mehmet it was a beautiful composer's trash bin. But the next week I found nothing in the bin, and the week after that, nothing again. Not one sheet of music in the trash, not even so much as a single note scratched onto a napkin, or a used-up rosin block, or even a banana peel with fret marks pressed into its skin from distractedly being eaten while practicing a vibrato. No, the old man must be sick, I thought, come down with a summer cold. It was a shame; I enjoyed collecting the composer's trash if only for the reprieve of tending to something precious, of being entrusted with the death of the beloved machinations of one's art. Trash, just trash, unadorned, unloved. Scorned because it announces decay, and decay is the product of time, and time is the fear of all living things. You look for small grandeurs in my line of work. A month here and you'd be singing odes to those rare, crumbless toasters.

"Do you think he's died?" I asked Mehmet. We were in the cab of the truck, watching Hamit drag a large bin full of sardine tins across the street.

"Who?"

"The old composer."

"Old men are in the habit of dying," he said.

SOMEWHERE A FAUCET was loosing dribbles of water over the flagstones of the alley and in a mirror of the rivulets, the muezzin's call to prayer slid over the grooves of the sky. Anything to beat the heat had me with my uniform off and over my head. My undershirt was soiled, the cuffs of my trousers slicked by the puddles. I dragged my cart behind me to the next bin: the composer's. I lifted the lid, expecting to find nothing once more and so resign myself to my worst fears, but instead, deep in the receptacle, I spied a small instrument laid gingerly over a pile of clean newspapers, more precious than a pair of china cups in packaging.

I pulled the instrument up and knew at once to save it from the trash, knew at once to do the only sin of a garbageman and keep this piece. The violin had obviously been loved. I took up the instrument into my arms. The patina held that precious luster of esteem that seemed to catch the light in even the darkest nooks—a compass for the sun, liquid as the glow of a freshly skinned onion. The top and bottom bouts were plump and milky and luxuriant. The border of the instrument was purfled with an inlay of ebony sandwiched around a thin strip of mother-of-pearl. Nestled into the scroll was a finely carved initial I couldn't quite make out. The only signs of wear throughout the whole instrument were in the peg box and the chin rest (which surely wasn't the original chin rest), as if throughout its life the violin had been conducted by a pair of spectral hands.

I had before prized a few items I'd found discarded, keeping them in a pocket or sneaking them into the cab of the truck only to find them broken and dingy in the new light of my apartment, and so I'd later place them in my own trash bin or leave them along the side of a road or buried under the retaining wall of a cemetery leaning down a hill. But when you come across a truly unbroken thing, it is a miracle, blessed, pure.

THERE WAS A new instrument in the composer's trash bin each week. I would, excited as a young girl on my birthday, run up to the composer's bin, peel off the lid, poke my nose inside, and fish out either an immaculate violin, or viola, or bow, or hand-carved music stand, or once even a cello, always placed delicately on a bed of clean newspapers. Mostly, it was easy sneaking them home—I was the last person to put anything in the back of our truck and would hop out of the cab as fast as an eel when we arrived to the dump so that I could retrieve my newspaper-wrapped treasure before anyone saw it. Then it was quick goodbyes, see-you-tomorrows, and I was off for home with my bundle in the seat beside me.

I lived in a closet-turned-studio in an old Ottoman mansion that had been partitioned into apartments many decades ago. There wasn't space enough for me and my thoughts in there at once; however, one claustrophobic afternoon, cleaning each crevice and corner in my studio, I had uncovered a small hatch in the top of my wall behind a layer of wood panels that were under a covering of stucco. I pulled down the hatch, revealing a ladder. The ladder led me up into the framing of the old house, what you might call an attic if there was anything but timber and shingles, indeed if there were even a few floorboards. I crawled from beam to beam like an insect. It was a cramped little attic, spreading out over only a small portion of the center of the mansion—most of the upstairs rooms had the roof of the building as their ceilings. Only in the very center was the space tall enough to sit upright. I resolved to make the attic the house for my collection of stringed instruments, and over the next few days, I took up a few plywood panels and a box of nails and installed my own floor directly over my studio and a few of the neighboring rooms. "Quite a racket the birds are making on the roof," said a neighbor. I agreed and speculated it might instead be a large owl or a rodent or even a child climbing around. I cleaned away the cobwebs and dust, brought up a battery-powered lamp, and constructed a display case. As soon as I finished my renovations, I tucked the instruments into neat and tidy order. I spent my evenings after work sneaking up into my attic and pulling one instrument down and back into my studio where I studied it for hours, with no thought in my head other than to marvel at its beauty.

One morning in the truck, I showed Mehmet a violin from the composer's trash. He told me the city's orchestras and philharmonics had been ordered to compose and perform with uniquely Turkish instruments. "Every day it's something new stolen away from us," he said. I thought he was being dramatic but I remembered now a few things—tampons, waffle makers, coconuts—and then just as quickly reforgot them. As we rode along the shore of the Golden Horn toward the dump, we passed a building that was not there yesterday. They must have thrown it up overnight, or else when my back was turned. Enormous gray concrete reached down from the sky to the water and threatened to eat up the lazy shoreline.

Next in the old composer's trash, I found an oud, then a saz, then a ney. I worried what it meant that even these traditional instruments were being removed. Was it an act specifically against the old composer or against composition itself?

THE CITY OF Istanbul woke knowing that books were now banned. We did not talk about it; we did not complain in the markets or at the office about how much this would put us out, but we felt it right in the sockets of our hearts. We simply rose from our beds and set about adjusting, some of us living now as if completely amnesiac to the reality of before, drowned in a blue fluid of forgetting.

Then the morning was filled with hundreds, thousands of narrow columns of smoke creeping up through the seams of the city to submerge the sky in black. People burned their books, but not everyone. Some forgot to do it right away, they were late for work, and so they burned them later at the stove while making dinner. Some didn't want to burn them, trusting them instead to the cycle of nature, leaving them to decay in their gardens or in the gutters of Istanbul, flowing then in scraps to the Bosporus and washing away into the sea. Frugal ones used their pages as toilet paper. Others still couldn't find a proper place to have a bonfire and so enlisted the trashmen of the city to handle it. Not all books had been banned. The last line in the presidential decree read: "Exempting all religious books, histories of religions, works by religious figures, spy thrillers, murder mysteries, and science and mathematics textbooks unless containing lines of poetry or else whole poems."

There rose for three days large columns of black smoke that painted the reflections in the Golden Horn very, very dark. I returned from work one evening to find the six or seven books I had space for in my studio mysteriously disappeared. Even the cookbook that was not an actual published book but merely a folder of my mother's and grandmother's recipes was gone.

I TRIED PICKING up the bin but it wouldn't budge. I squatted and tried lifting with my legs, but it was no use. So I dragged the bin into the alley from its perch, grating it over the flagstones and into the sun to have a peek. The lid popped off easily enough. Curled up inside, with his knees into his chest and blinking quickly in the light, was the old composer—at least, I assumed it was the composer; who else would be in his trash?

"I'm the trash today," said the old man.

"All right," I said. "But climb on out and get in my cart yourself or else I'll hurt my back lifting you."

The old man did as I told him, and after some huffing and grunting he was curled up in my handcart, not saying a word as I continued on my route, not complaining in the least as I made my stops and piled up more trash atop him. We went on like that until the rubbish was up to his neck, only his pointed head poking up over the pile. Though he didn't complain, he wore a harsh frown, one that doubtlessly took great effort and concentration to maintain. I'd just collected the last bin of the day when the old man said: "Well, off to the incinerator, I suppose."

"Yes," I said. "I suppose."

"Will it be quite hot?"

"Oh yes, quite hot," I told him, and this seemed to bring him relief.

"It's just been so damn cold in my apartment. I could do with a change of temperature."

"You might not fit through the slot."

"I'm not so fat," he said. He was very slim.

"It's a narrow slot at the incinerator."

He nodded with a strange sadness. The old man must have shrugged his shoulders because some of the trash around his neck curled over and fell out of the cart.

"It's terribly hot in my attic," I said, trying to console him. "You could go there instead." This struck me as a perfectly natural suggestion, in part because while we were going along, I was nervous over having to explain to Mehmet and Hamit, as well as our supervisor, why there was a live body in my handcart. It didn't seem like the sort of thing people wouldn't notice, or even ignore. And just how had I planned to stuff him in the incinerator anyway? The more we went like that down the alley with the old man in my cart, the more I realized he'd become a big headache because, though I admit I'm not very cognizant of the goings-on in my country, I didn't think having a composer in my trash heap was a good thing; in fact it might have been illegal for all I knew, dangerous even. That was the way things seemed now—it was impossible to keep track of what could get you in trouble. I resolved then to stuff trash all over the old man, to hide him from Mehmet and Hamit when they picked me up. I loaded him into the back of the truck myself, telling him to stay quiet, and I even offered to drive the truck back to the dump, dropping Mehmet and Hamit off at their homes on my way. It took some extra care at the dump, but mostly, nobody pays much attention to trash, and so with a quick bit of shuffling and waiting for the right heads to turn away, I had the old composer in the trunk of my car as I zipped home through the hills over Beyoğlu and into Kuştepe.

I pulled down the ladder to my attic and shoved him up the rungs. He was taking his role as garbage very seriously and hardly employed his legs or arms except in halfhearted motions. Stepping up into the attic, though, everything in him changed. The lights were out—the space was made darker by the single cataract of sunshine coming from the transom on the far wall preventing the eye from adjusting, but the old man started groaning like he'd seen a ghost. I pulled the latch closed behind us and heard, in the darkness, the small sounds of secretive, embarrassed weeping.

"You are safe here," I said, trying to console the old man, but he shook his head and slumped to the floorboards, reaching his arms out in front of him.

I had to crawl on my hands and knees to get to the light switch. When I threw it on, I found the old man bent over one of the violins.

"My violin," he said. "My violin."

He took it into his chest, clutching it fast and wiping his tears away from its body.

"I thought it had been burned, or busted, or compacted into a small cube. My violin . . ."

His cello, the other violin, the viola, the saz, the oud, the ney—they were there, waiting for him in the dark, waiting for him to notice each of them in turn and display his same tenderness of care in their reunion ritual, and he did so, not quite petting each of them, but running his hand over their bend and grain the way one reassures a lover of their presence.

———

DESPITE REUNITING THE old man and his instruments, I felt hollow on my route the next morning. It was selfish, but I was upset there was no longer the composer's sacred trash to tend. I was upset to lose this moment of joy and excitement in my routine. I couldn't play a single note, I wouldn't know how to hold the bow, or where to apply the resin, or even if something was out of tune, but there was no doubt his instruments were beautiful as objects, as things, as presences, as a taking-up of space. This sounds materialistic, but I think the opposite is true. Materialism would be appreciating them because they took up space, but I fell in love with the old man's instruments because of the way they took up space, the ease with which they entered the view of the eye. Even completely divorced from their function they were each a masterpiece, but as I learned during my evenings in the attic with the composer, especially in use, the instruments were devices of great beauty.

MEHMET HAD BEEN saying for weeks now that things in the city had become dangerous. I never listened to him. It's strange to me how much people want to talk when they are nervous. But then the grocer started saying it, and my neighbor in the stairwell, and the postman, and the baker—it was dangerous in Istanbul. They had all seen people taken up by police for having hidden things they should have discarded. They all swore they were witnessing more crimes. The baker said someone was smashing their windows. The neighbor said someone had mugged them. Maybe Mehmet was right, the city was becoming dangerous. He said it with a nervousness of the vocal cords, a chirp in their vibrations like the scrape of a coin over the ridges of a cello's string.

The composer didn't stop playing. Even in his sleep (which was infrequent and often upright in his chair), he made faint gestures of the bow over the strings. All week it was hurried, ravishing playing, making up for lost time, which of course is an impossible game but especially for the elderly. The old man, now discarded from the city, went about his life as garbage in my attic as though nothing had changed. He asked for paper and pencils, and then for the rest of his instruments, something I could not do because he was no longer in his apartment throwing them out. We speculated that perhaps the government (who had thrown him into the trash bin) might return to his apartment (maybe when they went to seal it up) and throw away the rest of his instruments, but until then he would have to be happy pent up in my attic, bent over and cramped with his salvaged instruments. That was until, when making my route through the veins of Beyoğlu that all led to the Bosporus, that great throat of the city, I came upon a violinist in a trash bin. Just as the composer had been, she sat hugging her knees to her chest. She said: "Hello, I am the violinist who lives in this building. They've thrown me out."

I knew immediately that I would sneak her back to my attic, if only to give the old composer a little company. After all, you always return to the pet shop for the second goldfish when you get the first one home and in its bowl and see how lonely it is, and indeed I admit I had begun to think of the old man the way you might think about your pet goldfish.

Then in other trash bins I found other wonders of music. A glittering snare drum, two honey violins, a dented oboe.

It was like this for weeks; I found more and more musicians and instruments in the trash and stuffed my attic full with them. They all hunched under the pitched roof; none of them (except for the cellist) could stand with their backs straight in the shallow attic.

On a Saturday afternoon I took a nice meze up to the attic to have a little celebration with the musicians. When I pulled down the ladder and stepped up into the space, an incredible symphony picked me up and swallowed me into the attic. Loud, oh so loud, as if I were directly behind the conductor at a concert hall. It was a brooding piece with heavy brass (where had they found a trombonist and a trombone?) and as they played, I felt I'd been made incredibly small. The walls of the cramped room sighed out and folded back a little. The musicians floated up from their seats. The objects of the room shrugged off gravity. The instruments wrote their songs into a growing bubble that threatened to consume the musicians and the composer and the meze and even me into its membrane, but I rubbed my eyes and the illusion dropped away, and seated at a stool right in front of me, the old composer spun the music out into a magnificent tapestry.

"Please," I said, setting the tray of food aside, "the house is very old. The walls are thin as threads of silk. Everyone will hear you. The whole neighborhood will hear you." But why hadn't I heard them as I put together the meze?

The musicians understood and nodded with somber faces. "But please, we have nothing else to do." The composer did not acknowledge me in any way. A shift in my stomach and I wanted to leave the musicians to their meze in peace. I descended the ladder as they returned to their music that shook loose the silt in the canals of my soul, but as I pulled the rope down, the trapdoor closed and made silent throughout the whole mansion what was in fact a dramatic symphony in C.

WE WERE IN the cab of the truck coming back from our route, with the windows down and listening to the birds hang their songs on the breeze, when Mehmet said that we'd be busy tomorrow, and the day after, and the day after that. He said they might even assign a fourth person to our truck, but where would we put them? He said the government had issued another, even more austere decree, and so people would have no choice but to throw away half of their lives. I asked Mehmet if I would have to throw away anything.

He and Hamit both laughed. "You don't own anything," said Mehmet. "I, on the other hand, will have to burn a few of my books. A pity, to have saved them only for this."

"You didn't throw them away?" said Hamit.

"No, but some went missing anyway, as if vanished by a ghost, and I wept all night for them."

Hamit, easily nervous, realized he, too, had kept some books, a few exempted spy thrillers, but it didn't matter to him. He should have burned them all, he said. He knew better than anyone about hoarding, which he defined as any attachment at all to an object. "Everything is eventually trash. It is the natural order. I shouldn't try to intervene." Hamit's thoughts, like an oil tanker, did not divert course easily, so he spiraled down a whirlpool of worry and proverbs.

"I'm afraid for my books," said Mehmet. He had hidden in his apartment, even from his wife, a few very special books, things he said were worth collecting, worth holding on to if only to allow another generation to view them. He went very quiet telling me that they were more than books, instead masterpieces of space, magnificent to behold.

"I didn't know you could read," I said, only partially in jest.

Disregarding my tease, he said: "It is not about reading only."

I took only a few of Mehmet's books at first. I promised they would be safe with me. I didn't tell him about my own books going missing, but I didn't think that was important since the attic (where I'd planned to hide Mehmet's books) seemed to have been spared the disappearings. I placed them on top of the display cases I'd built for the instruments. The musicians immediately began to read. In fact, the composer complained to me that now all his musicians were reading instead of playing their instruments. I told him not to worry, there're only a few books, they'll finish them soon, and they did, but then they asked me if there were any more. "These are marvelous, I haven't seen books like these in months. These are the good books from before everything was banned. Have you got any more? Haven't you got any more?" Instead, I brought back a few more instruments, and another musician. No one was throwing away books anymore. The musicians eventually went back to their symphonies, and the composer was happy again. He seemed to think life was better for him after being removed from the world. Still, I smuggled in an odd book or two from Mehmet, if only to give these poor creatures something more to do than play their songs. I worried somehow the word would spread that I had a tiny library in my attic alongside the concert hall. The musicians, you see, were very loud in their discussions of the books, and who knows how it is the government finds you. Sometimes I held my breath just to escape the anxiety. But the attic proved immune to the police raids that were now a regular occurrence for Istanbul's population.

WHILE I WAS away on my route, the composer had managed, don't ask me how, to install an upright piano in my attic.

"The floorboards are bowing," said the old man.

"They're only plywood."

"Plywood this strong, eh?" he said, happy.

I worried my goldfish were escaping. I worried someone would see.

From my window over the kitchenette sink, with a small cup of coffee at my lips, I watched three policemen get out of their van, saunter over to the median shaded by a long row of Judas trees, and handcuff one of the trees. They stood there, one of the policemen with his wrist in one loop of the handcuffs and the other loop around the lowest branch of the Judas tree, waiting for the municipal forestry department to send out a couple of men with a chain saw. I spent the afternoon at the window as the two men from the forestry department set to work felling the tree. The policemen took over from there and stuffed the tree into the back of their van but not before informing the tree of its rights.

I BID FAREWELL to Mehmet and Hamit and went leisurely to the grocer's on my block. Back at home I prepared a tray of boiled eggs, slices of white cheese, olives, and loaves of fresh bread, and balanced the tray on my head as I crawled up the ladder and through the trapdoor into the attic where I found not only the old composer and his orchestra, but also a dozen strangers. While I was away, the musicians had descended from the attic and into the streets, taking up as many things as they could. Already the only air in this tight space came from the lungs of the person next to you, and now so many more lungs thirsty for breath.

"I tried to stop them," said the old composer. He curled up onto his stool, as downtrodden as I was stupefied. The musicians had put up shelves in the far end of the space and stuffed them full with books. And now these strangers were joining them as they perused the books, discussed recommendations and prejudices, and laughed about how good it was to have company. It was dangerous to have the instruments, they made sound, but this was worse! Who were these strangers, I wanted to know—who knew if they could be trusted? But was this on my mind while a bile of anger slicked my throat? More than anything I was furious that my musicians had stolen away some space from my attic that could have been used to house more of these beautiful instruments, more of these magnificent musicians, and yet, as I went to the strangers to kick them out of my attic, I found that they were a long walk away, that the piano was no longer overflowing with sheet music and musicians, that there was now a semicircle of folding chairs around a podium somehow tucked into the attic, and beside me was even a table of refreshments and coffee. How had all of this fit into the attic? How had the seams of the roof not come undone? How had the eaves not shot right out of the building?

My attic had been turned into a concert hall/library/meeting house/pub/doctoral program, inviting visitors and residents alike. It was just an old woman at first, wrapped up in a ratty blanket that maybe her mother made decades ago. She stayed under the piano bench taking up very little space. But this one guest turned into two, who turned into three, then five, then twelve, then an artist who had watched his portfolios being dismantled by the police. "Each page of my drawings, each page of my studies. I thought they would set them on fire, but instead they took them gingerly into their own binders, marking each page and recording the contents before sealing them up in special containers they use with incredibly old documents, and that was worse, worse to know they were being preserved for the bowels of a registry. Who knows if they will use it against me one day, or else work to dismantle it in some metaphysical way, more permanent than burning."

And then resettled to the attic came a sculptor and a farmer and a baklava baker and two professors of literature and a French teacher and a pregnant woman and a man in a wheelchair and a family of Syrians, and on and on until the whole attic took on the strange and anticipatory pressure of a liminal station, and filled each of us to the core with an expectation, and the attic grew to meet this.

THEY BUILT THE massive concrete structure up another level. It was so tall now you had the sense that it was growing rather than being constructed. If you blinked too long, it would expand right over you, swallowing you whole. Not a window to be found. I heard a rumor they were trying to grow space in there. They were trying to compact air so incredibly dense that you could put it into your pocket and chip away at it with a chisel any time you needed a breath. I heard a rumor that in the building they were storing all the things that had been banned. "What about everything that had been burned?" I had asked the gossip, but she only shrugged and weaved her head.

I heard a rumor that it was a catacomb they were building, with each of us assigned a shelf.

Then, and you might not have noticed anyway with all the public works under construction for the past decade, all the trees were gone from Istanbul and the city was no longer emerald and azure but instead the temper of sunbaked limestone.

I WAS PICKED up by police in the morning, without much fuss. They found in my bag a tube of red paint I'd saved out of the garbage for the painter. It wasn't Turkish red, they said, by which they meant it wasn't the red of the flag, but instead a boring, lifeless red. It was on the latest ordinance's list of banned items.

At the police station, I was delivered to a special officer in charge of the contraband division. "What's with the paint?" he asked me.

I shrugged.

"You an artist?"

"They are banned," I said.

That wasn't exactly true: old Ottoman artists and nationalist artists from the sixties were still celebrated, their works remained in museums and galleries, while contemporary artists had been rounded up, their work removed from the public eye, their tools thrown into the sea. But the officer didn't argue this point. He sighed.

"I've got a drawer of paint myself," he told me.

"Evidence."

He shook his head. "I couldn't paint a straight line if I dedicated my life to it. Still, just having it around makes me think I could, makes it a possibility."

I understood him.

"Is it like that for you?" he asked, holding the tube of paint up to me.

"No," I said honestly. "It's just a tube of paint."

"Hmm."

He put the paint into his desk drawer, then pulled from a file a few pages and held them close to his face. I noticed he needed reading glasses but didn't have any. I thought maybe they'd been banned. It was possible; they made the population look old, weak, the opposite of what a Turk should be.

"There's concern in the department that your neighborhood is deviant," he said. "How'd you get the paint?"

I hadn't heard anything about the neighborhood in the gossip vines. Did he mean me? I felt incredibly naïve then, stupid for having believed no one had noticed the orchestra in my attic. But perhaps they hadn't. The officer told me about the tips they were receiving; the rumors had nothing to do with music, no one had complained of any sounds coming from my building. But it was standard to search someone's house after picking them up—there were probably police in my apartment now looking for the attic, or else just looking for anything. Undoubtedly, the musicians were playing, the artists were painting and hammering and molding, and the intellectuals were debating and laughing and writing, and the whole attic was a racket, racket, racket exploding just a few inches over the heads of a half-dozen policemen.

"I saw the paint in the trash," I said.

"You're a garbageman."

I nodded.

"Didn't you think it was there for a reason?"

"It's a habit," I said.

"You have a habit of taking things from the trash."

I invited only suspicion with my answers. What did he know about me in that file there? What did he know about my apartment?

"Not my habit. I mean, it's sort of an understood nature of garbagemen. We warn each other not to take things. It becomes hoarding quickly."

"And the paint?"

"My first transgression," I said, trying not to sound any particular
way, trying very hard to sound like I wasn't trying at all.

He nodded, I remembered the few books I'd owned that had disappeared from my apartment. Surely he knew, maybe even ordered
it, maybe even took them himself and had them now in a desk drawer
to show me. Maybe he knew about the attic. I was struck by the horrible idea that he had let the attic operate as a trap. I told myself that
they wouldn't waste time like that. If they knew about the attic, this
wouldn't be an interview. This wouldn't be about paint. I would be in
handcuffs in an interrogation room rather than in a chair across the
desk from the special officer.

"And where were you taking it?"

"Home," I said.

"You haven't got even a windowsill to put it on."

I nodded. Were there still police in my apartment? Would the
attic, now unbearably packed with people and things discarded,
come crashing down on them?

"Two years can feel like a long time," he said. "It would be a shame
to spend it in jail if there was someone else who belonged there
instead."

I didn't bother answering. The officer seemed somewhat relieved.
I'd spared him some extra work, I thought.

He put all the papers back in the file and said that because of my
inability to reduce my life along the guidelines of presidential decrees,
I would be sentenced to two years' imprisonment. He told me that
with the nature of everything there would be no trial, but there
would be a court date set in which I could issue a formal statement
for the record. I would be provided a lawyer to help me word my

statement before the judge, and then I would be taken to the prison and processed. I'd be held here in the police station until my court date.

Everything went pretty much how he said it would. My lawyer was exasperated, no doubt swamped with court dates for people like me. Instead of offering any help, he told me not to worry so much about jail, it wasn't so bad. All the people in there have changed. All the people outside have changed.

They put me and a dozen other people in handcuffs and drove us in a windowless van to the enormous concrete building along the shore. It was growing up the face of Istanbul, taking over the skyline like a creeper takes the side of a house. I looked for its shooting tendrils, its grasping fingers, but saw only straight lines, ninety-degree angles, concrete flat and flat and flat into the sky. How did it hoist itself up farther over the city?

Yet inside there was hardly any room for us. We stood single file down the hallway leading to the processing center. One of the guards pressed between the wall and our flanks to pass ahead of us. We were guided to a room with a camera in the corner. After some shuffling one of us would stand in front of the camera while the photographer crouched beside it and took our pictures. Then in an awkward bout of fumbling (the room was very small), we were each taken to another room where a woman with an inkpad and clean sheets of paper took our fingerprints, but the room was so narrow that we stood in the hall and put our hand on the door while she did this, each of us shuffling on to the next part of processing one at a time. After processing and a shower, we were given our jumpsuits and directed toward our cells. The main hold had six or seven floors of cells. Then we were split up. Despite being able to count the floors, I felt the ceiling was very close to me, shrinking even, eating up the space in its leisurely collapse overhead.

A guard escorted me down a third-story catwalk. Up ahead a

young woman with her face jammed between the bars, her cheeks red from pressure, called out to me: "Do not worry. It's your first day but don't worry, there are more criminals out in the city than there are in here. It's safer in here than it is in the streets."

The guard leading me nodded in agreement. "I'm practically getting my bachelor's degree just by hanging out in here—so many professors and writers, you know."

At last we stopped at my cell. The guard shrugged as he closed the door behind me. Inside was not all that large; in fact, when considering the space the building took up, it was surprising how small and how few the cells were. Despite its size, though, there were with me in my cell a few old women, a young man, a child, a backgammon board, a teapot, and a toy car—and I knew the items were in here with us rather than for us. In the nearby cells were a forest and a flock of academics giving lectures to each other. The guard who had escorted me into my cell was now halfway down the catwalk, stopping in front of another cell. A different guard came to him and shrugged and relieved the first guard of his hat and his baton and his radio before locking him up behind the barred door. Then that guard continued down the catwalk, stopping before another empty cell where another guard met him and relieved him of his hat and baton and radio before locking him up and moving on down to another empty cell, but I lost sight of anything else.

The Stray of Ankara

GÖKÇE WATCHES HER younger brother stride up the street to her flower shop in his only suit coat, carrying a borrowed briefcase. The coat does not have holes yet, but the hem of the sleeve has come undone, and the inside lining sticks out from overuse. The left arm is longer than the right. The suit pants haven't been pleated in years. No tie came with it, so no tie has ever been worn with it. It was made by the old woman who'd lived in the apartment above Gökçe's family for thirty-two years, back before she died, back even before Gökçe's father decided to fill his truck bed with the insides of their home and move to Istanbul (they'd made it seven blocks before he changed his mind).

Gökçe watches Levent shoo away the growling dog at the front step and escape into her flower shop.

"You're terrible, greeting your brother like this."

"It's not my dog. It's a curse from God."

The dog, with its matted fur and green-rooted teeth, barks and howls at the slight tremors of Gökçe's tulips in the shop window. Gökçe has chased the dog off with a spray bottle, she's thrown discarded rose stems, she's called the municipal officials, and still the mangy mutt, with its patchy coat and concave belly, always returns to her flower shop. She blames it for the decline in sales, but only because she refuses to believe that the men of Ankara have given up extramarital affairs, or that Turkish mothers have quit their games of guilt when birthdays pass unnoticed by their adult children.

"He's scorning you for the way you run things," Levent says, pointing at the dog. He adds a laugh at the end of it to make sure he can't be blamed for the criticism it is.

"What businessman are you impersonating today?" Gökçe asks.

"Mother would drown you in the river for the way you talk to me."

"Don't be a donkey's ass," she says. "Cut these stems." She points to a pile of tulips that need trimming for bouquets. She spits on the shears and gives them to Levent. She arranges a few shoots of violets into a bouquet of pink and red roses.

Gökçe expects him to remind her he's a grown man, but behind every grown man, there's undoubtedly a grown woman doing his dishes.

"Gökçe, Gökçe, Gökçesu, running amok through the riverbeds. Best thing she's ever done is flush the shit from the street gutters."

"Levent, Levent," she sings back. "Believed the crow and perched on a branch. He spread his legs and flapped his arms but he couldn't fly."

"We're no good at these anymore," he says.

"Don't stop cutting the tulips."

"You know, if I'm going to be your employee, we ought to discuss my wage."

Though teased for slow reading and poor hygiene, Levent has never been accused of lacking wits, and more certainly he's never been accused of having shame.

"We don't discuss finances in front of customers," Gökçe says. "Anyone could come in at any moment, and how would they like walking in on a money quarrel?"

"Has anyone even visited you this week?"

"I was closed on Monday, so that doesn't count."

"Gökçe," he says.

They stand at the countertop—a menagerie of tulips, violets, roses, lilies, orchids, baby's breath—pruning and trimming absent-mindedly until the stems are little more than stubs. They wrap the warped bouquets into newspaper cones. She uses the ones with Erdoğan on the front page for the ugly flowers, or the flowers that smell rotten.

"Gökçe, I need some money."

She ruins the violets, shredding them to ribbons.

"It's not a lot, maybe two thousand lira."

"What scam is this one?" she asks.

"No scam," he says.

"I don't have two thousand lira." She tosses her hands up over her head, as if to show that she's searched even the attic for a few coins. "I don't have twenty lira."

"Mom would have helped me," Levent says.

But it was their mother who'd squandered what money they had on psychics, tarot readers, and herbalists. It was their mother who had entrusted the shop to Gökçe over her brother. It was their mother who had a daughter first and then a son, which meant the daughter would feel always protective, somehow responsible.

The dog sidles back up the path from the sidewalk, curling into a ball under the shade of the shop awning. Soon it will yawn that squeaky, shrill yawn that puts her in mind of the grating of engine parts.

Gökçe throws her shears. They clatter across the countertop. "Pitch me," she says. "Pitch me like I was one of your marks."

"It's not a grift, Gökçe. I'm taking classes now. I'm enrolled at Bilkent University."

She laughs, wary of the confusion on her brother's face, knowing how frequently he wears such disguises. "What are the classes?"

"What?"

"What classes are you in?" she asks.

Levent sets his cutters and the flowers down and turns to face his sister like he's trying to speak through his eyes.

"You can do better than this, liar," she says.

Outside, the dog springs to its feet, riled by a passing squirrel or a pigeon. It walks itself in a circle and presses its nose against the door, leaving prints and smears up and down the glass that Gökçe will have to clean for the fourth time today.

"Cut it out," he says. "I'm not playing with you."

"Then leave, you good-for-nothing." She doesn't hesitate; she's seen this act since Levent convinced her to jump from the balcony of their parents' first apartment in an attempt to fly to the sun.

"It's oil classes," he says, reaching his hand out to her like he's got a little nugget of proof to show her.

"What, drilling?"

"Painting," he says.

"Ha! Drilling is too sensible for you?"

Levent pauses. He knows how to work the silences, the gaps between words, better than any poet—Gökçe has seen it a thousand times. He turns his whole body back to the task of trimming flower stems.

The dog presses its muzzle against the glass and licks until the bottom half of the door is fogged over. Then it scratches at the door-jamb, letting out small yelps.

"You're color-blind," she reminds him, trying to chip away his façade. "What do you know of art?"

"Ah, what do you know of anything, least of all taste. Maybe there is no money for you to lend, but it's not Mom's fault. It's your bad luck, your bad manners, your bad business."

"You wouldn't know which end of a brush to paint with," Gökçe tells him.

"It would be lauded as avant-garde if I used the other side!"

"They'd institutionalize you," she says.

The dog barks, looking back and forth between Gökçe and Levent. Bark, bark, bark, the dog is barking up a storm now. Someone in the neighborhood shouts for Gökçe to do something about the dog.

"And what do you do? Sit around all day playing these games of self-pity? At least I try. No one but me even cares you exist."

She smacks him with a rolled-up newspaper. "Who has more experience with self-pity than you? We can't all be crying assholes in need of hemorrhoid cream."

Levent picks up a vase and crashes it into the tiles at his feet because Gökçe's laughing, because she says that they both complain about the other's whining. He kicks about the pieces until they become dust, and then he kicks about the dust, and then he takes his briefcase and leaves. The dog growls at him on the way out until Levent clocks it on the nose with his borrowed briefcase full of bad checks.

Perhaps because she hasn't had any chocolate today as she usually does, or perhaps because Levent has reminded her there isn't a shred of proof outside this flower shop that she exists, Gökçe's attention wanders, and she overwaters the hydrangeas until water spills over the pot and down her socks. She jumps and knocks over the flowerpot, spills the watering can trying to catch the flowerpot, and soils her dress scooping handfuls of mud back into a fractured pot. Not in shock does the dog bark, but with a lackadaisical intent of spite.

"Stop fucking barking," she screams at the dog. But she doesn't move. Her whole life is a testament to the truth in Levent's accusations of insignificance. She finds solace in the knowledge that he matters little more than herself, cheating tourists out of spare change with his stories of sick grandmothers, destitute children hanging from his wife's breasts back in their shack, once even pretending to be a wandering dervish to a group of Brits.

Piercing as a smoke detector, the dog barks and barks and barks. Gökçe throws open the door of the flower shop, trying to catch the side of the dog's head. But they partake in this ritual too frequently, and it jumps away. "I'll kill you," she yells at it as it dashes down the street to Altınpark.

She leaves the mess. It's been a long day of waiting for customers and she is tired.

In the night, around the first time Gökçe gets up to pee, a breath of malice whispers into her heart. She lumbers down the stairs of her apartment into the back of the flower shop and opens her laptop. Outside, the yellow lights of old streetlamps boom in competing spheres, painting the road, and the shop front, and the cars and scooters in dingy Venn diagrams. The tile is cold without slippers, and she rubs her goose bumps away while her laptop loads.

She types "famous assassinations" in the search bar. At first it shows page after page of Americans, then Archduke Franz Ferdinand, then a Wikipedia article about the briefcase bombing of Tsar Alexander II. In an article about improvised explosive devices, someone in the comments section mentions how in the Second World War, Soviet engineers trained herding dogs to run at enemy tanks. Gökçe looks it up on Wikipedia. The Soviets spent a few weeks giving the dogs choice cuts of meat for running under their T-34s on command, and then they strapped kilograms of high explosives to their war dogs and let them loose. More often than not, the dogs, accustomed to Soviet T-34s instead of the German Panzers, ran right under their owner's tanks, exploding them both.

GÖKÇE TAKES THE pan off the heat and pokes the chicken around to keep it from sticking. She doesn't add any spices, in case that's bad for dogs. Stomach-guilt grips her for not slathering white wine, butter, tomatoes, rosemary, and feta cheese all over the chicken, and letting it simmer. It's a waste of good chicken, for a dog that has now conveniently disappeared. She scrapes the chicken breast onto a plate to cool.

She always was good at pastries and such, but living alone gives you just the two options of becoming a cook or going broke and fat eating out every day. Perhaps her body's ballooned a little, and maybe she doesn't have the savings she'd like, but she can't imagine what terrible shape both of those would be in if she did not cook so well.

The chicken's cool, so she wraps it in some napkins and walks down Gökyüzü Street, past a simit place, and into the alley. The alley narrows as she goes, until cars can no longer squeeze through. The elderly have set up tables for tavla and Turkish coffee in the shadows of the tall, square buildings. The men smoke cigarettes and play games while the women vie for the best gossip on their daughters and granddaughters, and everyone is distantly related.

"Thank heaven she never went to Istanbul," one of the grandmothers says about her granddaughter. "She'd be wearing short skirts and nothing up top."

The road ends at the edge of the park. There are plenty of fountains in the Ottoman style, a pond with an island in the middle, and a building on the island, and a dome on the building, but it's more of a nature center or something than it is a mosque—a mosque would have been too idyllic. But perhaps it will become one yet. *The mosques are our barracks, the domes our helmets, the minarets our bayonets, and the faithful our soldiers,* or something like that.

Short men who look like seagulls with their fat bellies straining their twig legs sweep up the patios of the cafés and restaurants. Slender men, dark from sun and dirt, sell simits and chestnuts. Mothers hooded in solid headscarves walk their daughters in patterned, colorful scarves down rose-lined paths and under acacia trees and through the playgrounds.

Gökçe follows a hedgerow away from the parking area to a secluded flock of shaded benches. She sits with her bait. The feral dogs are out chasing cats or pigeons or butterflies. Soon they will come to rest under the treetop awnings, out of the sun.

She waits at the park, with her cold chicken breast in one hand and Twitter pulled up on her phone in the other. A newspaper had tweeted about a former Miss Turkey this morning. She clicks the link because the woman has beautiful hair in a style she'd like to try. The woman is being fined eighty thousand lira and facing up to six months in jail for posting a satirical poem on Instagram. Gökçe doesn't need to see the poem to know it insulted President Erdoğan.

Until very late, after the afternoon call to prayer, she stays in the park, nibbling the bland chicken breast when her stomach grumbles and looking for pictures of the former Miss Turkey's hair. Her dog does not come. Not today, anyway.

FOR THREE DAYS she conducts this ritual: cook bad chicken, sit alone in the park, fail to see the dog, eat the chicken. She's considered enticing other dogs, bringing them home and training them, but it feels wrong. Perhaps the dog she wants is male, and that is why it's disappeared now that she cooks for it. But that doesn't make sense, because she cooks better than any housewife, and Turkish men love great cooks, so surely it is reasonable to think Turkish dogs also love great cooks. But no Turkish men love Gökçe.

So today, she sits on a different bench in the park with a jar of peanut butter instead. And it works like magic from *One Thousand and One Nights*. The dog, muddied and panting with a smile, comes to her ankles, silent and docile like the Roma children under highway bridges. She gives it some peanut butter, maintaining cautious eye contact while it chomps and licks and smacks its mouth clean. It starts wagging its tail and barking. Gökçe flings a scoop of peanut butter onto the ground and watches the dog eat it. When he finishes, she puts another lump on the ground, this time farther away from the bench, then another in the direction of the edge of the park. She makes a trail of peanut butter lumps in the style of Hansel and Gretel. The men playing tavla pause their games only for a moment to make a joke or call her a crazy witch. She cannot hear the old women's whispers.

Gökçe leads her dog to the flower shop, straight into the back room. While it feasts, she closes the door and runs upstairs to figure out what to do next. The first thing is to get rid of that awful screech of a bark.

DOG IS IN the back room, barking at a cardboard cutout of Erdoğan, when the bell Gökçe's grandmother installed on the front door erupts with clanks. She commands Dog to heel.

"Gökçe? Gökçe, are you in here?" asks Levent. "I wanted to say I'm sorry, Abla, about the vase. And, well, maybe not just the vase."

She throws the curtain to the back aside, startling Levent. "What are you doing here?"

"I didn't mean what happened to be so—"

"Is this about money again? I haven't got any. Get out."

Levent hangs his head because he's well practiced. She didn't mean to sting him, but she has a dog to train, a dog that has finally begun grumbling at pictures of Erdoğan. Levent approaches his sister, keeping the counter between them.

"I'm sorry I haven't come by in a while. My girlfriend threw me out."

"A pity," Gökçe says.

Brother and sister stand, palms on the counter, for a moment or so until Levent picks up cutters and starts trimming the new batch of tulips.

"Don't do this," she says.

"I wasn't kidding about the oil classes."

"Perhaps that's why it bothered me most."

"Not very useful, is it?" he says.

"It's a pity," she says. Levent doesn't stop fussing with the tulips. "You should go back to your girlfriend. She'll take you back for sure. She's not very bright."

"What happened to the dog out front?" he asks.

"Ha," she says. "Dog. Dog, get in here."

The dog takes his time coming in from the back, but Gökçe's proud because he's beginning to listen.

"You took it in?"

"I'm showing you that I can act. I can do things," says Gökçe.

"Don't torture it."

"I'm fixing him, making him into a martyr—or something important, at least."

"It looks hungry."

"I've trained him not to bark unless I want him to. Mostly trained, anyway. But look, he came when I called."

"I don't get it," Levent says.

"Sure, he looks hungry. Of course he does. The cabbies are stingy with food. I'll be taking him to the park soon enough. I feed him and groom him. I'll take him on walks when I trust him. I still have to buy a leash."

"Gökçe, you took in a dog instead of supporting your brother."

"It gets lonely around here, and he's cheaper to take care of than you."

"I'm not asking you to take me in, I'm not asking you to feed me. I'm trying to fix myself up, get a degree."

"They don't hand degrees out for single courses," she says.

"A goddamned dog. You hate that dog. You take it in, buy it leashes, spoil it, rub its belly, feed it, but you can't give me petty handouts even. Does he liven up the place? Perhaps he organizes beautiful bouquets."

Gökçe tuts at her brother, and Dog starts growling.

"I don't want you in here upsetting our training," she says.

Levent comes to the other side of the counter. He kicks the dog out of his way, kicks it right in the ribs, ribs that lack any padding. Gökçe tries planting herself between her dog and her brother to prevent further harm, but Levent shoves her aside and begins fiddling with the cash register.

She hits him in the shoulder, trying to deaden his arm like when they were kids in the neighbor's vegetable garden. "There's nothing in there, dummy. And if there were you couldn't have it, anyway."

He pries the cash drawer open and lifts the tray, but Gökçe meant it. "Where do you keep it?"

"There isn't any, you shit. I've told you we're broke. I'm broke. There's nothing." For the first time, she feels she ought to act more desperate, more debauched in the face of corrosive poverty, but then again, what is more depraved than training a dog-bomb?

Levent picks up the register because it's not anchored, or even plugged in, and heaves it against the tile floor because in the core of his soul is a boy-tumor who never learned not to throw his toys. This time is different, though. He keeps throwing. He grabs vases, bouquets, pots, watering cans, shears, trimmers, ferns. Dog barks and barks and barks and it pisses Gökçe off because she wanted to kick his barking habit. Frustrated with Dog and her brother, she jumps on Levent's back in a half tackle and he buckles for a moment, as if he's insulting her weight. He turns and, in doing so, swipes a shelf of beautiful roses clean with Gökçe's protruding rear.

"Where is the money?"

Dog jumps up on Gökçe's dangling legs. He scratches them in play. This is a game. This is one of the games brother and sister play.

Because God has a sense of humor, especially when it comes to siblings, a man with a beard, twill coat, umbrella, and angry wife comes into the shop for one of the bouquets that now litter the floor.

"My God," says the man, running over to the struggling siblings, testing the seams of his twill coat stretching this way and that to break into the fight. "Get out of here." He clucks his tongue and hits at Levent's head with the handle of his umbrella, catching Gökçe's once or twice in the excitement. "Shoo, get out, thief."

"I work here," Levent struggles to say. The weight of his sister's body, the scratches from the dog, the blows from the man, all squeeze the breath right out of Levent's pleas.

"Get out of here, jackass," Gökçe says to either Levent or the old man. The old man puzzles his face, then picks up a few daisies and leaves, shouting behind him that they're mad apes, ought to be locked up, sorry for taking the flowers.

Gökçe climbs off Levent's back because she needs to sit down, but he keeps kicking the vases. "A goddamned dog, better than me. A dog, Abla." He storms out at this notion, but Gökçe doesn't bother telling him anything on his way. She's no good at making up promises or poems anymore. But already she wants him to come back. Later, she wants him to come back and see Dog trained. To see her success before it's blown apart.

GÖKÇE KNOWS IT will be difficult to truly kill something, even a mongrel, so she practices—she builds up to it. First she kills the spiders in back of the shop. Some of them take two or three slaps with an old bouquet. She worries about whether they feel pain. She'll look that up later tonight.

Gökçe chases squirrels. She chases them through the north end of the park where there are fewer cafés but more vendors. She chases them with rocks, trying to get close enough to bash in their heads. She's concerned about maiming one and having to get down on her knees to finish the squirrel with quick and heavy blows. The vendors must say of this scene, *What is a fat woman doing chasing squirrels through the park?* The squirrels are agile and for most of the afternoon she can't catch any of them, but she's not trying her hardest; she's not running as fast as she can. She's scared of what to do when she does catch a squirrel. She's frightened about what it must be like to take a rock and bludgeon an animal, and she says to herself at least with a bomb it's less personal, but then she thinks about all the pieces of Dog that will be scattered about in the explosion, and she knows this is worse. And so she's running about the park with a shallow hesitation, thinking that if she can succeed without having to try her hardest, then it will mean one thing, it will mean conviction, but she doesn't think about what it means if she can't catch a squirrel.

She doesn't want to think about what it will mean for Turkey if she can't overcome this little fear now blooming in her stomach. She must keep practicing. Erdoğan is now adding a stable fitted for fifty horses—each costing more than fifty thousand lira—to his new palace, illegally funded and built in the Atatürk Forest Farm conservation ground. Courts have ruled for construction to stop. His staff have brought in gold-plated toilets. The electric bill, it has been claimed, totaled more than one million lira for the last month. Ten percent of the country makes less than fifteen lira a day. Hundreds of thousands of refugees live in tents. Erdoğan will hold a meeting soon with representatives of the Ministry for Women and Families. He will tell them rejecting motherhood is a rejection of humanity. He will tell them a childless woman is deficient and incomplete.

———

A STROKE OF luck, a miracle, a sign from God written on a flashing billboard—Gökçe learns that a simple bomb needs little more than fertilizer and kerosene. Fertilizer! Divine providence has made clear to her that, as a florist, she is on the just and righteous path. Yes, learning this goes a long way in settling her anxieties.

GÖKÇE LAUGHS AT the irony in her trouble finding a blind person in Ankara. They don't hold meetings anywhere she knows of. The first blind man she found after walking through malls and markets all day used a cane instead of a canine. It doesn't matter, though; today she forgot her shears. She thinks about the sorts of things the blind might enjoy: the smell of spring buds, the lapping of salty air against their skin, the tang of the surf, the sound of garden fountains, the feel of grass poking through trousers and picnic blankets. But there's no sea near Ankara, and she's checked the parks and gardens.

She'd tried buying a service dog vest online, but you need a permit to order one, so now she wanders the roads of the city, looking up ophthalmologists in Ankara. The first one is a doctor out of Güven Hospital. She stops at a vendor to buy some honey-covered lokma, then takes a taxi to the hospital.

"Are you pregnant?"

"I'm not married," she says.

The cabbie takes another look to see if he ought to be interested in her. She sinks a little when he turns back to the road so quickly.

She sits outside the hospital and eats her treat before going in and asking the receptionist where she can find the ophthalmologist.

"Fourth floor."

There are some stairs but she searches around for the elevator and takes it. She creeps into the doctor's waiting room full with a boy and his father, and a young woman with an eye patch.

"Can I help you, ma'am?" asks the short woman behind the counter.

"No, I'm just waiting for a friend, really."

"Which friend?" she asks.

"What?"

"What's your friend's name?"

"I'm just here to pick him up," Gökçe says. "He has a dog."

"Oh, you just missed him, probably went to wait for you downstairs."

"I must've kept him too long. I'm always late like this," she says.

Gökçe smiles at the receptionist, at the young woman with the eye patch, at the boy and his father, and she runs out the room and for the elevator. She stops at every floor on the way down because some shithead pressed each of the buttons and got off. If God did not bestow upon the world these people, it would be too much like heaven.

Gökçe runs out the hospital doors and bumbles down the street, huffing because she's no longer twenty. Everywhere are people shouting, walking, haggling, laughing, but she doesn't see a man with a dog. She hurries down the street in a desperate ditch, letting her senses take her past a Domino's, and a bazaar with small tea sets and cinnamon sticks, and a kebab place. She works up an unbearable appetite running after a phantasmal blind man.

There! Down the road a bit, she sees a tall man in gray pants and a navy jacket following his dog. She loses her breath she stops so fast, and then she pants like a hound. She can't stop hyperventilating, risking alerting the blind man, the thought alone making her breathier. But blind men don't care about winded pedestrians. She follows him down the street. Keeping a good distance back, she feels like a Bond girl.

For six blocks this dog leads this man that leads Gökçe before they come to a stop. The retriever slaps its tail this way and that as the two walk into the apartment complex. Gökçe's close enough now to hear the man muttering in equal parts to himself and his dog. She checks the address and takes a taxi home.

Next day, Gökçe stands outside the apartment block with a long pair of garden shears. But after an hour, people begin noticing her because of the shears behind her back, so she sets to work trimming the shrubs outside the blind man's apartment to kill time and blend in. But the shrubs are terribly misshapen and desperate for form. She takes her time trimming back mangy branches. If she had a ruler she could do it right. She sculpts little boxes of green at the foot of the apartment steps. She livens up the street and feels good about her charity. The line of shrubs down the retaining wall catches her notice. She sets to work trimming those as well, but soon enough the man with the guide dog comes out for a walk or an appointment.

She brushes a twig out of her shears and puts them behind her back, feeling stupid for hiding them from a blind man. She tiptoes behind her prey like the tigers from her mother's fables.

The man wrangles his dog and stops to pat his pockets. Like a djinn, Gökçe becomes ethereal and swift and descends upon the dog. Before either hears her and responds, she snips the leash with the shears. Remorse punches her in the stomach. This dog does not bark, or growl, or smell, as she grabs it to make off with it. Instead, it wags its tail next to its owner and has manners enough not to pant in the heat. Gökçe swallows back the flashbulb-guilt. There is a real villain to consider in this plot of hers. She throws the shears off into the garden of a nearby apartment block, picks up the dog, and sprints, wobbly, down the cobblestone sidewalk.

The man wails and swings his arms as violently as he can manage, whipping the cut leash around like a bull's tail. Once Gökçe's far enough away, once the dog stops writhing, she sits at a bus stop bench and fiddles with the special vest. She manages it off and runs back to the blind man as fast as she'd left. She drops off the man's dog and thinks to say something but nothing other than the word *anarchy* comes to mind, for no particular reason. She jumps into the apartment garden after her shears and digs them out of an overgrown tomato plant. "Good boy," she says to the dog. It barks, and the man cries, and Gökçe runs all the way home.

THE FUSE OF a firework is good enough, and it fits perfectly in the toilet-paper roll she has filled with fertilizer and oil-soaked cotton balls. Dog's in the back in his makeshift kennel, which is just a confined area cordoned off by flaps of cardboard, the flanks of milk crates, and part of an office chair she'd found in the dumpster behind her shop. Every once in a while, when he falls asleep, Gökçe tapes pictures of Erdoğan cut from magazines to the crosses of the milk crates and gives the office chair a good rattle. She feeds Dog when he tears up the life-sized cutouts she steals from political rallies, and throws treats to him when they watch the news and he growls. When it rains, Dog tucks himself under the counter in the shop and stays there until she plops down next to him and coos. When she goes out for groceries, he follows without a leash. She's gotten him used to the vest, and he listens when she talks in the empty shop between make-believe customers. He's getting fatter. They both are. They eat all day long. In a month, her trickle of savings will be gone.

Next week they will practice blind and guide. But they're running out of time. Elections will be held in June, and she can't trust the rest of Turkey to vote with reason. In ten days Erdoğan will hold another one of his rallies. It is her only opportunity.

"Would you like some sucuk?" she asks Dog. He says yes with his eyes. If all of Gökçe's life amounts to nothing else, if her meals continue alone, if her bedroom walls are never filled by the laughter of her own children, then she at least can claim she's trained Dog very well to drool upon command. In a year, she'll turn forty, a milestone for unmarried Turkish women. She will throw a parade alone, and drape herself in evil eyes and march to imaginary darbuka drum rhythms, and at some point in the night, she will deliver a one-line eulogy for her ovaries. *Good night, my sweet, unseeded organs.*

LEVENT STILL HASN'T come back to ask his abla for money or tell her she's a failure, and a loneliness settles in her stomach, the sort of loneliness that strikes when you quit smoking or skip breakfast. She turns in her bed like döner on a spit.

Gökçe has made the bomb and timed the fuse. She's sewn it up into the vest as best she can. She's practiced unleashing Dog on effigies of Erdoğan. She's practiced being blind. She hasn't made up a last testament because that feels like bad luck. She's locked Dog up in his kennel without dinner so that he will be savage tomorrow.

In the nighttime, just hours before she leaves for the rally, she cannot sleep. She becomes aware of all the sounds of the city around her, the clatter of drunken laughter echoing down alleys, the growls of railcars and taxis, the silent language of insects, and her throat swells with worry that these may be the last sounds clogging her ear canals. Every few minutes she checks her alarm clock to make sure that time is still passing, and its hands stop moving each glance she steals. She asks God to be merciful, to sprinkle magic dust in her eyes and let her sleep.

She casts off the sheets, careful not to gaze directly into the darkened angles of her room untouched by the drowsy streetlamps. She creeps down into the back of the shop, turning on every light she can safely reach along the way. She sneaks to the kennel, trying not to wake Dog, but closer she sees the lights have already roused him. She unties the office chair from the milk crates and scoots it out of the way, and Dog starts wagging his tail. She stands clear, and Dog goes to his food bowl immediately. Whispering, so as not to wake the djinn that might be hiding, she tells Dog no, to follow her upstairs instead. "Upstairs," she says again, but he doesn't know this word. She holds out her hand like she has something he might want. He follows her up the stairs. She turns the lights back off and guides Dog into her bedroom. The air feels fresher now, and so do the sheets. She pats the bed, and Dog jumps up to join her. She crawls under the sheets and pats next to her unused, second pillow. Dog crawls along his belly, tail wagging like a propeller, and curls up by Gökçe's chest and head. She thinks about staying here all night and the next day, and imagines that this is instead the start of her life, as nice as that is to believe. She puts her arm over his body and closes her eyes. Still, she cannot sleep, but right now, this is enough.

Soma

THROUGH THE HILLS sprout white turbines, lofted more than fifty meters into the air. In the breeze they swing languid arms in arcs across the sky, dipping the tips of blades beneath the horizon and pulling them back up like the strokes of a swimmer. They are propellers anchored to the earth, carrying it through its leisurely orbit. They are bright in the sun, these turbines, and at night their rotors glow from red safety lights, and we can't see the pillars or the blades, just the hubs sprinkling the air like cigarette butts.

The miners walk in the release of the moon, heading with their meals in pails and plastic bags, heading with their hard hats heavy in their hands, heading to the shaft elevator that extends some two thousand meters underground where they will work in golden pockets of electric light while the sun begins its sweep across the sky. After six hours they will ride the elevator up, stopping shy of the surface to let their eyes adjust before they breach once more into the world above.

As a boy I woke with my father and watched him pack his breakfast of spiced sausage and boiled eggs, and struggled in his arms as he lifted me and kissed my cheek, stamping it black with coal dust carried always between the fibers of his mustache. Then my mother would wake and wipe my cheek clean and perform her own ablutions before the morning prayer, and still hours before sunrise I would go to our apartment's balcony and wave goodbye to the miners. The moon was so big and bright I waited all night for it to explode.

Now eighteen, I still wake a little after four and go to the balcony with my coffee while my parents sleep. I wave to the miners as they walk through our village, and I make jokes: "Lock up your women. I'm on the prowl." They shout back: "Get a job, useless."

The file of men disappears behind the curve of the road, a scythe through the hills. For a half hour, at shift change, the town streets are empty and dark, and the breeze shakes the homes of absent men, as if the village needs only a little encouragement to leap up into the air and ride the wind far away.

Now those done with their shifts creep up the road quietly in a long column; the only sound is the shuffle of their feet. At the edge of the village they break rank and slip over stone streets to their homes, to their beds. I wave at my friend Mesut, who comes to the base of my building wearing his smile like a shard of porcelain in the dirt. I finish my coffee, grab my bag, and hurry down to him. Through the slopes of our village, I follow him, asking about the soccer match, about his shift, about the movie I lent him. The sun is on its way and I am restless.

We sneak out of the dawn and into his parents' apartment. The kitchen light displaces darkness, and from the hallway rolls his mother's snoring. Mesut goes to rinse the grit out of his hair, so I sit at the table, take out my test-prep book, and start working on the mathematics practice problems. Unable to focus, I pick at the seams of the plastic table cover decorated in daisies, coming undone. Mesut's mother keeps in a small white vase on the table a purple orchid—plastic stem, paper petals. I tap my pencil on the book, I flip the pages back and forth. I watch the windows growing full of light.

Mesut shoves my book off the table, replacing it with a plate of pasta his mother cooks up each night. "Swallow a big gulp before saying a big word."

I pick the book back up and set it next to the pasta. Mesut's a year older than me. He dropped out of high school and has been working the mine since.

"Win this race first, İzzet, then you can worry about entrance exams."

"I need both," I say. I tell him they don't give scholarships to idiots, no matter how fast they swim. My father can't afford university, not on his pension. I'm jittering my leg like I do every morning, waiting for the water. Everyone in the village moves in smooth, simple motions, their muscles spent from hours underground.

Mesut sits next to me. His father has already left for the mine. From the bedroom tremble snores growing louder, a testament to sound slumber. Mesut used to work the night shift with his father, but when one night someone ran off with a neighbor's bicycle, Mesut's mother cried worries of thieves and rapists. Now Mesut's father works by day to spend his evenings at home with his wife. Mesut tells me all their time together strains their marriage.

Mesut crumbles feta cheese over my pasta and gets a plate for himself, and this is what we do each morning: fork cold pasta into our mouths like furnaces.

Mesut's mother sleepwalks through the kitchen and into the TV room. She watches the local weather reports until after we leave, until she wakes up, and then she cleans away the dishes, the evidence of us, and goes to cook more pasta.

I clean my first plate and pile up another. We finish our meal in the silence of smacking lips and digestion, and then I fill a plastic container with another helping, and go change into my swimsuit, and pack my book back into my grocery bag with my goggles and towel, and I follow Mesut to the shed out back. The sun is up and already heavy in the sky so that it droops, long like an oval.

We climb into his dad's car, a relic from the sixties, and Mesut drives us out of the terraced village on narrow roads. I imagine calculating the village's slopes with my graphing calculator under the great expanse of mountain-fringed sky.

"Take the 240," I say.

"At this hour it will be slow."

For the last two months we've said this each morning, and I enjoy Mesut's route through Darkale, the winding descent. The way we travel is a delay of the sun, a delay of my eager nerves, my return to easy strokes. We take roads that cleave the mountains, roads from which we can count all the tumbledown shacks and hovels of the province falling over slowly, roads covered in shade, roads with streetlamps still on though the sky is lightly blue. Retaining walls squeeze our path, and we skirt around rocks fallen into the road and piles of trash people leave but no one picks up. And then before us opens the mountain range for just a moment, revealing Soma like a secret, tucked into the crevices, atop flat peaks, surrounded by gravel summits, pothole roads, telephone wires, and black trees that dance in the breeze. Far away are rain clouds. Half-finished houses in gradients, their terra-cotta roofs like steps into the air. TV dishes pimple up along the skyline. The minarets are ablaze with muezzins. The streets are built overtop a number of buildings; all are curved like funnels flowing down the slopes through paths of least resistance.

We turn east and head toward the thermal power plant. We curve around the field where squat cooling towers pop up in neat rows of six—olive trees growing in the shade of their steam clouds. Smoke drifts from the three slender chimney stacks attached to the plant like beautiful cigarettes. The plant fires the poor lignite dug out from the mine by Mesut and his father and every other able-bodied man in our village. The furnaces produce kilos of bottom ash every minute. The ash is mixed with water in a pump and sluiced away from the plant in eleven oversized irrigation pipes. We turn at the end of the olive grove and follow the pipes north out of the factory grounds. To our left are the eleven outgoing pipes; to our right are seven incoming pipes. Beyond these are the vineyards and groves and power lines and rusted-out cars and derelict houses, and farther still are the shops and restaurants and apartments and mosques of Soma where no one is yet on the street—all still ambling through their dreams. I practice my breathing exercises.

Mesut slows—ahead there is a dog with valleys in the space between its ribs, with gray hair around its snout, with shoulders sliding up and down like oil derricks as it crosses our path. He throws a bit of his sandwich out the window for it then speeds down the track of road that runs away from the plant in a beautiful line, the kind of line that's in my textbooks, the desire line, the most efficient line you ever saw, and I swear I can hear the water coursing through the pipes.

These pipes empty into a human-made dam to the north of town. Its bottom is covered in cement to keep toxins from leaking into water supplies. The ash separates from the water and settles along the cement like multicolored oils in chemistry. The empty water is filtered from the top and pumped back to the plant. We park at the road that runs along the side of the reservoir. Because of the ash and cement, the water is bright turquoise, as beautiful as the Ottoman palaces of Istanbul, covered in electric-blue arabesque.

I stretch, shaking my limbs to get the blood flowing. Mesut sets up a lawn chair in the gravel and begins drinking. I dive into the cold water. I backstroke toward the middle of the pond, keeping my eyes on clouds slicing the blue same as me.

"Keep your eyes closed, İzzet."

I close them. Open-water swimming depends on bearings, straight lines, knowing your way without looking. Mesut shouts when I begin to drift and says nothing when my vector is straight for the telephone pole on the opposite bank.

Other days I have practiced taking off while treading because

Mesut says they might not provide a diving platform. He wouldn't know, but it is good practice.

Before that, I practiced turns. He had me swim around buoys he set up while he watched my strokes underwater.

I used to practice swimming in groups. It's hard to navigate a race with hundreds of people cutting through the same small stretch of water. We'd made planks with short rudders and rope tails. Mesut rigged them all up into a network. I positioned myself amid the wooden swimmer-substitutes and swam toward Mesut while he pulled the flock of planks along, keeping pace with me.

Now there is only sighting left to work on. I keep conditioning, but I'm in good shape for the race. Mesut drinks his beers and falls asleep while I incorporate sighting into the rhythm of my strokes. When Mesut wakes, he takes note of my timing, my pace.

Nothing is jittery in my mind; my nerves are cooled by the water. Mesut shouts to me, his voice crashing with the crest of the water in my ear. I can't hear what he says. I reach the wall dividing the reservoir from the filtration system and push back from it. I backstroke for the beach, for the car. In the middle of the reservoir I look directly up, the blue of the sky converging with the blue of the water in my peripheries so that I am a point in an ineffable expanse of buoyancy. Here I have no thoughts. My limbs negotiate with the weight of the water through which I become weightless. I am deprived of sensation save for the color of the sky. I am miles in the air. My heart steadies. My strokes slow. The beach is close, though I can't feel it.

We pack everything into the car. My muscle cords twitch and scream beneath my skin. Mesut takes the 240 back to town because he knows I like to watch the turbines while I cool down, because I like to watch the great turns. We don't park, but he drives slowly. There's not enough of a breeze today; the turbines hang in disuse over the clefts of hills and fields.

"I'm going to be up there," I say.

Mesut gives a tired laugh. He's been awake, he's been working, he's been drinking.

"Right there." I point. "I'm going to straddle the rotors."

"What's the difference, eh?"

Instead of descending into the dark, I will climb into the bright day, into the sunlight.

"The same thing is done up there," Mesut says, "the gathering of electricity. So you are in the air, or in the ocean, or underground, whatever. I want to be flatly on the ground. Safe. I wouldn't mind taking in a little sun across a bed of grass, or under olive trees."

He drops me off at my house, and then he's off to bed. There are friends of his who go straight to bed after work, and most of the year they never see the sunlight.

At home, my parents watch television. In the kitchen, I study some more. My mom comes in. She cuts up a watermelon and leaves a plate of slices next to me. She sits across from me, watching the flicks of my pencil.

"I'm so proud of you, you know," she says.

What do I say to that? I could tell her it's not a sure thing. I could tell her I haven't even taken the exams, I haven't even swum the race, but what are these things to her? She looks at me, marble eyes heavy with pride.

"Is that watermelon for everyone?" my dad asks.

She takes it out to the living room, and they call for me to join them. On-screen is an American show. The cigarettes and cans of beer are blurred out so every few seconds the characters take swigs from pixelated rectangles.

"Have they asked you what you want to study?" my mom asks.

"I haven't turned in my application yet."

"You ought to get into architecture," she says.

"He's going to be like his father," my dad says, rosy glints of melon pooling in the corners of his mouth. He does this more and more, says I'm going to be a replica of him—like I haven't been training, like I haven't been studying, like the turbines are the same as the mine.

"I will be an engineer," I say.

"Do they work inside?" my mom asks.

"Four years of school just so you can wear a bigger hard hat? If you're going to fantasize, don't do it on a budget," my dad says as he stuffs another slice of watermelon in his mouth.

They eat watermelon and laugh at the television. My mom goes to the kitchen to start tea. Without looking from the television screen, my dad says: "What's that worth?"

He means *What can I do with it?* He means *How far will that take me from the mine?* He means he wants the distance in kilometers that I will escape into.

"I could be a technician for those windmills," I say. "Mom would like having me around as you two grow old."

"Who's planning on growing old?" My dad laughs a little. "Who wants to keep you here?"

"They make a living. It isn't the mine."

We sit like that until my mom brings out the copper tray of tulip glasses. We stir in cubes of sugar, the tinkle of teaspoons tickling our silence. The television is turned way down. My mom falls asleep. The engineers make six times what I would make in the mine. They live twice as long, I hear. They have suntans.

"It isn't the mine," my dad says, trying the words out for himself.

"There's a program that I could do. It specializes in . . ." But I don't know what to say. It's too late, and I can see that. My dad doesn't care about the windmills. We sit close to each other on the couch, the rough fabric scratching our undersides like bark. I'm jittering my leg. I'm feeling my body sink into the cushion. I want my dad to ask me about my swimming, how training's going, what Mesut thinks of my speed.

"I don't think you know what you're talking about," he whispers. "It *is* the mine."

There are cookies and a bowl of nuts on the tray. I swallow the tea as easy as sand, and my throat feels swollen. My dad keeps eating, plucking almonds from the bowl with fingers sticky from the watermelon. I think about going for a walk to get out of the house, but there's nothing to see in this town except retired men huddled around small tables at street corners, playing cards and tavla, drinking tea and coffee, their skin drooping like time because of their underground lives. There's nothing to see in this town but quiet women, running errands, beating dust from rugs, clipping cotton sheets to clotheslines, dripping soot from their hair at the bounce of each step. There's nothing to see in this town but coal-stained children like feral dogs through the streets, their lungs sucking all the ash from the air.

I go to my room instead. I try reading but I don't like the book and I'm a slow reader. Everyone I know is asleep or in the mine, like I'm a fugitive, like I'm the only unclipped bird in an aviary. I go to bed as well, with the sun in my window. When I wake, the sky is dark, the clouds cover the moon. I take my coffee on the balcony and shout to the miners until Mesut returns and drives me to the reservoir. We do this for two more weeks. I study when I'm not training, though I am exhausted and unable to focus. I think of every face in town. I book a small room at a hostel near the Dardanelles strait. Mesut gets the day off so that he can drive me to the race. The website claims more than six hundred registered entrants.

The morning of the race is here, and splitting across the sky comes a crash you can hear in your bones. It's flat, monosyllabic. The ground doesn't falter, the air is clear and blue, the grass shudders only in the breeze. If you could listen to the scrape of tectonic plates, if for just a flash of time there was the great flow of mantle and crust caught in your ear, it wouldn't sound like this. It's not at all like an earthquake. We know those here; you grow up knowing them. We know this too:

the silence, the absence of aftershocks, the snap of energy is a single, released moment, the space between heartbeats. It can suffocate you if you're not careful—the mine.

I've never seen the streets so full as they are now, though no one hurries. They compact themselves into one another, press close, hunch. More people from more homes. I break from my mom's grasp and run down to the street, her shouts chasing after me. Still we all pack tighter, our closeness brushing black dust from our skin. The crowd shuffles now, searching with stamping feet for the path to the mine. People talk in hushed voices, careful that their words are not picked up by the wind. The mine, everyone whispers, the mine. No one runs, no one shoves, no one steps on toes or heels. We walk deliberately down the curved path to the mine, our voices extinguishing as we near the mouth of the shaft. For a long time, long enough that clouds have moved to cover us, we stand there watching from afar a dozen or so men scraping at the pile of earth obstructing the main shaft—scraping with their hard hats like shovels.

I see Mesut come away from the mouth of the mine and run to him. His face is black and he doesn't recognize me. Behind me people start running for things, for shovels, for carts, for oxygen tanks, for picks, for stretchers, for a defibrillator, but we don't know what we're doing, we don't know what's going on.

Exasperated, Mesut shouts for help, shouts that the slope to the mine is blocked by boulders and soil. I follow him back down the ramp to the shaft elevator, my arms swinging wildly as I try to keep up. The keys to his dad's car must be in his pocket. People swarm around us, with buckets, with handcarts, with helmets, with outstretched shirts in vise-fingers. Others shovel rubble and dirt into every cart, every helmet, every palm to be carried away, up the tracks and into the sun. Everyone is shouting, cutting at the great barrier of earth between us and the shaft elevator with frenzied limbs. A scream of sirens, and the crowd breaks for a line of ambulances and the police chief's car. Mesut is throwing boulders large as my torso into carts, up and down, up and down, like a piston. I'm bobbing my head up and down beside him, screaming that there's no time to waste, there's no time for digging. There's a race up the coast, there's a race we must get to.

"Grab a shovel," he says between grunts, between heaves.

"Can I take the car?" I ask, because what else am I going to do? It's all set, it's my life at stake too.

He doesn't hear me. He shoves his fingers into the soil and unearths rock after rock like potatoes plucked for boiling.

"Do you have the keys?"

Mesut looks at me, confused. He keeps digging with his hands. He doesn't say anything. He scratches at the black soil with calloused fingertips. He's bleeding from a few cuts on his arms, between his fingers. There are hundreds of people now, a number of trucks with emergency lights, a bulldozer, an excavator, a dump truck. More people arrive, some with pots to help scoop dirt. No one's crying yet. I notice it, that no one's crying yet.

"Can I take the car?"

Mesut throws a stone back into the rubble. Screaming, he grabs me by the shoulders and shoves me into the pile. He yells to get a fucking shovel, to start digging. With difficulty I pull myself up from the rubble and rocks, and then there is Mesut's fist, fast and fleshy, striking me squarely in the jaw. I can't see for a moment in my right eye, the way the sight goes when I am swimming too long underwater. There's a pounding moving from the exploded capillaries of my face, through my jaw and temples to my ears. Mesut is on top of me as my sight comes back, his dirt-caked face shouting at me through the fizzling little dots on my peripheries. I grab at his collar, I try pulling him to the side, but he's bigger than me, pushing my chest into the dirt, shoving my head back so that I can feel the soil spill down my forehead. Desperate, I kick him off. No one around us seems to care. They are all singularly busy in their efforts to remove the rubble.

Mesut drags me off the pile and onto the cart tracks. He throws the keys to his dad's car at me and goes back to ripping at the rocks with his fingers. All around people are tearing into the mine. But I'm already packed, I'm already registered. I go to the car and drive away, north through the stalks of windmills. I listen the whole way for another explosion. I leave the radio off, and for the four-hour drive I listen carefully for another explosion, promising myself that if it gets worse I will turn back, but the four hours don't take long, not really, and I'm in Çanakkale, with a view of the Dardanelles from a square window in the hostel. There's an Australian named Bruce in the bunk next to me who asks me if I'm excited for the race tomorrow, who asks me if I got that black eye from swimming.

I don't say anything, not to him or anyone else while I lie in my bed until morning, thinking about the route I must take to cross the channel, thinking about the landmarks I will use for bearings, timing out my breathing with imaginary strokes. In the morning, I have a small breakfast very early and ride the ferry to the other side of the Dardanelles. I sign in and look around the beach for a good spot to start from. The water is choppy. It will be difficult to navigate. Where the strait begins to narrow, near Çanakkale, it is only a kilometer and a half wide. The current there is inexorable. I set up at the north end of the beach, go as far as I can, an extra two or three hundred meters up from most of the other swimmers all in their Speedos and caps and goggles, lubing themselves with Vaseline, slapping their muscles and shaking their limbs. I've done my preparations in the hostel. I don't like this bit of showmanship beforehand. The novices take places as far south as they can squeeze, as close to the first marker as possible, without room to maneuver with the current. The man next to me is very old for this race; beside him is a woman a few years older. They are married and from Liverpool. I ask what it is they are putting in their mouths. Salt tablets, they say, they are good for preventing cramps. They give me some. I take them with water and start up with my little ritual of splashing water from the sea on my forearms, shins, thighs, chest.

There's a starter's pistol, but we don't hear it this far away, in this much wind. We take the cue of the hundreds of bodies diving into the water, cutting at it with frenzied limbs, violent lungs, combustion engines inside thoracic cavities. I dive in and aim directly across, aim straight for Asia though the finish line is a few kilometers down, past Çanakkale. It takes some time to escape the breakers, and I haven't paced myself well, but soon enough I am out striding through the open water, I am beyond the sounds of shore, I am above a blur, a void, an ineffable divide. When I take a breath, I adjust my line. While I stroke, I gaze below me, watching the bottom until it dissolves behind the opacity of depth. But it is an illusion; the bottom is only a hundred meters at its deepest. There are men trapped now in a tunnel more than two thousand meters underground, and their lungs must be deflated balloons.

Most of the swimmers, especially those who started farthest south, are taken by the current of the water emptying into the Aegean. They broke too late, their lines too direct. They will not make it across. I make my turn and let the water carry me. In a long sweep I've aimed for the beach like a celestial body exiting orbit. There are a number of other racers who have done the same as me, there are a good number of them. But I am fast, I am calm, and I scrape at the crest of the water, I grip and tear and cut through it. Past the narrow I don't bother looking around me, I don't worry about nearby kicks or slaps. I don't bother opening my eyes beneath the waves. I look only during breaths, I look only at the expanse of blue above—I think only of my breaths, conscious, measured like the breaths of men who must worry over the factor of oxygen. I am not any distance above or below; my elevation is zero. I am on the flat of the earth. Every few strokes, as I turn my head, there is the boom against my eardrum from the breeze. I listen below me; I listen for explosions in the earth but can't hear anything over the slap and kick of hands and feet.

I ride the breakers to shore. A man takes a picture from the beach as I slip through the glinting surf. I can taste the salt in my smile. My back is burned from the sun and the brine. There are others in the water, the other swimmers. I am the only one on land, and my body feels heavy; the fibers of my muscles drip from my skeleton under the pressure of gravity.

Before my feet have a chance to cake with sand, a committee brings me a ribbon and a bottle of liquor. I ask for water and let someone drive me back to my room in Çanakkale, where I pack my things and send a text to my mother telling her I'll be back after dinner.

But when I get back no one will ask me about what I've done here, what it means for me. Will they think me vile? When I pull the car back into Mesut's shed, I check his house but no one is home. It's evening; the sun is an orange radiance spread just below the mountaintops. I walk through an empty village, my hand out, reaching for the sides of houses, brushing them with fingertips until I'm outside my own home. I walk up to my room. No one is here. Lights are not coming on in the other houses. I fall asleep and don't wake up until a truck honks in the street the next morning.

A procession of black cars curves around the truck, on their way to the square not far from Mesut's house. I splash my face with water from the tap and look for my parents. They are out somewhere. Maybe at the mine. Outside, I follow a small group of people walking after the procession of cars. I ask them if they have any news. If there's anyone still underground.

"They aren't sure if anyone's still alive. Already they've hauled fifty bodies."

"How are they breathing? How are they breathing that deep?" I ask.

A machine is still pumping air down the shaft like a large snorkel; the few miners left alive are struggling to sip from it. They are stuck, trapped, some with bodies broken in a dozen places, they tell me. They've pulled a few survivors from the mine; in a trickle are the miners surfacing.

"Is it a funeral?" I ask about the cars.

President Erdoğan is visiting. He's speaking in front of the old bey's mansion. In the square so usually stuffed with döner vendors and coffee drinkers are all the people I have ever seen in my life, every face to haunt the little village. More than that, even, more faces, more people from other villages, from the city of Soma not far away. They're hoisting banners, picket signs. They shout while the mayor introduces the president. He's taller than you think, with eyes like coal. He tells us that mining accidents are typical, they are to be expected. He tells us of incidents in Britain and France in the nineteenth century, talking to us like we are anachronistic, like we are suspended in the past. Since the mine was privatized, the cost of producing one ton of coal has dropped more than eighty percent. Our mines kill us at rates five times greater than in China, three hundred sixty times greater than in America.

Looking around, I am wrong. This is not everyone I have ever seen. This is only the semblance of the village. This is only the people not part of the mine. The people chant: *Murderer Erdoğan.* All around are men, some wearing suits, some in construction uniforms, some in miner's coveralls, some in fireman's gear, some with hard hats on, some with shovels over their heads. The women are in their living rooms, at the funeral homes, in morgues identifying bodies they barely recognize.

The president steps off the platform and immediately his bodyguards wrap around him. His limousine is blocked by the crowd, so the guards escort him to the lobby of a bank at the corner while rocks fly through the air. I pick up a rock as well and think about throwing it, but I don't deserve to, I don't belong here with a rock to throw at a car. The rocks these men throw are dug from the mine, from atop the bodies of their friends. A guard fires his rifle into the air. The crowd parts for the limousine, though their chants grow louder. The president is ushered into his car and driven away. A man tears from the crowd and runs for the car.

It's Mesut. He kicks the wheel. He kicks the fender, and right away two bodyguards in fatigues with rifles at their shoulders grab him and throw him onto the pavement. The motorcade takes off, cutting through the crowd of mourners, protesters, locals. They throw rocks at the bodyguards. The two men in fatigues try to wrestle Mesut's arms. A presidential aide in a suit pulls one of the bodyguards away. Fire in his mouth, he swings a sharp foot into Mesut's side. He swings again, he swings a third time, kicks Mesut in the ribs while the two bodyguards in fatigues hold him down on the cold pavement. They will arrest Mesut and hold him for weeks, maybe months without charging him. His father, if he is not in the mine, will not find work. His mother will spend mornings in the prison visiting him until she is detained as well. I do nothing. I don't stand out from the crowd. I've just won the race. I will pass my entrance exams. I go from the street full of people, down an alley, and I walk for a long way through a village I don't recognize, until I'm not far from the cemetery they've been taking the coffins to in truckloads.

Along the low stone wall stand relatives in long lines. A few politicians have stuck around; maybe they're from nearby, maybe they're up for reelection. The coffins are all covered with the flag, like the dead were soldiers, like they've just come back from the east, shot to bits.

They've brought in digging machines, three of them. The undertaker and his two sons can't keep up. They cut little rectangles into the dirt, long rows of them, you can't count how many, you wouldn't need to, the number will be on the headlines. The space between the graves is slight, out of necessity.

I think of the speed sound travels through water. There's a difference between salt water and fresh water. There's a difference between loamy soil and geode. Supposedly sound travels fastest through solid objects, but that can't be true. When I press my ear to the earth I still hear the whisper of methane, the crack of each molecule combusting, the slow fizzle. I can still hear the explosion in process.

Am I so different? Am I not just the other side of the coin, the man who will climb up a shaft two hundred meters above the ground, and tinker with machinery so far from the surface, tinker with the things of power, of energy? I will tell my children stories of my work the way my father has told me. I will tell them of the world of light, the world without gravity.

My father's mustache still leaks black powder, but mine will not. My children will ask me of the mine, will crawl onto my lap and ask why the fathers of all their friends have mustaches of pitch, have backs like mountain ranges, have stories they share, they know by heart, they lived through side by side. I will tell them of my life in the sky and they will ask me of the men I left in the earth. Perhaps they will ask me of the mine when they've outgrown sitting on my lap, ask me why the men of Soma walk like phantoms of soot through the dawn, and I will tell them of my love for the slow swing of turbines. Perhaps they will ask me of the mine when they've just come back from it, hands caked, cracks of white on their faces, ask me why I'm not down there with them, why I'm still climbing ladders upward bound. Perhaps they will ask me what I did during the explosion, and I will tell them about the race, about the beautiful strokes of the windmills.

Festival of Bulls

IN KAAN'S PICTURES of Istanbul, half the women don't cover themselves. He showed me them when he first got back from university. That was five years ago now. He had to drop out before his second year, but he talks about it, talks about his life in Istanbul as if it's some big part of him. He showed me pictures of the university grounds, and the coffeehouse he frequented, and the shops and restaurants and bars in his neighborhood. All those busy streets, and crowded stores, and beautiful monuments, museums, and views, but the first thing I notice in each picture are the women in crop tops, floral miniskirts, shorts high, high up the leg, and none of the women are wearing headscarves.

Kaan turns the truck and trailer north off the highway and onto a gravel road. We're on our way to a bullfight festival, but not like they do in Spain, it's not the bull against a team of people with spears. I must've looked worried, because he assured me that it's just one bull against another bull, and even then, they don't let the bulls hurt each other. He checks the mirror again. His friend is following us like he's supposed to. The trailer makes a racket coming out of the turn. Kaan slides his hand into his pocket and it looks awkward, like he's trying to pull his pocket inside out.

"Will there be any bulls from Istanbul?" I ask my brother.

He laughs a little and says no, it is too far away.

The sun leaks through thin clouds. Trees the color of dirt overgrow the fields without any hurry. The breeze funnels through the foothill silhouettes, shivering the branches. The world looks cold without stark gradients of shade and sunlight.

"Is it because they have their own festivals?"

"There are no bulls in Istanbul."

Kaan brings me along on trips like this so I experience the world. He tells me being cooped up on our ranch is the quickest way to rot my brain.

Kaan says: "Progress begins where . . ."

"Where the people gather," I say simultaneously, laughing. He's a broken record, my brother. His year away from home made him like this. He studied only enough to learn a few platitudes, without even bothering to interrogate their meanings. He heard a professor say the east is a backwater, so he is convinced his home is a backwater. He dated a girl for a little while who said headscarves were slavery, not piety, so Kaan thinks his sister is a slave like his mother was.

He thinks good ideas come from being surrounded by other people. He thinks wisdom comes from city streets, as if each person can only have half a thought and must share. Well, around our house is nothing but sun and rock-summit hills and slender acacia trees between cleared pasture. Farther north, by the sea, clouds linger around shallow mountains. People do not gather.

Empty crop rows run quickly from the road. The windows are down and the breeze is prickling goose bumps up my arm. I pull one of my mother's headscarves from my rucksack. It's thistle-purple and billows like a sail in the airstream crisscrossing the cab. She died a while back, long enough ago that I have gotten over it, but sometimes it's nice to pull out a few of her things and wear them as a way to keep her close. Kaan was finishing high school when she died. He passed the college entrance exams soon after, and then left—left me and Dad alone with our loss. Dad's still in a trance. He blames Kaan sometimes. Our grief attaches onto strange excuses.

With some difficulty, I wrap the cloth around my head. I check the mirror and tuck all the after-sunset shades of purple over my ear. I try smiling like my mother, but I have my father's large nose and fat eyes, and I feel his ugliness diffusing through my face with every second I watch my reflection.

"What is this?" Kaan says.

"What?"

"You're not old enough to need that."

"We'll be in public," I remind him.

"So? You're not an old granny or some peasant girl." He reaches for the scarf. I giggle as I slap his hand away, but he's not smiling.

"Would you say that to Mom?"

"Sevinç," Kaan says between grabs at my headscarf. "Sevinç, quit knocking around."

I slap his hand away, and each time Kaan returns it quickly to the wheel. The path is narrow, and I tell him not to kill us. The trailer behind us starts to drift a little to and fro between the ditch and the field. Kaan is strong and quick and snags my scarf between turns in the path. "Don't be reckless," I warn him. He tells me to shut up, and the car rides up the lip of the path, shaking our heads like the coins on a belly dancer's skirt. I try to push him away, but he catches my wrist and squeezes it pale. I scream for him to stop.

"Stop acting seven years old," Kaan says.

"Treat me my age, then," I snap back. I'm sixteen to the whole world but Kaan. He says it's not about that. He says I shouldn't be so willing in my ignorance, my backwardness, my perpetuations of misogynistic traditions. He says it just like that too, all in a row, all like a robot on repeat—like copper tokens he's picked up from a gutter while studying in Istanbul. And anyway, they don't mean much when he says them, especially the way he says them. He can't fool me. He's an older brother, a domineering older brother, a brute behind a mask of Western ideas.

I slip my arm from Kaan's grasp. He swerves the car, making it jump over the lip and straddle the ditch. My head whips hard into the doorframe. Kaan snags the cloth and unspools it from my head, closing the color into his fist. I touch my head where it slapped the door, and there's a small split at the crown of a forming bruise. Kaan's very still. The tears trapped in the corners of my eyes are cold in the breeze.

"What do you think Dad will do to you now?" I try threatening.

Kaan's eyes are darker than his hair and he whips them fast from side to side. He keeps patting his jeans. "Fuck Dad anyway," he says. He and Dad have been holding shouting matches each night for a week now. They do it out in the shed and think I can't hear them. Kaan squeezes the wheel and I'm scared he'll grab me again. I wait until we're far into the hills before I ask in a whisper for him to return the headscarf. "Others will see me."

"They have women all over the world. You're nothing new."

He's being obtuse on purpose.

✺

I TURN THE truck off the gravel road onto a narrow, dirt path between the trees and follow it for about ten minutes to a clearing. There's already a mess of people here, a collection of tents and trucks and cars. I park off to the side where there's a staging area for the bulls. I get out but Sevinç stays put, pouting and picking at flaking bits of ~aint from the ceiling of the cab. I go over to her side and put my ‸dow ledge. "If you think you're grown up, you ought these tantrums," I say. Someone's approaching, so down into her seat, hiding like an oyster. "It's just

Bartu," I say. He's not quite a friend of mine, more of an acquaintance. He worked as a hired hand for my father inconsistently over a few years. He's come along to help me manage my bull during the festival. "He's seen you around the house all the time, from when you were this big," I say, holding my fingers apart for a miniature space.

"Give it back," Sevinç whispers from the floor of the truck. I should, I know this. But she's still very young. She doesn't need to bind herself to old-fashioned values.

I go back to the trailer with Bartu to unload my bull. The tailgate slaps the dirt, letting out the heavy smell of manure. Bartu stands wide and waves his arms to act as a wall so my bull will follow me to a bit of rope tied around a tree. I leash my bull and pitch him some hay from a large pile in the middle of the staging area. I tell him to eat well and not to let me down.

Bulls smother the edge of the forest, all tied loosely to thin trees. The smell of grilled meats and stuffed peppers rises from the camps around the clearing. A draft brushes between the springtime buds, and the air is clear and beautiful. Struggling to be inconspicuous, I check the other bulls, sizing them up. They are large black masses. There're more than forty of them. The prize this year should be more than ten thousand lira. It's liberating just to imagine all that money. But the other bulls are immense and might as well be elephants.

"What's the matter with her?" Bartu asks, pointing to the truck where we see Sevinç duck back down.

"She wants to be a sheet-head," I say.

Bartu thinks hard, then laughs thickly to match his hands and arms and face. "Let her be a nice girl."

"Fuck off," I say, and he wraps my neck and head into his arm, laughing, and I have to hit hard before he lets me free.

"I'm hungry," he tells me.

"We'll find a vendor."

"Tolga is here somewhere," Bartu says. "He will feed us." Tolg

Bartu's cousin. He's the richest man I know of, but that doesn't make him wealthy. Still, he has capital, he can invest, he can afford a jeep, a nice car, air conditioners in every room of his house.

I go to get Sevinç from the car.

"They will all look at me," she says. I call her a coward, and she nods. "I want to go back home," she says.

"You need to get away from home once in a while."

"Please, Kaan, give me the headscarf."

"There are nice men who will feed us," I say. "They are too old to think that way of you. You mustn't worry about modesty."

"Please," she says. She thinks it's a sin to be uncovered; *indiscreet, indecent, impious,* these are the words used to justify oppression. I make her promise she will come along and eat, and I'm hopeful she will see the women who come and do not cover themselves. I give Sevinç the scarf. I wait for her to adjust it, and I expect an apology, but she does not apologize. I check for my phone, and for the hundredth goddamned time I reach into an empty pocket. My father smashed it in the shed with a mallet a week after I left Şehir University. I'd read an article aloud about Erdoğan's latest authoritarian policies. He told me to shut up but I wanted him to hear what his vote was responsible for. He took his mallet and my phone to his workbench, and in four swings he crushed its insides to bits.

Sevinç and I follow Bartu into the camps, through tents and tables, around children with dirt caked into the sweat on their faces, and past men with so many years behind them it all sits heavy, strapped to their backs. Bartu walks up to a tall, slender man, and they slap each other's shoulders and smile. I recognize Tolga's voice from our conversation over the phone. I had to go into town to use ⸻ce's telephone. I embrace Tolga and thank him. He's ⸻r me out about an investment.

⸻le gem?" he asks Bartu.

"My sister," I say. "Sevinç, come up and be kind."

"A lovely little girl," Tolga says.

"In some ways, I agree," I say.

Sevinç won't look at him directly after that, and he laughs and pulls us along to a grill and flame pit with a few other guests surrounding it. Steaming plates of köfte and pilaf are passed around. We all sit on a few cushions and rugs Tolga's strewn about his jeep. Bartu presents a bottle of rakı. People are talking and laughing. Sevinç keeps nibbling at her piece of meat, though the food is good and generous.

"Where are your manners?"

"Who is that?" she asks, motioning with her gaze at Tolga.

"He's helping me buy some pasture land and bikes."

"But Dad will give you the paddocks when he retires."

"Dad's not retiring anytime soon," I say.

"Of course not. You're not ready to take over."

"I know a few things, some things even Dad doesn't know."

She laughs sharply. "Dad knows all the techniques."

"Is that why he still does things the way they did before electricity?" I ask her. "Is that why we are poor and getting poorer?"

"Things are hard sometimes for everyone."

"Ah, what do you know. Lots of nothing you keep tied down up there." I tap my finger to my head.

She tuts at me and slaps at my arm but does so quickly and goes back to eating when Tolga looks over.

"What's he want to help you for anyway?"

I don't tell my sister, but Tolga might not help me at all. He's made a few vague promises, but Tolga isn't a charity. He expects me to come up with a share of the money. He knows I've got to have skin in the game. So I'm here with my bull a year or two early, hoping to win.

In the main clearing, a waist-high chicken-wire fence circles stamped-down dirt. Behind the fence, men and women sit in folding chairs and on cushions and rugs while they watch the tournament. Most everyone is wearing slacks with a few holes or long dresses tattered at the hems, shirts and sweaters with snags. There are a few tarps thrown up for shade.

Beyond the rugs, wealthier families have drawn up their flatbed trucks as elevated stands. They plant their fat bodies in folding chairs on the beds. The older women wear their bedsheets around their heads. A large flag of Atatürk in his kalpak hangs from a small construction crane behind the trucks. The countryside, full of trees and fields and hills, settles down for a nap under thin silver clouds lit by the afternoon sun.

Inside the ring, the bulls teeter their shoulders and haunches like the pistons in a motor. Like zeppelins, they boom their presence around the perimeter of the wire. Aariz, the official, guards himself with a stick as short as his arm. He wears an orange towel wrapped around his head as his mark of authority. Aariz and the other officials help keep two eight-hundred-kilogram ferocities from colliding with planetary inertia. Pressed up against the wire are the bodies of eager boys with fascination stuck on their faces. Nervous men with bets at stake stand with them, their impatience squeezing hands against the fence. I play with a string of evil eyes I bought from a vendor.

The bulls' horns are all ground down to little nubs to keep them from goring each other. It's prudent; these bulls are expensive to keep and many of them have work roles on their farms and ranches. It _____ financially ruinous to lose a bull. There's respect for them _____ —unlike dog or rooster fights, it's not about wounding _____ it's about bravery, standing their ground. They try _____ h like in a game of chicken, and the first to do

"Which is yours?" Tolga asks me.

"The black one."

"With the white ridge?"

I nod. "Sevinç calls him Domuz."

"Because he eats like a pig," she says to him, and grins.

Six months ago, I tied my bull by each leg to the beams of my father's little barn while he was still just a yearling. He shook some. I picked up a wooden plank from my father's scrap pile. The surface was rough. I whipped the plank across my bull's backside and stood clear as his limbs and head rattled around trying to break free of the ropes. It's how we get them ready for these fights, how we get them used to standing still, used to becoming like stones. Months ago, my bull was still writhing about each time I roped him into place in the barn. His guts expanded against his furnace-ribs and bellowed out hot grunts of air. I'd grab up the plank and start with pats against his haunches, then swing a little harder and harder still, hoping to work up to sounds too like loud slaps against sheet metal, but he never sat still long enough, so I spent the evenings running a coarse brush over his chest to calm him down.

A month ago, I'd ditched the plank and started standing in front of him, staring into his eyes, trying to excite and anger him, and played the games of wolves that hover over carcasses. I'd swipe a towel across the barn floor and kick up the dirt and stamp my feet, and my bull would do the same, and he'd shoot taunts from his snout so that I would charge him. And I did. I'd fan out my arms and yell and run up right to his nostrils to get him to shudder. Until a week ago, he had never stood his ground. I only weigh seventy-seven kilograms. Others train their bulls to be intimidating; they feed them into monstrous sizes and make them vicious creatures. The trick, though, is to make them comfortable with threats so they don't move. A bull trained to react to everything with aggression is unpredictable, just as likely to jump back as to charge, but a bull unfazed by other bulls won't go anywhere.

I pray for my bull to win, and repeat it for each evil eye on the loop. The bulls acknowledge each other with hisses from their nostrils, but they have not yet settled, not yet agreed to play the game.

Aariz, the official, steps back from between the bulls and the animals are free. They orbit around each other. My competitor's bull has charms tied around its shins. The crowd counts one. The bulls stop turning. They stand rigid, and I can see the grooves of strained muscle on their thighs and shoulder points and necks. The animals stare at the crest of the other's neck. Their penises are erect. The crowd counts two. My bull's back leg retracts, childish, a faltering toothpick underneath a cooked roast. I scream at him, and I can feel the rough grain of the plank in my hand, its fibers like a carpet. I almost pull the loop of evil eyes apart. I fall against the wire fence and make it droop, and I've lost the hopes of buying my own paddocks. I can see in Domuz's back leg the shiver of fear, and I know he will not charge.

The crowd screams and keeps on screaming, but at nothing in particular. Aariz does not notice my bull's flinch, and I am saved from disqualification. My bull settles, and his ears are back, and I clench my jaw like his. The weight of his muscles pours into the top arch of his neck, and he trips forward. The other man's bull reels back on its hind, then comes down hard, kicking up the dust on the trees and the shoulders of the crowd, and the crowd counts three. My bull, head lowered beneath the other's chest, loses confidence and the other man's bull routs mine back to the wire.

But Aariz has ended the match. The second official waves a stick at the other bull's tail, and the third official runs to stop my bull from jumping into the side of a truck. Aariz caught the other bull's slight flutter and disqualifies him for moving backward. My competitor screams over hands exchanging money. I release the breath I'd forgotten pent up in my lungs. The two young officials chase after Domuz, the bull now caught in the fence. I can hardly believe it. Bartu doesn't bother with glasses. We drink our celebration from the bottle.

❧

MAYBE SIXTY WOMEN are here today, and all of them cover their heads in self-respect. I want to throw that in Kaan's face but he's busy leading Domuz. Tolga, Bartu, and their commotion tag along. Tolga has given me fifty kuruş to buy simit from a vendor and I think to do so just to share it with him. Tolga is much taller than Kaan, and clean-shaven. He wears his hair long and swipes it back with his slender hands before he smiles.

"Sevinç," Kaan calls. "Sevinç, hurry up."

Kaan begins to tie Domuz up to one of the trees again. He gives Domuz plenty of slack to graze when he's hungry. Bartu hurries to grab the pitchfork and scatter hay around the tree. For fifty meters in all directions, dark trees anchor a herd of bulls like thin fingers holding on to black balloons.

"Come closer and listen," Kaan says to me. "I want you to sit with the bull."

"He smells awful, Kaan. You sit with him."

"The bull likes you, he is calm with you. He's too flighty today, and I need you to calm him down before the next round tomorrow."

I tell him I don't want to and I don't understand why he wouldn't stay with his own bull. He tells me Tolga and he must talk through things. I want Tolga to stay with me, and Bartu and Kaan can go talk through things.

"What things?"

"Business," says Bartu. He smells like the bulls.

Kaan shoots him a look. "Things for men."

"I thought you wanted me to expand my understanding," I say.

"You're still too young for some things," Kaan says. The three men start walking up the hill deeper into the forest.

"It is hypocrites like you," I say. I can't finish my thought; my voice leaves me.

Kaan turns back to me and walks slow, deliberate. I try to move away from his path but his hand grabs my arm, and again the pressure pales my skin as he drags me in front of the stupid bull and sits me down in the hay.

"Kaan," says Tolga. "She's just bored, poor girl." Tolga looks at me with pity and I feel younger, little, small. "We should celebrate today, huh? You take things too seriously all the time." He calls out for Kaan once more. Kaan returns to them. They disappear into the forest, lighting cigarettes as they walk.

Dried circles of dirt cling to Domuz's matted hair. I slide alongside him and sit in the hay. I try to pick out the dirt but he doesn't let me. I pet his head and ears. I keep brushing his ears back, and Domuz huffs and lays his head down. His head is as big as my torso. The rope tugs at the skin around his neck. He looks curious, but he's just a bull. I think then for a moment to untie the rope, just to give him a little more room for rolling around.

Domuz looks up over the small hill at a sound like laughter. There's the sound again. I think it's Tolga. He's probably told a joke he finds very amusing. I'm sure it is amusing. Then I can hear the rhythmic sounds of people talking, muffled, and far away. I find myself gone from Domuz's side, crawling up the shallow hill to take a peek. I want to join them, not because I will find their talk interesting, and not because I am lonely left here with Domuz, but because I want to see Tolga laughing. I want to watch him smile generously. I think he's handsome and imagine us beside each other tonight, laughing around a campfire. And then these thoughts strike me as foolish, childish, and I'm reminded again of my age, a strange beam between childhood and adulthood I'm left straddling. I want to join the men on the other side of the hill, but Kaan will grab my arm and drag me back to my spot in the dirt next to his bull. Yet perhaps Tolga would stop him. Perhaps he would scoot over to make room for me around the fire now lifting smoke in thin slices up the channels of the forest canopy.

⚡

"FEISTY ISN'T THE right word," I say.

"She's a pain in the ass," Bartu says.

Tolga laughs hollow but only for Bartu's sake. I agree, though, and tell them how she pines over the shit my father says, buying into the politics of ignorance.

"She's just got too much conviction for Kaan," says Tolga.

Bartu's laughing almost every chance he gets, and I wonder if he's had too much rakı, if Tolga's had any.

"Blindness is all it is."

"And you've learned so much in the West," Tolga says to me. "I don't wish any bad blood, Kaan, but you must let her decide for herself the customs she desires."

"But how can she choose with only the knowledge of a single option?" I say.

I know Tolga wants to say I too am ignorant, too concerned with my own discontent at the way of things, but Tolga is smart, quiet, and nods.

"Honestly, I'm wondering about Sevinç," says Tolga.

"She's half your age," I say, knowing how Tolga means it, and I feel bile swelling in my throat.

"She's growing up."

"Not grown yet," I say.

"Maybe, maybe," Tolga says, smiling. "Your father ought to start looking for a man." Bartu can't help but laugh about that.

"She can find her own man."

"There are some things that just must not change," Tolga says. "Perhaps I can talk to your father about her as well."

"You'll come to regret it, my friend. I won't abandon my sister so easily."

Tolga has a hollow laugh. "I am only teasing you. Oh, Kaan, you are a funny man. Your sister must be her own woman except if it offends you. You're too easy to tease."

"We all have our blind spots."

"Speaking of blindness, your father still refuses to sell me any land. I've offered more than it's worth, and I've offered to buy the sheep along with it, yet he says he will not sell. Meanwhile, even from my house all those kilometers away I can see your place is in disrepair. In the village everyone says things aren't going well for you."

Tolga is right about my family and the ranch. We are hemorrhaging money and it's my father's fault. He drives the sheep south in the winter, renting depleted crop fields for them to graze. With proper housing and straw supplies, we could keep the sheep nearer to our land and save on renting out poor fields of stubble in the winter. I mention this sometimes, but he tells me that his own father did it this way for a reason, that his grandfather did it this way for a reason too. He asks me if I truly think I'm the first person out here to want to change everything.

I shake my head. "He won't retire. He'll die in the pasture twenty, thirty years from now." I can't wait that long. I can't keep watching him impoverish me, my sister, our futures. I have plans. I have my own hopes. I have half a degree.

"But then it will all be yours," says Tolga.

I take the rakı bottle from Bartu and drink. Tolga's smart. He makes me an offer: if my bull wins the fights, and I put up the prize money, he'll buy me my own pasture, my own sheep. He'll pay for winter housing for the first two years. He'll pay for hay, and alfalfa, and even corn to feed during the snows. He'll get me a motorbike, and Bartu will help me tend the sheep in the pastures. He says for all of this, I'll give him my father's land when he dies. He says it's a good deal, and I'll take it because I am under my father's thumb and I can't stand it.

The land is worth more, but my father's reckless and getting worse. He's using farmland as pasture land, and isn't bothering to grow his flock. By the time he dies, he'll have racked up so much debt the bank will own everything. I say this to Tolga. "There won't be much land left when he gives up shepherding." I say it almost to convince Tolga it isn't worth it, almost to change my own mind.

"All the better for you," he says.

I nod.

"Then we have a deal, my friend. All that's left is for fat Domuz to win." Tolga has another hollow laugh about that. We shake hands. I pray my bull can go on to win.

"Ah, it is too late, but I should have negotiated your sister into the bargain," Tolga says with a very clean smile.

Bartu splits his sides and shoves an enormous laugh through his tight mouth.

I grimace. I search for my cellphone. Empty pockets—I swear the next time I'll bite off my pinky to remember.

Tolga grins. "It was just a joke, Kaan."

At the top of the slope behind us, outlined by the generator lights of the camp, a small minaret of purple cloth pokes above the mangy grass—Sevinç.

I jump up, knocking the empty bottle over. The bulb of cloth disappears down the other side, and I run up the hill, my boots slopping a suction pop through the mud. At the top I lose my balance a moment and realize how much I've drunk. I think people are saying things to me; I can hear them not very far away. At the base of the hill, Sevinç scrambles to get her lap under my bull's head. She's petting him and watching me with wide eyes hiding under her scarf.

"What're you doing?" I ask.

I don't let her answer. I stumble down the hill, the uneven ground and the rakı tripping me up on my way. I can hear Bartu behind me saying to bring more rakı from the car. Sevinç stretches her arms over my bull's neck, fastening herself to him.

"Is he calm?" I ask, a little way from her.

She nods at me, lying. My bull's back legs are already tense. His eyes train on me, and, in a trance, I sprint the rest of the way, rushing the two of them, yelling that Sevinç is an eavesdropper.

My bull doesn't move even though Sevinç is nervous next to him. Her body rattles up against his shoulders. I run right up to Sevinç. She stares at my boots, tightening her grip on my bull's neck. I crouch down, trying to look her in the eyes, but her eyes are slippery and hard to hold. "Were you eavesdropping?"

"No," she whispers.

"Are you a liar?"

She can't say anything. I ask again, but she remains quiet. I pat my bull's head and go to the car. I grab more alcohol and some rope. Bartu and Tolga have come at the sound of my shouting and are waiting by the bull for me.

"No," Sevinç says. "I swear I'm not lying."

"I told you to stay with the bull."

"I am. I did. I'm not going anywhere. Domuz is quiet, see?"

"Stop this," Tolga says, more like a question, wondering what's with the rope.

"Hands out," I say to Sevinç. She's reluctant, worried what'll happen if she shows me her palms and what'll happen if she doesn't, but in truth I'm not sure of what I'm doing. I'm not thinking about the next step because I'm worried. I'm not thinking about how I'm reaching for her wrists now to tie her to the tree because it could still just be an act, I can still stop.

"I'll stay put," she pleads.

"What're you doing?" Tolga asks.

I tell him and Bartu not to worry. Sevinç hides her fingers in my bull's coarse hair. I snatch her wrist up and start looping the rope around it while she wriggles her whole body to get it free. I have to sort of sit on her to keep her steady. Domuz isn't moving.

"I hate you. I hate you."

"When will you learn?" I ask her.

"What sort of brother have I got?" she shouts at me. "A pretender. Progressive, sophisticated. Ha! You pretend all these things even while tying me up, huh? Is this how to treat modern women?"

Tolga says something I don't hear over my sister's shouting. Everything feels slow and drowned out. I can't bring myself to make another loop around her wrists.

She says I am a tyrant to do this to her, that I am evil to abandon my father, and I feel this fuse in my spine catch and crackle up to my brain where it becomes heat in my throat, my nose, the sockets of my eyes. She says that I should just go back to Istanbul, that I should leave before Dad finds out the kind of man I am. She says it was stupid of me to come back if all I want is our father dead and his land in my pocket. I pull hard, burning her with the rope. She lets out her whine. "What did you hear?" I ask.

"Stop this, Kaan," Tolga says. "She'll be fine."

"What did you fucking hear?"

Sevinç cries as I wrap up her other wrist. The color leaves her skin and I hesitate.

"Kaan, cut it out," Tolga says.

"She'll tell my father about this. Think I'll still inherit anything then? Do you think he'd be happy I'm making deals to sell his land?"

"It would only break his heart," Sevinç says.

I laugh at that because it catches me off guard. I laugh because I hate my father and now this weird sense of pity strikes me that has nothing to do with him. I'm hurting my sister and all she thinks about is him, and it makes the ground tilt under me—I can't explain.

"Kaan. Kaan, she won't tell." Tolga keeps on talking and Sevinç keeps on shouting, but I let go of the rope. My bull is sitting still. The whole time he hasn't flinched. I think maybe he can win after all. I unwind the rope from Sevinç's wrists.

I crouch beside her. "Listen," I say. "Listen, can you listen?"

Sevinç settles a little.

"Can you pay attention? You know me, Sevinç. I won't tie you up. But you have to do something for me."

Sevinç slaps me across the face. I'm drunk and the sensation of it stays put on my cheek, the tingle. She slaps me again, not as hard, and then she's smacking my shoulder and arm with successively weaker blows until tears come to her eyes and she stops.

"Listen close. I'm sorry."

Sevinç sucks in deep breaths like she's drowning.

"Listen to me. I'm sorry. Now promise me you won't tell Dad."

"Be reasonable," Tolga says to Sevinç.

She watches Tolga nod at her, coaxing her to agree.

"I'm not abandoning anyone. I'm not leaving you," I say. I am here for her. I am back to save her from my father. That is what I have told myself over and over again but now I'm not sure how true it is.

"Fine," she says.

I reach out to pull her head close, to kiss her forehead, but she jerks away. She won't look at me now, she won't meet my eyes, but I am satisfied. Sevinç isn't one to lie. I go to Tolga, picking up the new bottle of rakı. Bartu's already disappeared, likely trying to find some food or a woman. The smell of fires fills the forest, and the rakı will soon taste like a lullaby.

⁊⋞

THE MEN SLEEP with their arms tucked around their chests for warmth. Kaan lies across the bench seat of the truck with an empty bottle between the pedals. Bartu is in the bed of it, his arm propped straight up by the side. Tolga has a tent to himself. Inside there must be a dozen carpets to keep him off the dirt, and a dozen pillows to pick from. He turned out the two lanterns on the beams a few hours ago. Someone burns incense.

The bulls, too, are sleeping. Their exhales rumble like muted thunder. The northern hillside is spotted by the dark bodies rising and falling with lazy breaths. Kaan expects me to sleep here in the hay with Domuz. There isn't room for me in the truck. I could crawl to Tolga's tent and sneak through the flap. He would understand. I can't sleep in the mud. Here. He'd point to a large sleeping bag laid out atop a thick cushion. Tolga would tell me I'd had a tough day and he'd make me tea. *Dad really isn't such a bad man,* I'd say. *I know,* he'd say. *Dad just wants the best for us,* I'd say. *I want the best for you,* he'd say. He'd use his slender fingers to brush the bit of dirt from my cheek, tenderly.

I am careful shifting around Domuz so he won't startle. I'm worried the other bulls will wake and start bellowing. I crouch low, bending so carefully I hear my knees creak in the still night. The stars are sleepy behind the treetops.

The rope is still slung, painful, around Domuz's neck. I check my wrists for marks, but I can't see any in the dark. What kind of brother do I have? Love for him is what others call oppression, and oppression what others call love. I nestle myself into the curve of the bull and think of the star on the Turkish flag, protected by the crescent. I scratch with light fingertips the scruff of Domuz's chin and draw a line down his throat to the base of his neck. I hook my finger in the rope. Domuz opens his eyes, and I jump, and he startles because of me. But I calm him before he can make too much noise. His smell bullies out the incense, and he shoots his breaths at me. I call him fat and smile. I pet at his fur and hum a little melody made up on the spot.

I pull at the rope. Domuz shifts his weight around and leaves his eyes on me, and it feels heavy to be watched by the bull. It feels the same kind of heavy to be watched by Tolga. But what is he doing now with my brother? He looks kind and gentle, but he is making a secret deal with Kaan. I couldn't hear it all. I didn't understand it all through the sounds of the forest and the camps, but the two of them were plotting against my dad. I want to tell Tolga I love my dad, so that he will stop his secrets with Kaan, so that Kaan will leave our dad alone. I want Dad to drive Kaan away, back to his precious Istanbul, his precious life across the country from here, back to where he is safe from insulting us and cutting open our hearts to bleed away.

I bring my hand around to the knot on the rope. Gingerly, I pry at it with my fingernails. I'm careful not to rile Domuz. It takes minutes before the rope slacks and unwinds. In the moments afterward, I stare back at the tents and cars to make sure Domuz is all clear. I tell him to run. I tell Domuz not to play these games anymore. I hit Domuz on the hind end, and he grunts. He pours the heat from his exhale over the cool earth and he stands up. He matches the night with his black hair. I hit him again but he doesn't move from my side. I pick up a stick and poke him with it and lead him farther into the forest, but still Domuz won't leave me. I snap the stick across his hind end, and Domuz starts off on a trot into the trees, and I imagine he'll continue until the trunks become so dense he can't squeeze through them. He disappears and I stay looking into the night for a long while.

I Am My Country

WE SLIPPED THROUGH the city in an old taxi, under booming streetlamps that devoured the night. Jet lag dripped from the corners of our eyes. My mom cooed at my brother and me nestled under her arms, just the three of us. Beside us, the water of the Bosporus stole by—silent as blood through the body, dazzled by the glint of Istanbul. Already, along the avenues and squares, the street vendors were unpacking their carts.

I drank in images through heavy eyes. If you looked carefully, you could see the silhouettes of domes and minarets, of high-rises and palace towers, of castle spires and suspension bridges, all like paper on the horizon. Horses pulling carts passed us. The cabbie tootled the horn. The masts of a thousand and one sailboats swayed slowly in the water.

My older brother whispered things in his sleep. The taxi dipped into alleys that splayed like irrigation ditches through Istanbul. We would soon be at my grandma's apartment, stuffing our mouths with watermelons, worrying over the fates of seeds in stomachs. Our aunts and uncles, still children like us, will come with the sunrise. We'll play games I don't appreciate because I'm the youngest. We'll speak the private language we share that none of my classmates back home, or the saleslady at Macy's, or the bagger at the supermarket understand, the language only my family seems to know.

It took me a long time to realize my father had an accent, my mother too. It took me a long time to understand what it meant that my father couldn't pronounce the letter *w*. Childhood friends of mine laughed about this, asking if he was from another planet. I didn't want to sound like him. I wanted to sound like a person that knew their language.

We slept from morning to evening the first day. All my relatives were out of the apartment running errands by the time my brother and I woke up. There was no television, so from the living room windows we watched sleepily, as if in a dream, the people in the road below.

A man sat on the bench in the street, the sun flat over Istanbul. He wore nothing but his boxers and a cap, and his fat belly sat plump over his lap. A few meters from him, children in bathing suits played with a hose, their mothers watching from balconied apartments. The air smelled of hot, stale water. It smelled like the sprinklers that shoot into the street in our neighbor's yard in Kansas. The old man on the bench peeled oranges. The sun illuminated his round belly, skin tight over the fat. His hands were getting sticky from the rinds. There was a shout of children's laughter. I looked and, in my mind, I expected to see the swing hanging from the tree beside our driveway, but there were no trees in the street. When I looked back at the old man, I was left watching our neighbor in Kansas, sitting on his porch shucking corn.

WE ALWAYS WENT to Istanbul a few weeks ahead of my father, and stayed a few weeks after. Phone calls from Dad came at strange hours then. Mostly it would be afternoon, and he would joke that on his end it was only morning, he was getting ready for work. But sometimes from the shop below the phone would wake us, ringing through the pitch of night. My mom would throw on a robe and grab the key the shopkeeper left her. I would listen through the floor of my bedroom and hear her ask how work was as though he was just finishing up at the clinic at this hour.

To make a call back to Kansas, we had to take a few lira notes down to the shopkeeper in the basement of the apartment building. In Kansas, there were two phones, one in my parents' room and one in the kitchen, and we didn't have to pay for them. The shopkeeper said it would take a few minutes for the phone to warm up and that I should play with his daughter while I waited. She was beautiful— teeth like pearls and gilt-gossamer eyes. I thought of my brother telling me I had ugly eyes like our dad, ugly eyes for a girl.

While I waited for phone calls, I would go out the back door to the alley with the shopkeeper's daughter. I carried the ball and the toys because she had to cling to the wall for her lame leg. We rolled the ball back and forth. If she missed it, she would take a long while to limp after it. It upset my stomach to watch this. Soon I ran down the ball for her. Soon I gave her the prettier dolls.

I went to the shop and asked for one phone call please, just so I could play with the shopkeeper's daughter for a change from my brother, my aunts. The shopkeeper came out and said the phone was ready. I placed calls to made-up numbers. One time, after playing with the shopkeeper's daughter, I dialed my dad. He mumbled sleepily; he sounded like he was watching TV from another room. I asked him if he was a good doctor.

"Maybe."

"Can you fix what's wrong with the shopkeeper's daughter?"

"Don't be a jackass. There's nothing wrong with her."

I wondered if he couldn't see the limp, or if he even knew the shopkeeper had a daughter.

————

MY BROTHER WOULDN'T touch his bowl of cereal. "It tastes different," he said. "The milk here is wrong."

Putting on her robe, my anneanne came from the hallway with her face screwed up. "Wrong? What's wrong with the milk?"

In English, he said, "I don't like it here. The milk's gross. And it isn't even working. I'm supposed to be strong."

"What's wrong with your boy?" Anneanne asked my mother.

"Does American milk make you strong?" my mom asked. "If you had American milk, would you eat your cereal?"

My brother nodded. He loved complaining. He thought he'd found his ticket to complain our whole visit.

My mom went downstairs to the shopkeeper's phone. She called my dad without having to wait or pay. She talked fast and said that their son needs American milk or he will never be a strong weight lifter, a strong wrestler, a strong boxer.

TANKERS SLICED THROUGH the Bosporus as we took a cab back through the streets to the airport—this time in the light of day, this time without jet lag so that all the shapes of buildings, ruins, palaces were crisp, sharp enough to cut your finger. Men at every corner sold kebabs and roasted nuts and ice cream and simit.

It was my mom and my grandpa and me in the back of the cab. My mother wore a scarf over her hair for style, a taffeta dress beneath her raincoat so that she looked like those women who cry at airports in movies. But she wasn't crying, the sun was out, Dad was arriving, not departing. Clucking his tongue, Büyükbaba told the cabbie to stop at this grocer for a moment. He went in and came back out with a large paper sack. In the car, he peeled labels out from the bag. I thought I saw milk jugs.

We pulled into the waiting area at the airport. The windows were down and everyone in the car smoked. Büyükbaba stepped out of the cab with his paper sack and whistled. We looked out the right side. My dad—in a sweater with his raincoat on his arm, with prickles around his jaw, with his briefcase and suitcase—walked out into the daylight, squinting. He looked old. I realized then that my dad was much older than my mom. When I will tell people later that my grandpa and dad served in the army together, they'll ask if he bought my mom. I won't understand.

My dad embraced Büyükbaba, and they put his bags in the trunk, but not before Büyükbaba put the sack of milk bottles in Dad's suitcase.

A WEEK LATER, we took a bus to Antalya along the south coast of Turkey. I slept most of the trip while my mom and dad smoked, and my brother played tricks with the other children. I'd wake up, still asleep, and see some young girls, a little older than me, sell treats up and down the aisle. The bus driver's son was on his lap, smoking a cigarette, hands at the wheel just under his father's hands. People departed along the way, at each stop we'd lose a handful of passengers until it was just us and an old man near the back.

In Antalya, we had lunch with a friend of my father's from his days in the army. After the meal, we boarded his boat for his house in Cyprus. It was a long trip that proved to me the immensity of the sea. We drifted into Cyprus under the high mantle of night. The town was dark. We carried our luggage up a slender staircase crammed with golden light from a single bulb at the apex. I pleaded for a party, but everyone was tired. "And besides," my dad said to me, "there's no booze."

From the balcony of the house the next morning, I could see all of Cyprus. It was still too early for my mom and brother to get out of bed. I sat on the balcony of the house with my dad and his friend with the boat, all of us in our pajamas, drinking orange juice, eating cherries, spitting the pits over the railing, trying to hit the passersby who lived here.

"What do you think of Turkey?" my dad's friend asked. His name was Rüstem and he had an oiled mustache.

"My dad says it is Cyprus."

Rüstem looked at my dad, who shrugged and sipped his morning coffee. Rüstem wore a gold chain at his neck; his white chest hairs would catch between the links and I worried they hurt, but he didn't seem to mind. Rüstem pointed toward a fence in the distance. "Over there is Greece, and over here is Turkey." Soldiers walked the fence. People here worried about fences. "They think they should make this island a province of Greece. They think since I am Turkish my voice matters thirty percent and theirs seventy."

"If that's the way the votes work," said Dad.

Rüstem huffed, patted his chest, and left to buy more cigarettes.

"It's British, the island," my dad told me, always ready with a history lesson. "It was. Now it's Cypriot, which is Greek and Turkish both, which is perverse in the eyes of people who think a thing can only be one thing."

"How can it be everything?" I asked.

"There are things in this life that mean a great deal on paper that will mean nothing to God."

I wanted Dad to stay in this moment with me, to stay seated on the balcony in his undershirt and his trousers stained with sticky cherry juice, to stay still until I was old enough to understand his riddles. I didn't like these games, these things he'd say. They were of the world of adults, where a sentence you speak can mean seventeen different things. I wanted Dad to explain who I was. I wanted Dad to tell me if God was Turkish, if that meant God wasn't in America, if that meant we were lost souls outside of our summers. Despite my age, I wanted to understand these labels, to be a part of them, affix them around my neck like bricks so that I would stay grounded—I had in me a great worry of floating away in the breeze that did not worry these adults. But I knew things only in concrete terms. Of Turkey, I knew the cherry pits, the white-sliver cigarettes, the gold chain in the morning sun. Of Kansas I knew the grid roads, the prickle-wheat, the inky clouds like watercolors.

I blamed my dad for a long time after this, I blamed him for leaving me behind as he spoke, I wanted him to stay there and wait for me to grow up, but what sense could he have made to me?

※

IN COLLEGE, I worked the help desk at the library because I thought I would meet people. No one ever needed help so I reshelved books to pass the time, books I would never read, books on horticulture, geodes, Soviet society. No one ever checked out novels at the state ag school.

I passed the time teaching myself about Turkey. Reading about Istanbul was like reading about myself. Reading about Turks was like fortifying my own Turkishness. Reading a line like "In 1561, Sultan Süleyman had his son executed for treason" and thinking: *I didn't know that about myself.* How do you explain this to someone who isn't bisected?

In one of the study alcoves at the library, I watched a man read maps with his fingers. His name was Max. He wasn't blind, he just knew this was the way to read maps; he said they had to be felt, traced by the tips of your fingers. He stayed like that for a long time, turning pages slowly—with pages that large, that heavy, you could rip little lines along their edges with fast movements. He looked so intent, I worried if I turned my back he would disappear into the topography of the Sinai.

Not long after we started dating, Max said he loved my family. "They have history."

"We've only just immigrated."

"But they know where they come from." He said it was good to know your port of origin. He loved asking me questions like who built the Blue Mosque? How did the carved heads of Medusa end up in the sunken cisterns? Have I ever walked the city as an act of inheritance?

For a long time, he would sneak into our bedroom when my mother called. He'd pick up the second receiver, covering the mouthpiece with his hand, his breath making dewy the peaks of his knuckles. We spoke in Turkish about our days, errands we were running, who we saw at the supermarket. Eventually he stopped hiding. He'd pick up the receiver and sit on the couch with me and watch me talk with my mother about this and that, about Dad, about prayers. He liked listening to my language. He told me each time I spoke Turkish was a ritual in communicating with the dead. He told me I must hold on to that in this country where we can barely communicate with each other. He doesn't get upset when I tell him through a smile that history is boring, when I doodle sailboats over the maps in his issues of *National Geographic,* but I can tell it drives him crazy. I am his country and he will not betray me.

"Take a look at this," Max said.

On the table sprawled a large sheet of paper, a phone book, an atlas of the Balkans, a Turkish-to-English dictionary, a book on the Ottoman Empire, a book on Islam, a book on this and that and some other thing, so many books he'd ordered from libraries far away. He told me he'd been working on a project, been calling everyone we know on my side of the family. This was it, he'd compiled a history of the Duysak family. There was a tree, there was an annotated map, there was a list of names I'd heard before in dreams or memories hanging like apples from this tree.

1. Great-great-great-great-grandfather Ahmet, efendi of Monastır. Ruled for three years before being killed by his brother, who ruled perhaps more justly.
2. Great-granduncle Mehmet, imam of Monastır. Promoted on merit. Engaged more in politics than religion. Instrumental in a settlement between Christians and Muslims in the town. Would later be killed by Serbs in the First Balkan War.
3. First cousin twice removed Captain Hayrettin. Fought in Damascus against the British. Sad end in Iskenderun.
4. Third cousin Kırk Caylan. In railroads. Acquired a small fortune before distributing equally among his four spendthrift sons.
5. Grandfather Orhan Sezik. Tank driver turned taxi driver after the Second World War.

No one has the name Duysak. Max tells me that it was given to my dad in 1934. He went to the name bank and applied for a last name when the government made residual titles illegal. On my mom's side, he said, there was an imam of Yerebatan Sarayi who served the sultan.

"Did you know there's a statue of your dad?"

I laughed. "Did he and his friends make it and put it in a square?"

"He was the mayor of Gölmarmara," he said, pointing to a place on a map. All these maps had points on them, had meridians drawn through borders of empire.

My dad had brought electricity to the town while finishing his schooling as a medic for the army. He was made muhtar for a season. This was apparently before his time smuggling American fridges into Turkey for sale on the black market.

"He never told me." And for a moment I hated Max for finding this out from under me.

———

IT WAS THE summer before my last year of college, and I was going to Turkey alone. I might not have really noticed it—after all, Dad only came sometimes, and Mom always stayed in the apartment right next to the window AC—but now in the apartment were only Büyükbaba and Anneanne. My aunts were busy, they lived in Ankara now. They didn't bother using vacation time to come to Istanbul just for me. My uncle, born only a few years before me, was still in the city but had taken over a warehouse through a friend of a friend and lived in the flat above it. He drove me down the Bosporus in his black car he said a friend gave him out of gratitude. We passed the old fortress Rumelihisarı where some fishermen smoked thin cigarettes in the sun. "When will your father come back, huh?" he asked me.

"Dad's busy, you know." Dad hadn't been back for six years. Ultra-nationalists had started disappearing anyone who they thought was threatening Turkishness. People drove past the apartment in a white sedan the last time he was here. We knew they were there to seal him up. They drove slowly, so slow they might have stopped—so slow they could still be there, outside the apartment in Galatasaray.

We passed communist graffiti and my uncle cursed them. "These people have no appreciation for hard work."

My uncle was in plastics or something like that, working out deals with exporters. He was taking me down to his storehouse to sit around with the good Turkish workmen. He said I was getting to be old enough that I ought to be a bride. I was sure my father had told him about Max back at university, but I pretended to be excited about the day ahead anyway, the afternoon spent playing tavla and drinking tea in a plastics storehouse, a few bulbs hanging from high rafters, large loading bay doors flung open to catch the breeze.

We sat around a pallet raised to waist height by a forklift. They had three tavla boards, games going on each of them. I smoked though I knew Max didn't like that side of me. The men in pale-blue-

and-gray coveralls asked me why I wasted such a gorgeous day with them.

"My uncle works so hard," I said, smiling. "If I want to see him, I have to visit his warehouse."

"Can't you just see him after work?" asked one.

"No, she lives in America," said my uncle.

"What's in America?"

"When are you moving back?"

I told them I wasn't moving back; this was my last week in Turkey for a long time, at least until the dust settled. There was an assassination every week. There were groups of students running around with guns and torches, shooting other groups of students. Once in a while a bomb went off in the city. Violent and splintering political factions—ultranationalists, soviets, Maoists, Turanists, Islamists—beat, maimed, and killed themselves as much as one another. My dad had to prescribe anxiety pills for my mom. There were pictures sent in the mail to us by Büyükbaba of neighbors without arms. We passed them across our dinner table as we scooped spoonfuls of peas and mashed potatoes into our mouths; outside the only explosions were thunder and fireworks.

One of the warehouse workers shoved my uncle in jest and said: "Her last week in Turkey and you've got her stuffed in a warehouse."

My uncle brought out a bottle of rakı, and we all drank it warm, without water. More bottles, and we got drunk on a lazy afternoon in Istanbul, with the heat like electricity through the air.

The men said they were getting hungry. We all walked out of the warehouse without bothering to lock up. My uncle had one of them fetch his car and meet us at the restaurant on the corner where he knew the owner. We stuffed our mouths full of pilaf and yogurt and köfte. We drank wine, more wine, then whiskey, and we all realized, together, that it was very hot in the restaurant, that no matter where we were, it would be hot.

The man who fetched the car honked the horn and we all piled in with the roof down, me in the back, sitting on the storage compartment, the restaurant owner climbing in as well, my uncle driving with too much alcohol in him, speeding along the Bosporus and passing other drivers in a way that sent a thrill of shivers through me. At a streetlight, a worker in the back told a joke that had everybody roaring creaky, choked laughs. He was telling another joke when a car pulled up beside us. Suddenly the laughter ended, though the voices were still loud in my ear. My uncle and the workers started arguing with the people in the car beside us. I couldn't tell what about. Drunk, and getting dizzy now, it seemed as if the two cars melted into one with a dozen people packed into it, all of them yelling and cursing, and then one of the other men moved in such a way, flashing a revolver he had tucked under his jacket. In an instant, the two cars split apart once more, and almost everyone shut up, except the one or two people who were still talking were screaming now. The other car tore off down the street, taking with it all the anger and shouting and leaving us here with the end of a joke that had us all croaking our cracked-throat laughter as my uncle sped up the road again.

And just like that it was over. We parked a few blocks from Büyük-baba and Anneanne's house, and the men said that it was time for me to be going.

"Leave those men alone," I said.

"They pulled a gun on us," one of the men said.

"I hadn't noticed."

"You're American," said my uncle. "If I let them, they will keep doing it."

I kicked the side of his car in frustration, leaving a small dent.

The car tore off down the street shaded by tall apartments with clotheslines strung across them finding the breeze in their laundry sails. I stood there on a street corner in Istanbul when the muezzin started calling out on the speakers throughout the city again.

This voice is everywhere, this beckon. The man seems to call to me that I am an impostor. He seems to stretch his voice across the sky to say: "You are not Turkish, look at you jump when I sing, look at the hairs standing on end." And the muezzin is right. There are no minarets in Kansas; I am unused to the swell of prayers. I never asked my father what to do at times like this, these five times a day. They rattle around inside me, these questions for my dad, and they hurt because they have been left unasked for too long and now there is no longer a chance.

MAX WAS AT the airport when I landed, and I fell asleep while he drove. When I woke it was four hours we'd been driving. We sat parked at a small cemetery behind a church no bigger than a combine. He took me through the graves and told me the life each represents, told me his grandfather didn't speak a lick of English. In the church, he showed me the pictures of the men and women who built it, who sawed the panels, hammered the nails, stained the glass for the small window in the steeple, and he told me of the guilt he keeps bottled in his marrow for not being a farmhand like them.

They lived long lives. He took me by the arm through the headstones. The dozens and dozens of stones shared maybe a handful of names; they were all German. Max said they spoke German, even his own father knew a few words as a child, but that ended with him. His grandmother was from Germany. She immigrated when she was twelve and never went back. All their lives these Germans, having come across the world to this bit of earth with sand and limestone, never strayed from their farms. Max looked at me and said in a voice that was somehow both proud and disappointed: "Not like you. You still have a language. You still are a country." His history was over, he said; the line had been severed and he was now nothing but a boy made of Kansas soil.

We went back to our college town. The semester was starting in a few days. Exhausted from jet lag, I must have somnambulated my way into my room and under the covers. Max brought in my suitcases, and made tea, and joined me in bed. He traced the lines of my skin the same way he traced maps. Over my palms, my forehead, the backs of my knees and elbows, he dragged his fingertips. I thought of him melting, becoming water to course through sluiceways carved along my body. In bed, in those moments just before sleep, he would say things, speak sentences I mirrored with my own lips to taste the way they felt in my mouth. Sentences about us, about our own history, our own nationality we could create. I told him ours is a language made up. I told him that in Kansas our muezzin is the tornado siren. He laughed and asked me to keep talking. He loved the thoughts I tucked away, but I didn't say anything more.

AFTER COLLEGE, AND then grad school, we were married on my back porch. Actually, we were married in a courthouse, and then two days later we had a ceremony at my parents' house, with white lace sashes strung between the pillars of the deck and gazebo, and lights on wires around the fence and pool and eaves of the house. His parents didn't hold it against me that it wasn't in a church; at this time what was Islam to them but something that happened elsewhere? Years later, they'll grow scared. After all the bombings, I don't blame them, and I'll think about how we should have been married in a church. I'll think about it as a moment that could have proved I belonged, proved I wasn't going to cover my head, proved I wasn't made from the desert.

I took a job in Kansas City working for an ag company. Plenty of room for growth if you didn't mind being a woman in a man's world, if you didn't mind talking about corn, beans, and sorghum until you had them dribbling out of your ears. We had a boy, and another, and another, and Max stayed home with them. I had the better salary.

I didn't teach my first boy Turkish. I didn't teach the second or the third boy either. I look through a reference book for a word that means the loss of a trait, the end of a string of inheritances passed through generations. At best, my boys will know the words şeker, nasılsın, anneanne, iyiyim, teşekkür ederim—vestigial: having become functionless through the course of evolution.

SNOWFALL THICK AS cotton gathered in my three boys' hats. Huge flakes clung to eyelashes. Max carried the youngest at his side. I guided the other two with draped arms toward the front door of the Athol church just outside Smith Center. The bony stover of the dormant cornfields ran in lines away from the light of the church. Large blades of gold—the light—spread across the night in thick cataracts. Christmas Eve in central Kansas: you could hear the crush of snow, you could taste the numbness of cold, you could smell the starlight on the barren crop rows, you could feel the expanse of the world jump away from you in all directions, a shout filling an infinite jar.

We took our place in the procession sweeping by the pastor, the other members of the congregation, neighbors, relatives—all exchanging greetings, blessings, and words of disbelief at the rate boys grow. I remembered their names, every single name no matter how distantly related. I talked easily and laughed generously and shrouded myself in the local lexicon so no one could suspect Max's wife didn't belong. Not that people stared or avoided my company. Max had always said I didn't need to come if I didn't want. I didn't have a choice, is what I wanted to tell him. But it was a selfish thing too. I wanted to take a peek, I wanted to be a part of a religion that wasn't locked in a jewelry box, or left on the bottom of a bookshelf to collect dust.

We shuffled down the wooden pew, well-polished from use, and sat on a long crimson cushion running its length. I was just short enough that my legs fell asleep if I sat too long between standing songs.

My poor grandmother, if she had seen this: her little girl's little girl standing with these imansız, talking herbicides in buffet lines, eating potatoes and corn with every meal, abandoning her children for an office stuffed with suits. "That father of theirs will have them baptized while you're discussing clients and diagrams," she would say. So what if he did? I think of my father, and him saying along, "So what if he baptized them?" but it is my voice coming through his mouth, and I want to ask him what I am, aren't we something together, outside of us? I should know better, he would say. You and I are the whole of it.

The pastor's voice, like honey, asked us to rise. I made it a point to only sing the songs without Jesus, but in a Protestant congregation these aren't many. I made it a point that my boys followed their dad up for communion while I stayed seated on the crimson cushion, ruddy faces all around passing by, covered in smiles. After the World Trade Center, I will make it a point in my life not to mention the Prophet Muhammad. I will make it a point to vanish my spiritual heritage. If you listen to the blood in my veins, it will sound secular; it is the type of Turks we are anyway. I will spend my life pretending to shirk a religion I was never part of from the start.

I REMEMBER MY father used to growl at covered women. He'd see them on the street in Istanbul, and he'd make coarse noises with the grit of his throat. It hadn't dawned on me that he was Muslim until

I was maybe eleven or twelve and I found in his study a string of prayer beads stuck between the pages of a book. I took the string of beads, hid them in my bedroom so that they could be sought after, so that my dad would ask me where they went and I could ask him what they are, how they operate in relation to the universe. I hoped he would reveal such high regard for them and help me understand. But my father just bought another string of beads. I've looked but now can't find them.

SOON AFTER MY father died of a heart attack, I visited my mother with my three boys to keep her company in that large and empty house. My father had this ability I never fully appreciated to make the house into a reflection of himself. If he was quiet, so was it, no matter how hard you tried to drown it in noise. And if he was loud, or angry, or excited, the house too seemed to vibrate in excitement. And now in his absence so too did the house and all its contents feel absent, ethereal.

The boys, fed and tired from playing, fell asleep watching *Power Rangers*. In the kitchen I helped my mother clean the dishes, and perhaps a bit abruptly I asked her if Turkey is so great, why are we here in Kansas. I asked my mother if I was supposed to hate Greeks, if I was supposed to hate Communists, if I was supposed to hate Islamists. I asked my mother if my ethnicity is a trinket to be displayed in a glass case, or if it is a reliquary-ensconced idol for worshipping, or if it is some simpler else: a freckle on an arm full of freckles. And she knew better than I why I was being blunt—there are questions so large that the only way to ask them is in obtuse ways.

She said she missed Dad, too.

We used to go to Turkey every summer. But after the 1980 coup, we never went back. How is my uncle? How are my aunts? I hear they have children of their own. I wanted my husband to see the sights. He would love the Ayasofya, the Blue Mosque, the cisterns. In an alley crowded by vendors, Max, guidebook in his back pocket, camera slung around his neck, would look at our boys, then back to me. He would give me a look that said: "But why didn't you teach them Turkish? But why did you cut them from your lineage?" He would have said: "You hated not understanding your father, you hated not knowing what he meant on the balcony in Cyprus."

And I would have said: "Don't pretend to know something."

But I still think about it, about my boys asking: "What are they saying? What does it mean?"

❧

SO HERE WE all are in my mother's living room in Leavenworth, huddled around a birthday cake, singing for my oldest boy. His action figures decorate the fireplace. Toy cars line the windowsills like cliffside stunt sets. My husband is putting a Band-Aid on my other boy's shin. My brother is chasing his own kids around the house. My mother is crying tears so small you can barely see them, the burn of the candles glinting the corners of her eyes like remnant riverbeds.

We sing and clap and my boy blows out the candles, and he says that we all ought to go ahead and dig in and he'll join us when he's had time to digest his dinner. I love the way he talks, my little man, only seven years old.

My mother claps her hands together in front of her face, "Ay, my darling," she says. She's still crying the kind of tears like gloss. It's been only three months since Dad died. I pass out the cake. There's a basketball game my husband and my brother shout to each other about. The children scream too, like tinkling cups, like laughter from a copper pot. My mother cleans up the kitchen table. We think of my father.

We have heard recently of Prime Minister Erbakan's policies, his opening of many religious schools, his repression of political parties, the growing concern of his Islamist agenda. Inflation is nearing one hundred percent. Büyükbaba calls to say he sees too many women in headscarves, and my brother laughs with him.

"So what do you care? You're not a woman." I regret this.

"Do you remember what Dad used to say?" my brother asks.

"They cover their heads but not their asses."

We laugh together.

"That was before such tight pants too. Dad knew even then— people are only getting dumber," my brother says, but what he means is he's nauseated about Turkey, about all these changes. What he means is he doesn't want to talk about it though there's everything left to say.

"Do you remember the shopkeeper's daughter?" I ask him.

"What shop?"

"The shop below. You remember. The girl there."

My brother shakes his head.

"She was beautiful. She was my age." I am watching my little boy as I ask this. I am watching him and I think: *The girl was so beautiful, but with that limp in a country like that.* I think about this a lot lately. I think about how she could have been beautiful in America, how she could have been beautiful anywhere else, if only she'd gotten out of that little shop, out of that neighborhood where boys pushed her over to pass their time. For a long time, I was mad at my father, thinking him inconsiderate, negligent of the shopkeeper's daughter. For a long time, I thought him the cruel one, but age has revealed to me I was cruel in seeing something broken rather than something whole. I am old enough to know better, but I will still hold it against my father for not doing something to help her. I know he could have. I hoped he could have.

"I don't remember anyone from the store, just the telephone on the wall, the thick receiver like a nose. You know, in the right light the telephone looked like a face. That's the only face I remember."

"The girl would yell up to us when there was a call from Dad."

My brother laughs and leans in to separate us from the birthday party whirling around the house. "Dad was something. You know he'd call ahead to see what kind of milk I wanted. It tasted strange over there, you know. Not pasteurized or whatever. He'd call and ask me what I wanted and then he'd cross the Atlantic with two jugs of milk in his suitcase. What kind of a man is that, huh? What kind of love is that? Bringing milk through customs. Dad was something."

"Don't be a child."

"What?"

"He never brought any milk. He and Büyükbaba would buy it from a grocer by the airport and put it in his suitcase."

I say this because for him there is a magic still left in his childhood and I am greedy. I want it too, I want that film to stretch over my memories. I say this because for a moment I am angry with him that he so casually holds Turkey in his hands like a precious shell from the shore.

My brother leans back, looks around the room for his own kids. He tuts. "Well, anyway . . ."

Our children are riding on my husband's back across the blue carpet. My mother sits at the table. Pictures in gold frames cover the mantel and side tables. Kansas is a land of vegetables, without fruit; Turkey is just a part of the brain—unrevisited.

Three Parts in Which
Emre Kills His Daughters

{PART I}

HERE IS A man named Emre who lives in the Kasımpaşa neighborhood of Istanbul in a small apartment with two bedrooms—one for him and his wife, Mirhiye, and the other for his three grown daughters, Adalet, Necla, and Ece. Adalet, the oldest, is tall, tall as a tree, with lips that can't help themselves from frowning. Necla, the middle, is dark, much darker than the others, with teeth that gleam like mother-of-pearl. Ece, young and thin with limbs like a sparrow's legs, is just finishing high school.

Today, like any other day, while his colleagues file reports on various insurance claims, Emre is trying to finish reading his book about the brigand Black Mustafa. But Emre must keep shutting his book away in the desk drawer. His supervisor is puttering around the office trying to get reports in early so everyone can go home before the riot police close the block. Emre hunches his shoulders over his small treasure to protect it from his supervisor's gaze, then flips back to his place just as Black Mustafa is laughing at a girl he has snatched up from the nearby village. The girl is trying her hardest to climb a tree and knock free a hive dripping with honey, but the tree is too smooth. She keeps falling, while just beyond the hill, the police are shooting a storm of bullets into the sacks of sand Black Mustafa has dressed up as a decoy gang of thieves.

Emre's supervisor places his hand on Emre's shoulder. "The police are shooting gas into the street," he tells Emre. Looking up from his book, Emre half expects to see sandbag dummies with haphazard grins along the windows of the building, but instead the office has emptied of his colleagues, and even the supervisor has left the floor for the elevator. Along the street, he hears the stray popping of canisters firing from short tubes. Emre keeps his finger in the book and rushes home without even stopping to look at the riot-squad wall. Growls like an earthquake pass through the city. The sun like boards on his back, Emre winds his way around Beyoğlu and cuts through the small stretch of green that is Sururi Park before finally reaching the steps of his apartment building, his lungs rattling like boiling kettles. He slips in the front door and walks in on his daughters arguing.

Young Ece is standing at the kitchen table with a spoon in her hand, waving it wildly overhead. Dark Necla is at the counter stirring sugar cubes into her tea and spinning spools of hair around one finger. Tall Adalet is lying on the couch with her feet hanging over one end and a book held closely to her face.

"It wouldn't matter if you were bald," says Ece. "These guys would pin you down and wrap your head up because they can't control their penises otherwise. In two years, that's where we'll be: squads of men on headscarf patrol."

"So what if a woman wants to cover herself," says Adalet.

"I'm not immodest," says Necla, "but these women are uncomfortable." She gives up the cord of hair in her hand and touches her shoulder like she is cold, like she should be worried someone is watching.

"Necla, you've got good hair," says Ece. "All I'm saying is that if you only concern yourself with how your hair looks instead of the concerns of the country, pretty soon it won't matter because all us women will end up wrapped in veils and scarves looking like round pushpins stuck across Istanbul."

"Oh! with your frenzy," says Adalet over the top of her book, but she is not reading anymore. She can't focus because as preposterous as she finds her sister, there are many sirens pleading down the street, many shouts and broken bones not far from them.

"Jealousy is an ugly shade for you," Necla tells Ece.

Ece is worked up now, talking about chains to beds, multiple wives, child-birthing factories. Emre uses her commotion to tiptoe past the creaky floorboards of the hallway.

"What's all this got to do with a few trees?" Necla asks of the protests happening in Gezi Park, the demonstrations that set Ece to boil in the first place.

Young Ece tells her sisters they don't get it, they've got too much air in their heads. If Necla could look through a window instead of a mirror, if Adalet could read a newspaper instead of a fairy tale, maybe their heads would sink from the clouds.

At first, the Gezi Park protest was a handful of environmentalists preventing the bulldozers from clearing away one of the last strips of grass and trees in the city. Then the students heard, then the antigovernment groups, then the academics and lawyers and journalists, then anyone with a son blown up in Syria, then anyone with a sibling in jail, then anyone who hated the Kurds, then anyone who supported the Kurds, then anyone against animal cruelty, then anyone with a grievance as small as a pothole unfixed in the neighborhood— they all heard that you could go to the square and expel in one grand catharsis every issue taken with the government until one half of the city watched on their televisions the other half of the city shout and chant until their throats were red, and sing songs, and grill kebabs by bonfire as a form of protest.

Ece had never seen anything so beautiful, anything so worthwhile. She is young, after all, susceptible to the heartstring-strokes of freighted moments. Everyone everywhere had dust masks or scarves or shirts tied over their mouths and noses or around their heads. Thousands of phones constantly rang with alerts from Twitter and Facebook. Journalists shouted into microphones as swarms of people with TV cameras captured the boil. Oh was it loud, oh God was it a clamor without bounds that filled you up in the chambers of your heart! Everything seemed grand, as though the protest threw long shadows over the square and its people to make them look giant and changed into a booming magnificence of red sheets, white crescents and stars.

Behind the noise, policemen stood in knots with great gravity, some waiting in blue uniforms and some in black body armor with white helmets and shields, some waiting with truncheons and some with rifles. Their liquid movements were out of a dream. Residual smells of tear gas blew across the square. Behind this, the handful of gray police tanks with water cannons atop their turrets waited in the white sun. She was there, Ece felt so bound up in the television, the headlines, the notifications from social media, the racket rumbling down the street, she felt she was there.

"Stupid girl," Necla says to her younger sister. An ambulance screams by and the three of them measure their breaths.

At first, they don't notice Emre sneaking down the hallway to his bedroom. He throws off his jacket and bag and shuts himself away in his room. Then, Emre's daughters, having sunk into biting silence, hear him sniggering at his book, and they (curious about his early return but equally relieved not to be alone in the house) come scratching at his door, the three of them mewing along the gap underneath, asking him, "Aren't you coming out of there? Tell us what happened at work. What's going on outside?"

He shushes them and sticks his nose right back into his book. The police are on the trail of the brigand, the mountainside erupts in gunfire once more—volleys cut trees and split rocks.

"I have a new dress, Daddy," says Necla. "I had my friend make it, but you'll think it's wonderful. Come look at it. I'm going to have some people over."

"Is Ayla in there with you?" asks Adalet.

"What are the streets like?" asks Ece.

As Emre reads of the brave police captain steadying his rifle, taking careful aim so as not to hit the young girl, who should spring ghostly onto Emre's dresser but Ayla the housecat, cheerful and mischievous. The cat swipes her tail this way, then that. The cat watches him, her mews mixing with the voices of the sisters through the door: "Dad, I said: didn't you bring any more books back from the library . . . ?" "Enough fiction, look outside . . ." "It really didn't cost so much to make, but the pattern . . ."

Craving attention, Ayla the cat stalks over to the flower vase on the dresser and nudges it to the edge. Emre wags his finger at the cat as if she would understand, but she nudges the flower vase again, so he hops out of bed and springs to the cat. "Pesky, pesky," Emre says to the cat as he picks her up, swings open the door, and tosses her into the hall, her mouth opening and closing silently. Adalet catches Ayla as, in a chorus, all three daughters continue their entreaties for their father to join them.

"Where is your mother?" asks Emre.

Emre's wife has gone to the spice market for cloves and cinnamon with the other wives of the building, who will then retire to one of their homes for afternoon tea, their tinkling teacups keeping time with the conversation like a metronome.

The windows shudder in their frames from the force of far-off clashes with police. The daughters—one body with a mess of henna-black hair, three heads, six arms, six legs, six eyes, ninety-six teeth like pearl hammers beating Emre's eardrum—stand in Emre's doorway, demanding his focus, demanding his abandonment of paperback bandits.

"My dress, Daddy . . ." "You promised we could go watch today." "Come read with the cat and me."

"Enough," says Emre to all of them. "Out, out of here. Leave me be, huh? I came home early for peace, and let me have it." He lies down on his bed and starts reading again.

Necla, the middle child, turns immediately, hiding her face from the others, no longer concerned with the flow of her yellow floral dress as she runs out the front door, probably to her friend's apartment. Adalet, the oldest, puts the cat down and follows her sister out of the apartment. Ece goes to the kitchen table to pout, as this is the place with the most commanding view of their home. Like a bellows she will keep huffing, will boil the air between them into thick blocks of suffocation. She finds it distasteful to be so captured by fiction. She shouts down the hall to him that there's a country out there that needs him. All this reading and he doesn't know a thing. She sends him articles and videos and images, but the emails sit unopened. She's asked him to subscribe to a few policy and cultural magazines. Yesterday he promised to take her to the park to watch the demonstrations (she can't go alone, no, they are dangerous). He promised to read her college entrance essay.

Emre is enrapt with the story playing over the black of his mind. He stands in the crowd gathered around the firing squad. The brigand Mustafa is strapped to a post, unblinded, falsely accused of shooting the muhtar. Emre starts to hear a hum—in his kitchen, behind Ece, the refrigerator starts humming. Outside, you can hear the buzz of bees weaving the air. They are hungry. The buzzing swells. Like thick raindrops, dense bees begin pelting the window. It sounds like small shouts. They grow in number until a little cloud of them blocks out the window completely. A grist of bees is somehow leaking through the insufficient squares of the bug screen. They will get in. They are bottling up between the screen and the panes, busy and cramped like a cross-section of a honeycomb. They will press through the glass, squeezing like water drops.

Then they are no longer there; the bees have disappeared. In the room, the humming becomes silent, an apian vibration only felt, imperceptible to the ear. Emre looks back from the window clear as day. He's been turning the pages without reading, and he is filled with that deafening type of silence that comes after listening to something very loud now gone quiet.

"Why don't you come along?" Ece asks. "Don't make me walk the neighborhood alone."

He doesn't say anything to his daughter—did he hear her?

"Don't you care? Are you afraid?"

What could he tell her? She would never understand this small pleasure. Emre's father never learned to read. His whole life he would sit at the breakfast table before going to a job site, watching his wife with the paper, asking *What? What is it?* each time she furrowed her brow or snorted in disgust or approval at the latest political event. He ate each breakfast nervously like he was being left out of a joke. He made Emre read to him at night while his wife cooked dinner. If Emre read too fast and capably, his father would smack the side of his head. His father was dependent on someone else for everything he did not personally experience. Emre reads now with the greed of making up for the poverty inherited, to do with vigor these things his parent could not. How could he say to his daughter: *Dearest, I am full of life.*

"Don't you hear me?"

She thinks about what he might do at the protest in the park. She thinks how out of place her father would look with a mustache and reading glasses and a blazer with worn elbows—lost among the dark bodies painted by the sun, lost among the gyre of the crowd wearing fatal smiles. She's asking him to join her in this ideal, to take an interest, at least for her sake, in the tragedy of their country. *Don't be melodramatic, Ece,* he would say. So she steals one of his paperbacks from the bookcase along the wall and very carefully begins tearing pages from it and ripping them into little squares.

"I'm going to the protests," she says.

Adalet comes through the front door then. She kicks off her shoes and dumps her tote bag on the kitchen table. Ece huffs weaker than her mother's tea. It is a desperate huff, encasing pleas that cannot be translated. There is a dictionary that exists for the performances of the heart, but alas, Emre has not seen this volume.

Adalet takes a novel to the couch where Emre cannot see her. The sky outside is a flawless blue—a promise—above a cloud of fog or smoke in the alleyway. There is the flick of conversation like scraps of paper still in the air, still being thrown at Emre. He's sleepwalking through life, spellbound as he reads. The slam of a door is hardly noticed, and he's alone again.

The phone in the living room rings. Emre puts down his novel and answers. A soft click comes crawling through the receiver. It repeats a few times, then stops, replaced by a pressure. Emre thinks to call out to his wife, but the pressure is distracting, muffling, slipping through his ear and into his throat to silence him. The pressure is cold, smells of snow. The phone clicks again, and the pressure evaporates. There's nothing, not even the sound of a dead line. Emre hangs up. Through the window, he can't tell if it is evening or overcast afternoon, and there is in him a great dread of the passing of time.

Adalet is reclined on the couch. The cat is on her lap, purring.

"What are you doing?" he asks. "What happened to all that talk of action?"

"Huh?"

Emre looks at his daughter, trying to find that greed of life flicker through her.

"Ece's gone. Out the door as I came in."

Emre looks at the cat a moment. He points at Adalet. "You and I were talking."

He thinks to join his daughter in the living room now that she has calmed down, now that she has gone back to their shared pastime. His wife arrives with a bag of groceries and says they are expecting company. A cloud of tear gas quits the alley.

THE POLICEMEN COME for him like any other retrieval, with a few short knocks at the door so that they could be anybody—the building manager or the upstairs neighbor with an extra plate of börek— but no, they are policemen without gifts. They say they are sorry. "Your daughter, Ece, was taken to the hospital in a bad state. There's nothing they could do, you know?"

Yes, yes. Emre must have known that these policemen were coming with malice on their tongues. He wants to tell the two of them that of course he knew his daughter was dead; what kind of a father wouldn't know, wouldn't feel the void the way a sleeping limb has gone dark to all senses? But this is not true. He looks up at the policemen and realizes that he didn't feel a thing in the last few hours but the gravity of a folktale. There is a mistake then, these policemen are at the wrong house, collecting the wrong father. Emre's daughter is still out at the protests, sitting on a park bench in the sun taking in the view, he tells them. "What could she have been doing at a hospital?" he asks them.

The two policemen lift him to his feet and take him to the squad car parked downstairs under the shade of an acacia tree. They take him alone because his wife, Mirhiye, is out somewhere again, temporarily severed from this confusion. A third man is in the car, sitting in the back with Emre, which makes him think about opening the door and flinging himself out onto the highway.

They are at the hospital in no time. They take him to the morgue in the sub-basement where the light feels heavy, poured from a crucible. A doctor and a technician are waiting for him by a metal table where draped under white sheets is the body. The doctor and the technician remove the sheet and ask him if this is his daughter. They tell him how things played out.

With the end of a pen the technician describes the fatal curvature along the body's skull: the impression of a gas canister. With the end of a pen the technician describes the bruising around the ankles. A man dragged her away from the police, by the legs, along the gutter of the street. Everywhere people were dragging bodies with eyes open to the blue-soaked sky. By the scrapes and the damage to the brain they say she must have convulsed the whole time, she must have rattled right there in the gutter.

"Is it because she is young?" Emre asks. "Is it because she is too young, you think? Too young to be going to the protests?"

"Always the young go to these things," says the doctor.

"The old too, though," says the technician.

This can't be his daughter, the first stone of his kidney, lying on a slab of metal before him. His daughter is ferocious, and this body is static. His daughter is surely back at home now, having come safely from the protests. She will be curled up by the AC unit, tearing strips of paper from the pages of a book and holding them up to the light with scrutinizing eyes. Who is this before him? He knows—it is his daughter with her skull caved in, red like a split watermelon in the sun, but there is no room in him for such grief.

NEXT WEEK, EMRE is walking to work. The city is born every morning in the sunlight that blooms over the domes on the Asian side. The glass buildings of the city dazzle high overhead. Emre hums a tune like those of the brigands from his books. He stops in the bakery at the end of his block and buys simit and cheese. Back on the street, their cat, Ayla, mews at him, her tail slinging in slow curves back and forth. Emre tosses her a bit of cheese and tells her to head home, but the day is so lovely that she follows Emre all the way to work.

At his cubicle he hides his book in the open drawer of his desk, stealing time to read it while he hears his coworkers in other cubicles say things like: "The tear gas is incredible." "It's like a village there. All of them acting like Romani, like they've got to be so melodramatic, so sentimental. It makes you wonder, I suppose." "People want to live decently. Is that sentimental?" "They've blocked YouTube. Twitter too." The government will go on to censor newspapers, ban Wikipedia, close up dissident outlets, arrest a few journalists, and play videos of violent protesters on the state-run news channel.

Emre wants to hush up his coworkers, tell them that he can't focus on his book with all their prattling on. Between the cubicles, Ayla slowly pads. The talk dies down when people start to notice Emre. He shuts the drawer and pulls a file from the stack on his desk. He goes over a claim report that has already been read by three others. He's halfway through when his supervisor comes to his cubicle.

"Is this your cat in here? She's terribly loud, you know."

Outside a streetcar shambles by with a screech of its wheels. Taxis zip through alleys. People are talking without care. Somewhere in the city, a person is screaming and waving a flag.

"I know it's a tough time, but there are people here with allergies," says the supervisor.

Emre closes the file, keeps his hands on his desk, and watches his supervisor with a polite amount of attention.

"Really, you should be home, Emre. Think of your family."

Emre thinks of his wife. He thinks she is probably preparing a light lunch right now, still making a serving too many—it has been only a week, after all. But she is not at home; she and some people from the apartment building are going to the supply closet in the basement to look for old pipes, bottles, rags, and gasoline.

{PART II}

IT HAD ONLY been a month before Necla began to throw parties again. They started intimate. At first it was just neighbors, then friends from work or school. They would come in the evenings, after dinner, with bottles in each hand. They drank the wine, then the Scotch, then the rakı. With the wine, everyone laughed, their mouths always open in wide smiles. With the Scotch, everyone shouted; they could hardly hear over one another and the honking of the taxis floating up from the street through the open windows. With the rakı, they danced and sang and played games that they made up on the spot, and everyone was very young while they drank, with life in their mouths, their skin bursting into flames under the gold lights of the kitchen, the living room, even the bathroom. They grew anxious as the long summer was coming to a close. They behaved with abandon in the streets on their walks home. Some of them stopped coming. Some were arrested. But those who kept coming brought more friends and more liquor.

Many of Necla's friends complimented her hair or her dresses or her shoes; she could blush on command. But with the liquor and the dancing came, for Necla, a stillness in her heart, a sense of failure, depletion, an insatiable desire for affection. Emre would be in his room during these get-togethers, or he would be hustling out to the grocer's for bags of ice, his presence noted only by the glint of the ice cubes as they melted under his arm, the plunking of them dumped into the sink. All the while, Necla, the perfect hostess, would move between bodies attentively, spastically like the flickers of electricity.

Tonight, Necla is throwing another party. In the small apartment are packed forty, maybe fifty bodies, slender and stuck to one another. The floorboards creak with the shuffle of feet and the vibrations of jazz through the speakers. Glass clinks constantly, and there is a little pop of a cork or the plug of a bottle being loosed every so often. Her sister pulls sweaty cubes of ice, one by one, from the sink to run over her red cheeks, the back of her neck. Her mother is crying tears like champagne bubbles lighted by the city's glow pouring thickly through the window. Necla breaks from the glut of people and sneaks into her parents' room. On the bed, Emre rereads one of his favorite books about a little boy who runs away from home in a hot-air balloon that drifts too far from shore.

"I knew I'd find you here," Necla says.

Through the door, they can hear jokes, then the voice of a popular singer. Necla goes to the foot of the bed and sits on her knees.

"I thought you would cheer up with all these people here," she says.

Emre is in his book.

"I'm worried about you. I'd love to see you smile. Anything just to see you smile."

Outside you can hear the scrape of a vendor's cart, the kiss of stars against the sky. The nightstand lamp throws blades of gold and gray across the room, and Necla dips her fingertips into the shadows over the floor.

"I feel terribly lonely in there, Daddy. In the party I feel like I am a breath you can't catch. It's not such a big party, though. I could invite more people. We could really fill the apartment. We could get everyone squished together so that we could hardly see, hardly breathe. Everyone would be stuck to their spot, pinned there, unable to float away. You know, I have this idea. Promise me you won't laugh. I've had this idea of throwing a never-ending party. Have you ever read a book about that? What are you reading now?"

Someone burns incense, you can hear the skitter-crackle of the stick like bumblebee wings.

"I wanted you to meet Hasan tonight. You would like him. He's from Ankara. Promise me you will come out and meet him?"

Emre looks from his book and nods and says he will come out to meet Hasan.

Necla stands and straightens her dress. She remains briefly, like the afterglow of a television just turned off.

Much later, as the party slips into silence, Emre comes out from his room to the kitchen, creeping past the dozen or so people still drinking. He searches for his youngest daughter, Ece, in the crowd. He searches for her in the corners and under the couch and behind the doors. Necla watches him do this, but he doesn't notice. His wife, Mirhiye, is wrapping a tea towel around her face as a mask. Adalet is still spreading ice cubes over her skin.

EMRE CARRIES A large cardboard box full of newspapers from the office under the crook of his arm. He knocks on his daughters' door. He fumbles it open and finds Adalet fanning herself by the window because it is so hot. He sets the box down by her bed. He takes yesterday's *Zaman* and puts it in her hand.

"I don't want this."

"I have subscribed you to a dozen newspapers," he says.

In the box are *Milliyet, Sabah, Hürriyet, Cumhuriyet, Bugün, Vatan,* and others. He takes them out one at a time, stuffing them into Adalet's hands. She makes unaccepting fists that crumple the paper. Emre dumps the box in the room, shooting sheets of newspaper across the floor.

"Stop this."

Emre says the paper boys will deliver each edition through her window every morning. They have installed a rope and basket and pulley just for this. He is proud that he has created an analog internet for her to use, uncensored and unblocked. He is proud to have this little evidence that he had listened to her, he'd heard her. Then he sees the novels on the bookcase by the bunk beds. He goes to them with his box and in three sweeps of his arm scoops out the contents of the bookcase like watermelon from the rind. He says she won't need these anymore. He says that these fantasies are beneath her. She grabs his arm to stay the box, to keep it from disappearing through the window. She's yelling at him, but he doesn't listen, can't understand what she's saying. She takes hold of his other arm like concrete, and there is a ferocious burn as she squeezes. He pulls free of her. She takes up the scattered papers and hits him with them. She crumples them into balls to throw at him, she rolls them into bats to beat him with, she folds them into bees to sting him until he drops her books and slaps her and breaks immediately into sobs.

Adalet runs from the back room for the front door. Emre is fast, despite his age, and catches his daughter by the arm. She struggles in his grasp, her limbs and hair whipping into violence, but Emre calms her down. He wraps her up in his arms and goes limp, the weight of his body dragging her to the floor. She kicks a chair over, the clap echoing out into the courtyard full of daylight.

Emre is trying to calm her down. Adalet cries. She tells him that she wants to leave, she needs to get out of this house, she can't breathe, he's constricting around her.

"Relax, Ece. Relax."

"Stop it."

"I'm not letting you go out there."

"Ece is dead."

Adalet is screaming now. Somewhere astray, a dog barks in response. You can hear the neighbors turning on their vacuum cleaners in their flats to drown out the noise. Emre tells his daughter he will read her entrance essay; he'll help her with it.

NECLA MARRIES HASAN the following spring. What does he do but listen to her? What does he do but call her *darling, sweetest, dearest*? What does he do but shower affections and attention upon her? So he wants to go back to Ankara, and she will go with him. How lovely is it that he says to her she has a good face for smiling, says to her he likes the way she wrinkles her nose at him, pulling her lips up and flashing teeth she no longer cares are too sharp.

For a time, they joked about having to schedule the wedding around Emre's walk to work—he ventures out so rarely otherwise. Then Necla couldn't stop thinking of this, a wedding parade marched through the streets of Istanbul. From the minarets would come the vows, shouted to them by beautiful muezzins. They could hire the open-air tour buses for the guests to ride along beside them, put the string quartet on a platform truck, rig a large bolt of velvet carpet to the back of a car that would drive ahead as she and Hasan walked hand and hand into their union, Emre doting along, in his work clothes on his way to the office. The city would watch her. Hasan has a grove of oranges somewhere in Anatolia he's inherited. He believes himself to be a businessman, a budding tycoon.

She watches him with eyes curved like crescents. When he talks, his fists can get away from him, but he's still a good man, she says. Sometimes, when there is a dried-up well in your chest where there is supposed to be a cistern of affection and care and attention, any font that aims to fill it is a welcome one, no matter if at times it stings with poison. This was Hasan to Necla. It's not so hard to understand, even abuse is seen as love by those whose lives are trained on the trellis of neglect.

It was an accident, their wedding night, when he stuck a fork into her arm. She had said something about Ankara, about staying here in

Istanbul, and he wouldn't have it. Then she said the people here were kinder, they were open-minded, so he grabbed up the fork from the room-service tray and stabbed quick into the top of her arm. They left it in, both of them surprised. Necla didn't feel a thing. Hasan was in a clean shirt, his jacket on the chair, his bow tie come undone. She still had her heels on. She was on the corner of the bed. He had been bringing her the tray from room service. What had they said to each other after? What had they explained of themselves? She forgets, but she likes the memory of the fork, silver, glinting, and cold, breaking suddenly from the contour of her warm and sunbaked arm. She felt noticed.

The phone in the living room rings. Emre gets up from his bed, puts on his slippers, and scratches over the tile floor. He answers. "Hello?" he says again.

"It's your daughter," says a woman.

"Ah, Ece? Ece, is that you?"

Emre looks around the room for Ece. There is a large territory of his heart expecting to see his daughter come out from hiding. He casts glances under the tables and along the skirts of the couches before he feels foolish. "Stop that now. I miss you, Daddy. I miss you so much. Mother said you would come out to visit me, and it's been all autumn since she said that. She says she can't peel you away from your books. Daddy, just once come out and see me? There's something we need to talk about."

"Oh?"

"Hasan wants to meet you, Daddy. Perhaps if you talked to him . . ."

"Ece, is that you?"

Emre walks around his flat with the phone pressed warmly to his cheek, peeking into the corners of mirrors, the cracks in the crown molding, the space between the windowpanes.

"Daddy, stop it. I miss you. Don't you know that? Can't you feel that? Isn't there a bit of blood left in you, a scrap of soul in your marrow?"

"Ece?"

A crackled sigh comes through the earpiece. Then the click and the soft void of a silent line. Emre creeps back to his bedroom, turns on the light, and opens his serial to another tale. His wife leaves the apartment most days. She dresses in all black with a tea towel over her face. She behaves like a hoodlum, throwing bricks through police car windows and building bonfires in the middle of intersections.

Emre spends the rest of the day filling out a college application form. He fills it out as Ece. He is applying to be a political theory major at a university in Budapest.

AT HOME, MIRHIYE is in the kitchen boiling something when the phone in the living room rings.

"Daddy, I need to speak with Mom."

"Who is this?"

"Please, Daddy. Please. Hasan will be back soon."

"Ece, is that you?"

From the kitchen his wife asks who is on the phone.

"Ece?" Emre asks.

Mirhiye smacks Emre with a plastic spoon. "Shame on you. Shame. You cruel, cruel pig."

Mirhiye takes the phone. It's not long before she is crying. Emre thinks he hears sobs on the other end as well, and he wants to ask what all the fuss is about, what is so terrible? Who is that on the phone?

It is Necla, her last phone call. Hasan is coming in through the front door, he is going for a knife, he is dragging cuts along her skin. Mirhiye is screaming.

Not long after this, the police come for Mirhiye—they have photos of her at protests tossing gas canisters back into the columns of the riot squad. The police are machines in their routine, they have done this dozens of times. They turn Mirhiye, tell her to be careful not to struggle, snap the handcuffs round her wrists, hold her by the tender, fatty part of the back of her arm. She shouts at her husband for doing nothing. She screams like her lungs are ripping open while the police guide her down the hall. They leave the front door ajar and Emre can hear his wife splitting the paint of the hallway with her screams all the way down to the bottom of the building and out into the sun-soaked street.

{PART III}

IT IS A year later when Ayla the cat disappears. For a long while, Adalet searches Kasımpaşa for her. She puts up posters. A neighbor finds the dead cat, stuck in a crevice in the rock wall that surrounds a nearby graveyard. Her neck was broken. They put the cat in a shoebox. Adalet thinks of the lullaby-purr coming heavy from the curl of fur on her lap. But what should they do with the box? It is a big city, overstuffed and overstacked; you can't just leave the box somewhere. There are only a few tufts of grass in public parks. They had no plot of land. There is no such place as the boneyard of lost pets. Adalet calls her friend and asks what they could do. "With fish it is simple," says her friend. "You can't flush a cat."

Adalet goes to the hall closet for packing tape to secure the box, but all she finds is blue and silver gift wrap, which she uses instead.

"When did you ever care about the cat?" Emre asks his daughter.

Adalet takes the box to the Bosporus. The sky is flat. The water laps slowly at the shore. Fishermen shrivel in the sun. She drops the box over the rail, but without enough of a push. Both cat and box spill into the strait and are lost beneath opacity. The lid floats with the currents as they empty into the Marmara. Adalet watches the lid until it becomes a speck in the sea-glint. All over Kasımpaşa, the lost-cat posters still cling to lampposts and telephone poles, and they will remain until the weather strips them down.

Emre wakes in the night to a few dogs barking. They are fighting hither and thither, perhaps over scraps from a garbage receptacle, perhaps simply for dominance, as this is the game of street dogs. Then he hears the weeping of dogs. Emre goes to the kitchen and rummages around the fridge. He pulls out a jar of fig jam. He takes from the pantry a half baguette and a spreading knife. He sits at the table and eats with a smile. Watching a black room is like watching a photograph develop—bleeding into existence is the shape of Adalet's body on the couch, head to foot flickering like a shadow, but he thinks it is Ece come back from the park after the protests, and he is terrified to see her head split open like a watermelon. An ambulance siren cuts the sky, and Emre finds himself trapped looking out the window into the night. His daughter comes up beside him.

"Don't go out there," Emre says.

"Can you even hear me?"

You always ask me that, he wants to say. Why won't she call him a coward? Why won't she tell him she loves him, that it's not his fault?

"Come, Ece."

Emre sits his daughter in a chair at the table. He goes over to the couch and pretends to ignore her.

"Come on," he says. "Tell me I'm a coward. Tell me that you want to go to the protest."

She shakes her head.

"You can do this for me," he says.

Adalet cries and shakes her head and her father leaves her be.

In the morning, Adalet packs her belongings into a few boxes. Emre hadn't noticed. He simply remembers one day seeing four stacked cardboard boxes sitting in the hallway, thinking, *What could these be for? Have we more cats to dump?*

Now in his apartment there are only three empty beds shaved thinner each day by the passage of time, and a man guessing stations of the sun by the light of the windows.

There's a moment in life after a loved one is gone when everything begins to fade. First it is the fingers and toes, the extremities of the body. Next it is the frame, the shape of it embraced. Then finally there is the memory of the face, until eventually one morning as you stir the spoon in your coffee, you realize the memory is not buried but gone, and no amount of excavating will bring it back.

EMRE IS IN the compass of the Ayasofya, chilling his bones in the brisk and brinish breeze from the sea. He has grown a beard along with his mustache now. As if sleepwalking, he finds himself at the patio of a café ordering tea. His hands shake while lifting sugar cubes. Many people pass him by, some taking pictures, others eating finger foods. There are certain streets in the city where, if you wait long enough on a Sunday, you can watch a parade of detainees being escorted into the police stations.

All around him there are the very still people of the park, the people who move only with the sway of branches. They seem a head shorter than a real person. They seem to be painted in watercolor, their edges blurred and indistinctive from the air around them. From this group, a young woman who recognizes him approaches.

"How is Mom?" Adalet asks.

Emre looks around, waiting to wake up, but there is no relief. Adalet orders a tea from the waiter. She sets a tote full of books against the leg of the table.

He thinks he sees Ayla the cat licking herself in the glint of a vendor's cart. He is about to ask Adalet what she is thinking, but she starts anyway: "I was thinking about the first time I suspected I was a ghost. I was walking the shop fronts along Bebek, bounded by the gleaming façades of Ottoman villas. I barely took up two fingers' width of the sidewalk. I was thin as smoke. An old man in a cap was going the other way; he would pass me by. He hadn't noticed—the narrowness of the walk, the breadth of my body—though he was looking right at me, he stepped into me as if I were nothing but mist. The old man was blind, that explained it. When I turned to watch him carry on, I could tell he was blind, but for a moment, without this rationale, the notion that I was a ghost, lost to the realm of memory, whispered into my heart.

"The second instance in which I suspected I was a ghost happened not long ago, this winter. It was snowing all day, snowflakes slanting through the air so that the minarets seemed to be heaving. The domes of mosques, blanketed, looked weightless like a crest of clouds, as if at any moment they might disembark from the earth and dissipate upward. I was just stepping out from my apartment. The day was strangely bright. I was cold in my bones. I crossed the street, the crunch of my footsteps echoed in my ears, everything else was made silent by the blanket of snow. In the middle of the street, I stopped. I realized then that there was no one else out. For a little while— perhaps because we do not often get snow like that here—I was alone in the street, and the still and silent city became completely empty of everyone except for me, and I worried I would stay that way, trapped."

Adalet takes her tea glass in her hand but does not drink. A honeybee crawls up the spoon from the bottom of the tulip cup. It flutters its wings but they are too heavy with red liquid. It crawls to the tip of the spoon and can't escape.

"Is it like that for a ghost, do you suspect?" Emre asks. "That you are alone? That maybe you can't see any of us, just as we can't see any of you?"

"What sort of a thing is that to ask?"

"Are you trying to say—I mean, if only I'd been . . ." Emre reaches across the table for his daughter. His fingertips brush back her hair. "What are you thinking with that head of yours?" he asks.

With this head of hers between the cages of his fingers she is thinking: *The third time is now. I think I am a ghost you are trying to anchor with your hands, poor Dad. I am an apparition, temporal in your arms. There is all the world between what I am and what you hold.*

She places her hand over his, slides it to her cheek. She misses her father. He misses his daughter.

"I am not blind to you," says Emre, because in his blood he thinks it is the thing to say.

She picks up her bag of books and walks home through the bustling streets. Emre loses sight of her quickly.

Walking in a patch of sunlight that spills over the buildings, Emre thinks about fig jam. He stops at the grocery. The grocer says hello to him, but Emre is in his trance of small pleasures. He pulls out a few lira while into the bag go the fresh bread and jar of jam. Through the haze of his routine, he hears someone shouting "Ayla!" and he turns to look out in the street for his three girls.

Mule Brigade

IN THE MOUNTAINS on the way to Iraq, the lieutenant's jeep pulls over. He hops out the back and takes a few steps down the hill. He has to piss again.

"Is that healthy?" Corporal Kayaoğlu asks.

"Could be diabetes, right?" I say. "My old man has that."

It's a bright day in October and we are hunting mules. "Accessories to crime," Sergeant Ali calls them. "Kurdish brides," Corporal Kayaoğlu says. Mules, I call them because I don't have a sense of humor. It's cramped in the armored car: packs, rifles, radio equipment, water, boxes of rations that have been sitting here for God knows how long. Private Yilmaz is out the hole in the roof, manning the machine gun. His bottom half is stuck between me and the front seats. We're sealed in by plates of armor not quite thick enough for these mountains. "We're not in Syria, at least," Sergeant Ali likes to say.

The lieutenant comes back up the hill, and we continue for the village. The country is mostly gold, streaked white with snow, speckle-green from shrubs.

We follow the lieutenant's jeep down the highway from Şırnak, where we've been posted for the last few months, where there is a curfew. Our squad was involved in daily roundups of suspected terrorists. We were good at it. No one saw those people again. I got used to what was left of the city fast. I slept in the bombed-out buildings because militants only target clean, official stations. It's all just a pile of rubble anyway. "The sun is down, go back to your pile of rubble!" we would say. There were the little echoes of bombs we felt in our bones, there was the sound of small fires burning black, there was the flat skyline of mountain peaks very, very far away. But out here there is the sky ripping open overhead, there is the complete absence of gray like I might only see colors for the rest of my life.

Sergeant Ali is worried what it means about our squad's reputation to get stuck with a mission like this. He takes soldiering seriously. He finds the lieutenant unbearable. It doesn't help that the lieutenant keeps pulling over to pee, that we keep getting lost on these roads on our way to the border where—unless it's some colonel's strange idea of a joke—we are to round up and execute every horse, mule, and donkey in the area. Ask ten different people why and you'll get ten different answers. The government says we're here to prevent the spread of animal diseases brought over from Syria and Iraq. The generals say we're here to cripple smuggling and black marketeering. Sergeant Ali says we're here to protect the integrity of Turkey's borders against separatists and terrorists. The Kurdish villagers say we're here to starve them slowly, mule by mule, livelihood by livelihood.

Corporal Kayaoğlu turns around and looks at me through Yilmaz's legs. He's got a finger pressed up to his grinning lips. He swings his fist quickly into Yilmaz's balls and croaks out a harsh laugh. Poor Yilmaz gets woozy on the machine gun. He's the Kurdish interpreter assigned to us while we're out east. Most people here don't speak Turkish well, and everybody's got a brother or uncle who's a guerrilla in the PKK, Kurdish Workers' Party. We've spent the better part of the season ducking PKK bullets on patrols, or huddling under door-frames when a truck packed full of explosives destroys a neighbor-hood block. When Yilmaz speaks Kurdish there's that tic inside us that translates to bloodthirst and nerves on the fritz.

There's the village at the base of the mountains, already in the shadow of dusk. We are driving down the dirt path in no time, between tumbledown shops with tarp roofs and centuries-old build-ings with cracked TV dishes tacked to their eaves. At the well, an old man drops his bucket and runs from the sound of our engines. Four children in bright sweaters full of holes chase after us with smiles until their mother shouts at them, and they stop one by one: red, blue, yellow, white. Under the shallow awnings stand men with thin cigarettes, watching us. There's a mule tied to the trailer hitch of a water tank just outside what looks like a coffeehouse. A group of men are smoking and playing tavla under the awning.

We pull over and everyone's out of the jeeps in a hurry, so I climb up to the machine gun and watch the rooftops. My hands shake from the cold. The men all look happy under that awning, wearing coats and drinking coffee. I think about our nights on deployment in the little town of Şırnak, about coming down from great heights of adrenaline and wishing I could make a cup of coffee just to keep my fingers warm.

Everyone's got their rifles up as they approach the coffeehouse, but the lieutenant's disappeared again. Scanning the street, I see him ducking behind a shed with a petrol ad.

"Whose mule is out there, tied to the water tank?" Sergeant Ali asks. None of the men under the awning move. Yilmaz says some-thing in Kurdish. The men's faces register something, and a few of them look at each other. Then the nicest-looking guy, a real sweet-heart of an old man, stands up from his game of tavla, smiles, and nods. "Mine," he says in Turkish. "Yes, mine. Mine." And he points to it with pride, like a father points to his strong boy.

Kayaoğlu walks up to it, pats its neck, scratches its ears, and smiles a wide smile back at the men of the coffeehouse. He's got a rifle slung around his neck, finger by the trigger.

"Tell him it's our mule now," says Kayaoğlu.

A bit of translating and the old man laughs. He nods and laughs.

"I don't think he gets it," says Yilmaz. "He says it's not for sale."

Sergeant Ali cares about showmanship. Sergeant Ali wants everyone here to get the message very quickly, so he kicks the small table by the old man and little porcelain cups go shattering across the floorboards. He grabs up the old man by the collar of his sweater, points at the mule, and shouts at the crowd of men in the coffeehouse that it is our mule now.

The village men are shuffling closer to us.

"I think he gets it now," says Yilmaz, pulling on Sergeant Ali's arm.

The village men slowly close the distance between them and us. They keep absolutely silent, and I'm nervous about where to train the machine gun, whose hands to keep my eyes on.

"Sergeant," I say.

But he doesn't hear me. Sergeant Ali throws the old man down, and with a bit of fuss like he's suddenly overexcited, he draws his pistol, brandishing it about his head as he yells at the people gathering around, filling up the street now too, and coming out from their homes until we're encircled by all these people with empty faces, and any one of them could have a gun in their pocket.

"Sergeant," I insist, but he's yelling so loud that he won't hear me. Yilmaz is translating fast as he can, as calmly as he can, as Sergeant Ali shouts to the whole coffeehouse that it is now illegal to have a mule, and looking at the faces of these men you wonder if they even speak Kurdish or if this whole town is deaf.

People from the village come out into the main street to watch the commotion. My gaze is darting here and there as doors open and out spill wives, children, grandmothers, and just as fast I'm training the machine gun on each new movement until they stop, startled as much as I am.

The old man crawls to his knees and starts begging. He shakes his clasped hands before Sergeant Ali like it's his own life on the line. I've seen people less upset about us taking their uncles. He tugs at his sweater, holding it out to Sergeant Ali as an example of something, saying *Look at it, look at it.* Yilmaz talks to the men very calmly, like he's not even translating for Sergeant Ali anymore. The men under the awning are talking now, they're talking to Yilmaz and I wish they'd go silent again. The things they say have Yilmaz looking around, looking at me, and I've got my thumbs off the handles and onto the button-triggers of the machine gun. Everyone keeps talking and I can't understand a word of it, and Kayaoğlu points his rifle at the men around the coffee shop, and I shout because I feel like something inside me will break: "Hold on, Sergeant."

And Sergeant Ali looks at me.

"We could use the man's help."

We don't know the area, we haven't got a place to stay, we don't know who has mules and who doesn't. It makes sense, I guess, as I keep talking. "You've got to get a few locals on your side," I say.

Sergeant Ali tells Yilmaz to get all that across, to ask the man if he's got a house, if he'd do us this favor.

"Yeah, he has a house," says Yilmaz.

"We're going to be staying there," says Sergeant Ali.

The man stays on his knees, and nods and nods and holds up his hands.

"He says he'd love to host us."

We quarter with the old man. His name is Hamdi. He leads us up the village road into the hills like sharp folds of paper to his house. It's a squat, red thing with a few windows and a telephone pole right by it. He tells us a little story about how he tried using the wires once as clotheslines. There's a shack behind the pole and a little clearing between it and the house. He parks his mule next to the shack. Inside is a large cog and wheel used for milling.

Sergeant Ali orders us to secure the area and there's that momentary jump in our blood again, but no one is here. I poke around the shack and find nothing. I nudge Yilmaz and we go inside the house.

"Tell him to start a fire," I say. "Please."

Hamdi introduces us to his wife, who begins crying when she sees us. She's an ugly crier, but she is smiling the whole time. He pats her head and sends her back into their bedroom. He's rushing around the house to start the fire and a pot of tea and make sure we're comfortable and happy. I sit in front of the stove warming my back like a cat. I unsling my rifle and put it on the floor, and for the first time in months it doesn't feel like an extension of my arm, and I'm not scared to be without it.

Yilmaz sits on the couch and sighs. Kayaoğlu and Sergeant Ali are still talking outside. Yilmaz says something to Hamdi and points to a few photographs hanging on the wall. Hamdi speaks quickly, telling Yilmaz they are his daughters. "But they have been gone now for over a year," Yilmaz translates. Hamdi doesn't miss a beat scurrying all over the house, even when he starts crying.

Yilmaz takes off his helmet and his rifle and his vest and he helps Hamdi in the kitchen. They make a large pan of meatballs and fried potato slices in tomato sauce. Yilmaz offers him a cigarette that Hamdi turns down. Out the window, the daylight is waning. It's all just dust and mountains, dust and mountains, some snow, a low sun in the sky as yellow as fried egg yolk, thin air—cold, cold for the lungs.

THE FIRST FEW days are slow. What can we do? Sit around in the village until someone walks by with a pack animal, which of course no one is doing because the whole village knows we're here.

Sergeant Ali blames Hamdi, saying he must've telephoned everyone he knew, everyone in the village, everyone in the whole province last night to warn them. Sergeant Ali says every villager here is a PKK terrorist.

Sergeant Ali tells us that we're important. He's good about that—keeping up morale—so long as you don't think about how he's really just talking to himself about himself. He says that for every mule that goes to Iraq and comes back, that's two thousand lira in the hands of terrorists. They make a fortune selling cigarettes on the black market. He says out here, in the badlands along the border, a mule is as good as a truck, and that every Kurd with a mule is a smuggler bringing contraband into Turkey, cheating the country out of billions of lira in tax revenue every year, and putting that money to use buying bullets and rifles for traitors and separatists. There's got to be three, four, maybe even five hundred mules and donkeys and horses in the mountains around here. He says the villagers rent them out like cars at the airport, he says the PKK are nothing more than beloved vigilantes out here; he says we're doing good work.

WHAT A LOT of nothing there is out here. You could get a few land surveyors out into the mountains and have them take samples and measurements, and they could do it for years without ever coming close to cataloging all the nothing they've got out here.

We sit around with Hamdi most of the day. The lieutenant and his men have taken the armored car and gone into town. They've shacked up in some local ağa's decrepit villa. They're setting up a large pen outside town for the few mules our squad is out catching. We've found three mules and a donkey all week, and Sergeant Ali is getting upset. We deflate the tires of every car we see, hoping it will force people to ride their mules around.

Corporal Kayaoğlu throws Yilmaz's helmet down a well as a joke.

The joke is that Yilmaz's mother is Kurdish. And I'm the one with no sense of humor. Sergeant Ali reminds him he must wear the helmet at all times. Hamdi gives Yilmaz his wool hat to wear under it so his head won't freeze. Hamdi is like that only with Yilmaz. Sure, he feeds us all well and smiles at each of us and fluffs the cushions of his couch before we sit down, but there is a difference in the way Hamdi takes care of Yilmaz.

Hamdi brings us a small tray of meatballs wrapped into half loaves of bread. His wife pours out cups of strong tea for us between sobbing fits. She's still sobbing, though we've been as kind as soldiers could be. We've said how lovely the home is. We've grinned and nodded at all the tea. I have Yilmaz tell her to keep her face in the steam so her tears don't ice up when she comes out to serve us. He says something to her, then something else to Hamdi, and then Hamdi and his wife go indoors.

SERGEANT ALI HAS just come back with Corporal Kayaoğlu. They were driving through the nearby hills, and unless they've got them tucked into their back pockets, they've found no new animals today.

"They're warning each other when we're on the move," Sergeant Ali says.

I look at Yilmaz and Hamdi, who are popping olives into their mouths like on holiday, first Yilmaz, then copying his movements with a little giggle, Hamdi, each of them spitting out the stones in turn.

"He's warning them," Sergeant Ali says, pointing at Hamdi.

"He's got no telephone," says Yilmaz.

Sergeant Ali lights a cigarette and squats in front of the house. Kayaoğlu and I take the jeep around back to the fuel tank and fill it up again.

"There's got to be a whole hillside packed with mules," Kayaoğlu says to me.

I shrug. I picture a peripatetic herd of mules fading in and out of existence across these mountains.

Kayaoğlu grumbles about what we're doing. He leans against the jeep and smokes a cigarette and says that we're fucked. He's glad to have a reprieve from Şırnak, but we are fucked, going nowhere now, and it's only a matter of time until we get stuck here as a kind of border patrol, until we become a permanent station in the middle of nowhere. We bring the jeep back around.

"If we don't get a mule today, it'll be his we take next," says Sergeant Ali, pointing at Hamdi.

Hamdi has abandoned the bowl of olives and is scurrying between us with a tray of tea glasses and nuts and cookies, flashing smiles, keeping our bellies full and our hands warm with fresh tea. His wife is inside by the stove, her skin ruddy from the warmth. Yilmaz whispers something to Hamdi. He whispers it over and over but it's nothing any of us have said. It sounds like pleading.

Sergeant Ali drops his cigarette and goes to the shack beside the house. Hamdi's mule is eating a little bit of hay. Sergeant Ali unties it from the mill and leads it before us. He fastens it up to the jeep while Hamdi watches, smiling at me and smiling at Yilmaz, who keeps repeating something under his breath. Hamdi goes into the house and hurries back out with a fresh pack of cigarettes, offering them up to Sergeant Ali. Kayaoğlu takes one of the cigarettes.

"He wants to know what you're doing," says Yilmaz.

Sergeant Ali is doing his job, anybody could see that.

"I don't think that's a good idea," says Yilmaz.

"If you're not careful, people will assume you're interfering," says Sergeant Ali.

Hamdi looks like a chicken, running around, clucking madly in Kurdish. Kayaoğlu should be laughing but he isn't. Maybe he's just too cold like me. Maybe he and I should go inside and sit by the stove with Hamdi's wife and let these three sort things out. Maybe Kayaoğlu and I should get in the jeep and drive down to the coast and all the way back home.

"He says he knows where you can find another mule," Yilmaz says. "He says if you leave his alone he can tell you where to find a replacement."

Sergeant Ali smiles. He's clever. That's why he's Sergeant Ali.

"What wonderful news!" Sergeant Ali says, throwing his arms out wide like he might embrace Hamdi and give his cheeks two kisses each. "What a wonderful host we have, isn't he?"

Hamdi settles down but his gaze doesn't leave his mule, not even after it's untied and returned to the mill, not even while we're all loading our packs back into the jeep; only when Sergeant Ali barks at him does Hamdi return to us. "He's coming along," says Sergeant Ali. "He's going to give us the whole tour." Hamdi tells Yilmaz he can't go; he has to stay with his wife today. She's very sick, can't we see that? He says please to let him stay here. Yilmaz is convincing, so we take down Hamdi's directions. We ride off in the jeep.

At the farm, we park away from the house, fan out, and reconnoiter. Kayaoğlu walks the ditch road bordering the small field. He's looking for any other animals. He's looking for a kid with a gun. I can see, even from here, the steam of his breath scatter in small, pale puffs. All clear, we go inside where Yilmaz and Sergeant Ali and I talk to a farmer. The man is telling us his mule is like a brother, in fact it is better than his brother who is a drunkard that smells worse than his mule's asshole. His brother wastes the days away, stealing small handfuls of lira from his family and spending them in the back of the coffeehouse that doubles as a rakı and gambling den. We should be taking his brother, he's the one breaking the law, not the mule. He's the one gambling, drinking, shitting wherever.

"He says his mule is so hygienic, it even shits into a trench he's dug out," says Yilmaz.

I kind of want to see this trench.

"He says he's never been involved with the PKK and certainly never smuggled anything."

The farmer is desperate, and Sergeant Ali is a resourceful man. In no time, we've got a few locals helping us out to protect their own mules and donkeys, a network of informants. Kayaoğlu says that's what's wrong with Kurds, so easily they give up their brothers. Sergeant Ali tells him to be thankful for that.

WE'RE OUT BY the stream today. The water is low but it will flood with the thaw. It's scrubland all around, dusted from last night's snow. Our bootsteps sound like cracks in the earth. We're out by the stream because the owner of the two mules we collected yesterday turned in the old lady who lives here.

There's a donkey with a big smile waiting to greet us when we pull up. He stands by an empty trough dry as a bone. The old woman runs out to us. She's wearing a red headscarf and she's missing a few teeth. Yilmaz and Hamdi talk to her. Hamdi's with us as a guide. He tells uneasy jokes as I drive. The old woman looks worried, but who wouldn't? She and Yilmaz talk. She invites us into her home. Kayaoğlu laughs and starts pulling the donkey to the jeep.

Inside she has two little boys sitting on a cushion by the wall, her grandsons no doubt. They sit in front of a busted radio taking turns playing with a candy wrapper. The old woman and Hamdi talk about the weather, I guess. She starts shaking her head. There's nothing in their house but the woman and her grandsons and the odds and ends that pass as their possessions: a cushion, a radio, a copper serving tray, cracks in the walls, calluses on their palms, and wide, clear eyes good for staring. The boys stare at me and Yilmaz. The woman shakes her head at Hamdi, and he says something like: *Please.*

"He's telling her he will bring her a crate of figs for the boys," Yilmaz tells me.

"He doesn't have any figs," I say.

"Maybe he does. Maybe he will. He'll be the richest man in these hills after we leave."

What he means is: Hamdi will be the only one with a pack animal.

"They're all supposed to be rich," Yilmaz says.

"What?"

"They're supposed to be making thousands of lira a week off these mules."

Sergeant Ali keeps telling us each trip a smuggler makes will turn a profit of eight hundred lira per mule. But look around. I mean, where's the money? In the empty tea tin?

The woman sits down behind the boys and pulls their heads to her chest, smiling, still shaking her head.

"Hamdi's telling her they are handsome boys," says Yilmaz.

"She looks jealous," I say. She holds them tighter with every word out of my mouth, like she's scared we'll take the boys as well as the donkey.

Kayaoğlu comes in and says he's got the donkey tied to the jeep and it's time to go.

The woman becomes upset. She says no over and over. She looks at Kayaoğlu, saying something you don't need a translator to understand. Her face is cracked from the wind, and this makes her look more sinister. She's shouting after Kayaoğlu as he leaves out the door.

Hamdi keeps saying it: *Please.* He tells her to stop, that's what it looks like. He's telling her to keep it down or something worse could happen, but she doesn't care, she follows out the door. Hamdi smiles and says in Turkish to Yilmaz and me: "Everything OK, everything OK."

Sure, Hamdi, everything's OK.

I get in the jeep and the wind slips down my collar, whispering chills into my bones. Yilmaz stays with the boys with those clear, wide eyes, innocent to movement, and the three of them sit still as stones in a creek.

The old woman grabs Kayaoğlu's arm and he spins around and hits the woman to shut her up. Kayaoğlu doesn't have time for this. He's got a lot of work to do today, we all do. I start the jeep's engine. We have four more stops to make before we lead the train of animals to the lieutenant's pen. Yilmaz doesn't even look to see the commotion; he and the boys stay turned to each other, watching one another. Hamdi helps the woman to her feet, dusts her off, and takes her inside and starts a meager fire for her. But Yilmaz doesn't move, he stays with these boys, letting them play with his knife until I honk the horn and he climbs in.

Just a few decades ago, just half a century ago, this was nothing more than trade, the routes through the hills. Borders are there to be crossed, I think. Even if you squint into the morning sun, you can't see the thick line over the mountains demarking Iraq. And it is a thick line; in places like this it is a very thick border so that your whole body, a whole village can occupy this vague limbo, as opposed to the thin lines of places like Germany or the Netherlands, where your hand can be simultaneously in three different provinces.

At the end of the day, I park behind Hamdi's shed. Hamdi gets out sorely; his *Welcome, Turk!* attitude is gone. Yilmaz pets his hand over the mane of Hamdi's mule. He pats behind its ear and gives a little scratch.

"What's the matter with him?" I ask Yilmaz, motioning to Hamdi's house.

"He thinks I should have done something to help the old woman."

I think about this, but not too long. The sun is down, and I am cold, so I say: "We do what we can."

WE HAVEN'T SEEN the lieutenant and his men in six days—they've stayed in the village eating and drinking and sleeping—but no one's complaining. Sergeant Ali seems at ease without the lieutenant, even laughs a few times while we eat. Night falls and Yilmaz and Corporal Kayaoğlu take the first shift of guard duty. Sergeant Ali and I are inside, standing in the living room with our backs to the stove just watching Hamdi and his wife on the couch. They watch us right back. Hamdi keeps nodding with a grin on his face. He's nodding, saying with his grin: *Don't kill me, don't kill me, don't kill me.* Hamdi's wife is still crying those silent, heavy tears, so heavy there is no break in them, there are just two lines of liquid down her cheeks like swollen veins.

Hamdi's wife offered us tea but Sergeant Ali scoffed so I couldn't take any either. "Wouldn't you have liked tea?" I ask him. I throw another log into the stove and give the bellows a little squeeze.

"Pull yourself together."

Sergeant Ali is a poor man with high aspirations, stuck in charge of us degenerates. He cleans his rifle again. He's going nowhere. How long until he sees that?

HAMDI AND HIS wife have gone to bed. We hear them as they roll in their sleep. I want to tell Hamdi's wife not to worry. I want to tell her everything will be fine, but I don't know what everything is.

Sergeant Ali takes over Yilmaz's shift a little early. Yilmaz comes in from the night with frost in his mustache shining red from the embers of the stove. He becomes nothing more than his shadow in the dark. He spreads out his mat next to mine on the floor. I half pretend to be asleep, but I feel just as much that I am pretending to be awake.

"I'm going to kill that Kayaoğlu," Yilmaz says. When the two of them share a shift, Yilmaz and Kayaoğlu, the jokes aren't jokes anymore. Kayaoğlu is enormous, his hands are twice the size of mine. He's a good soldier, Sergeant Ali tells us so. He's killed sixteen terrorists. He doesn't worry about anything, and he doesn't hesitate, and everyone thinks that means he's brave, but what it really means is that he'll use any excuse to point his rifle into the nearest house or grocer and fire. He'll wait for someone to run out, terrified, and he'll drop them because they're Kurdish.

"I'm going to kill him," says Yilmaz again.

I stay quiet, but he knows I'm awake. "Man, don't say something you can't do." Soldiers fight, and sometimes accidents happen, but Yilmaz's mother is Kurdish, and everyone would say: *Yep, just as we suspected all along, a traitor is a traitor is a traitor.*

"I mean it," says Yilmaz. "Next time he looks at me I will shoot him right in his chest. Easy. One, two, three."

"One, two, three," I say, but it isn't easy.

Back in Şırnak, Kayaoğlu put Yilmaz in a stranglehold. We were put up in a ruined hotel for a few days' rest, and while he was showering, Kayaoğlu strangled him until he blacked out. He was bruised horrible the next day. We all saw it. Yilmaz could hardly stay upright. The doctor said he'd slipped on the tiles.

"You could use your knife," I say. "At least it'd be quieter."

Yilmaz props up on his side. "Will that look like an accident?"

I sigh. "Is that what you're planning? To get away with it?"

Yilmaz thinks. I can't see more than the boundary of his shoulder and neck in the dark. I've been staring at the embers in the fireplace and my eyes won't adjust.

"Shit. No, man, that's not what I plan on doing."

"He deserves it," I say, but it sounds apologetic, like I don't believe in Yilmaz.

"It's about justice," he says like a defeated country.

"It's cold. Don't you think?" I ask.

"What?"

"It's cold." I don't have anything to say. He lies back again. He drifts off to sleep then, or maybe I do. I'm thinking about a beach near Mersin. I'm thinking of peeling oranges and tanning in the sun, and then nothing.

THE NETWORK OF informants has been successful beyond the lieutenant's expectations (or so we guess; he still hasn't turned up after two weeks). Sergeant Ali chalks it up to the general stupidity of the locals. Kayaoğlu and he are with the mules now. Two hundred of them in a large pen we'd built near the shepherd's house. I thought about how the shepherd might use his flock to smuggle cigarettes in their wool, but some things you keep to yourself.

Yilmaz and I are packing up our rolls and rations into the jeep. We load the MG 3 into the back. Hamdi's wife smiles at us, following behind as we go in and out of the house. Yilmaz asks Hamdi something. They see I'm curious.

Hamdi grins and holds up a hand and disappears into his house. I look around and his wife is gone too. Yilmaz straps down the MG 3. Hamdi comes back out with a thermos I hadn't noticed before. He gives it to me. "Tea," he says. "Hot, hot. Now you go."

Yilmaz laughs a weak laugh.

"Thank you." I take the thermos without guilt. This is his only valuable, a quick look at the house would tell you that. I sip the tea. It is strong and honeyed. I thank him again and say to Yilmaz: "Did you teach him that?"

Yilmaz nods. "All week he's been practicing how to say 'Now you go.'"

Hamdi nods and smiles and backs away into his house. I take another sip. The tea is hot, but once I sit behind the wheel of the jeep I'm shivering again, and I can feel the cold of steel through my clothes, on my arms, my fingers, my thighs, my ass. I start the jeep. Yilmaz hesitates.

"You'd better hurry," he says.

"They won't be happy about you sitting this out," I say. He's running the risk of being called a sympathizer, or, worse, a spy of the PKK.

"If I go, I'll shoot Kayaoğlu."

I shrug. "He deserves it."

He waves me off, tells me to pick him up after. I drive down the dirt path through the village that looks deserted in the low autumn sun. The only pack animal left in the whole municipality is Hamdi's old mule, breathing steam into the bright day.

At the edge of the village is the rest of our platoon, leaning against the bars of the fence they've set up. I back the jeep up against the pen full of mules. We have all the time in the world to unstrap the machine gun and mount it and feed the belt into its hungry maw and slap the cover closed and chamber the first round. We swing our rifles off our backs and switch off the safeties. We spread out, ten meters between each of us so that there is plenty of space for the discharged brass, plenty of room for the wind to bite at us.

Sergeant Ali tells the lieutenant we're ready for the go-ahead. Some men are steadying their arms on the fence and aiming their rifles. One of them throws a bottle into the pen to try to spook the animals. A laugh here, a laugh there, suddenly everyone is full of jokes. The mission will be over soon enough. We've achieved another victory. Tomorrow we'll be heading back to base. But still, we have this last part of the job to do, and now it gets quiet, and no one is looking at the animals, and no one is looking at each other. No one seems to notice Yilmaz's absence, not even Corporal Kayaoğlu. They can only think about themselves; they can only look at their own boots.

Some of the mules still have their packs strapped to them; a few still have their reins hanging from their muzzles. One still has the strip of cloth tied over its eyes that keep it from going dizzy while walking circles round the cog of a well pump. Some are well brushed. All are well fed like members of the family. None of them had sacks of cigarettes tied to them. None had rifles or shotguns hidden in their troughs. One had an owner with a collection of bootleg DVDs. Three hundred seventeen animals out there, huddled together, close as pebbles in the dirt.

Sergeant Ali gives us the order lazily, says with a smile: "All right, boys. Go on. Shoot them."

So it is with lackadaisical thirst that we fire the opening rounds: two in the dirt, one through a cloud, another into the haunch of the nearest mule like an accident. The mules all jump, their muscles rippling under their skin in shock at the sound. They are unable to move, to turn and run even the short distance to the edge of the pen. A few short bursts. We are acquainting ourselves to the act. How many of us have ever killed a thing? And the mules are looking at us, saying: *Don't kill us, don't shoot us.* And we are saying back: *Don't move so much, just die easy, OK?*

Disappointed in us again, Sergeant Ali takes his handgun from his hip and fires into the flank of a nearby mule until the gun is empty and he reloads and empties it all into the dead mule again so that we get the idea, so that we follow suit, and I don't want to, but everyone will notice, so I fire a few bursts from the MG off to the side, high so no one will see I am missing. I fire one long burst, and I think of Hamdi and his mule because I have done good. I think of Yilmaz because, like him, I have spared some small piece of myself from being a killer. Steam pours from the barrel of my MG, and I realize I can feel my hands, better still I can feel heat through them. I hover my hand a few centimeters from the barrel and I can feel the warmth in my veins again, and I smile at this morsel of summer I am holding between my fingers.

Sergeant Ali tells us to go nuts, to have fun with it, to shoot like they were the devil's own. And I guess it makes sense to the others. They tell you that if it weren't for us, Turkey would be a dangerous country, and you believe them. And then they tell you what a Kurd is, how they are not Turks, they don't want to be, and that having this many Kurds is dangerous. Then they show you videos of PKK attacks, of bus bombings, kidnappings, assassinations, and you go along with it, it makes sense, they are dangerous, they do want to kill you. Then they say to round up families, collateral is important, but you know that by now, they hardly need tell you. They say the PKK is strong because of smuggling, because they terrorize and extort the east. But then they put you in a jeep and drive you to a village full of old men and women and say none of it's enough, now we have to kill these mules because they too are dangerous—do not be deceived! They are threats to the state, they are accessories to treason and their trials will be quick, their executions summary, so you drag the mules by rope to this pen, and you pull the trigger, and most of them don't even move, they just look toward the boom of gunfire with those eyes, black and round as cherry pits stuck into the sides of their faces, long lashes batting away stray flies, and only now am I asking myself what dots weren't connected along the way—but what could I do?

The steam dissipates. The wind will have the barrel cooled soon. I fire another long burst, the rattle pouring through my bones. I shoot the already dead mules but the thud-slap of bullets puncturing them is an addictive sound. I shoot a standing mule this time and watch the ripple of muscles under its flesh stop and be still. They will grow suspicious, my brothers; I have to hit the target to keep shooting.

The barrel is a bonfire to stoke, and I am relieved briefly, my shoulders slack; I become aware of how tensely I have shivered until now, and all that is gone in the warmth.

YILMAZ ISN'T AT the door of Hamdi's house waiting for us—neither is Hamdi. I hop out of the jeep as a buffer between Yilmaz's absence and any number of eventualities piled into the jeep behind me. I call out to Yilmaz, hoping he will peek through the front window with his broken grin. Kayaoğlu shouts his name too, shouts that they carved out a whole mule pussy just for Yilmaz, they've got it intact he says, and I believe him. The lieutenant stands up in the back of the jeep, looking at the clouds. Sergeant Ali jumps out after me. The men in the armored car are arguing.

A scuttle of feet. Sergeant Ali turns in time to catch Hamdi's arm in motion. He's wielding a knife aimed right for Sergeant Ali's throat, and in a quick bit of momentum, Sergeant Ali yanks Hamdi through the rest of his swing into the dirt. Hamdi screams when Sergeant Ali stomps on his wrist. He drops the blade and begins squeaking like an injured sparrow. Kayaoğlu is quick out of the jeep.

Sergeant Ali pulls out his handgun again. "Where's Yilmaz?"

Hamdi is shouting at us, cursing us.

Kayaoğlu calls out from the house. We turn and see him dragging Hamdi's wife by the arm into the open air. She's stopped crying; she's bleeding all over the place, dirt sticking to gleaming patches in her thigh. She's got a tourniquet tied above the hole but it's bleeding through, it's her femoral artery. None of us are medics. It'll be a minute more maybe. She's already losing consciousness.

"PKK," whispers Kayaoğlu.

Hamdi pulls on the sleeve of my fatigue. Hamdi points to the shed by his mill. I realize the mule is gone. Hamdi points beyond the shed.

Kayaoğlu is doing his best with Hamdi's wife, giving her a little morphine, reapplying a bandage, telling her nice things, wonderful things like how she is going to be all right even though he is now covered in blood too, even though the wound is slippery and it looks like she is coming undone.

I lift my rifle, sights just below my eyes. I take nervous steps toward the shed. Sergeant Ali follows me with his own gun, with his own pair of hungry eyes. On all fours, Hamdi starts crawling to the shed, he's crying now, and standing up, and then he runs in front of us, and his quick movements have me terrified, terrified I might pull the trigger and shoot him, terrified that without meaning to, I might kill him. He runs for the corner of the shed and behind it. Sergeant Ali tells me to wait, wait until we have secured the area, but I run after Hamdi and see him climb up the rock terrace around the back of the shed, and up the escarpment of dirt to the top of the hill. I shout after him, asking where is Yilmaz, but he's crying and choking on his own gasping breaths. I drop my rifle and clamber up after him. Sergeant Ali curses me.

I get to the top, and I'm about to grab Hamdi and hit him and beg him to tell me where Yilmaz is, when he points out across the countryside, out into the cold foothills with their shoulders huddled together. I look in the direction he's pointing, and I can see, on the back of Hamdi's little mule, Yilmaz riding for the mountains, for the border.

The Smuggler

KEMAL AND THE pregnant woman drive along the border away from Kobani in silence. She's barely fifteen, more girl than woman. Kemal knows some girls or friends with sisters around that age, and none of them are fit for rearing a child, domesticating a man, creating a home.

They ride in silence because Kemal doesn't know how to ask her if it's all a hoax, if her claims of virginal conception were merely an attempt to pacify her shamed family. She keeps quiet, Kemal guesses, because her Turkish is bad, or because her family tried to kill her, or because she is tired from running away.

Along the road to the north, a barbed-wire fence runs the length of the Turkish border. On the border, Kobani behind them is decimated, besieged. Here the road into Turkey is closed, so they drive west for Jarabulus. Soldiers, half of them boys fulfilling their six months of military service, populate the guardhouses and checkpoints along the fence. They watch over the barren landscape of rocky hills and spiny, dried plants, so near the Euphrates that they wonder how a river with such an ancient contract of fertility could forget to nurse its soil.

There are more of them than last week, and more arriving each passing day. It's all anyone can talk about. Turkey's started operations along the Syrian border, committing thousands of troops to a direct military intervention in the raging civil war, so now the only things in the news are the Suruç bombing, ISIL, PKK. Syrian and Kurdish refugees waiting in long lines along the border fence with the remainder of their possessions packed tight into arms and hands. One soldier dead. Two injured. The guards in their posts watch the border with weary eyes and fickle trigger fingers. They make Kemal nervous.

Kemal smuggles cigarettes, beer, and movies across the border with Syria to make a living while he practices drifting in the parking lot of his old high school. He and a few other men from the village, who pour every last kuruş into their cars, race and gamble their days away. There's not much here for them unless they want to be farmers or shepherds. Kemal's gone back and forth across the border dozens of times, but this is his first time smuggling a person, and it has his body feeling a little unwound from itself.

Kemal tells himself he doesn't believe this girl's fantasy about being a virgin mother because he isn't superstitious, because of all the times and places for such a thing, it wouldn't be here in this godforsaken place, it wouldn't be now, in the middle of a civil war. But Kemal assures himself of his disbelief so often he can't help but grow suspicious.

"Your parents didn't believe you?" Kemal realizes he sounds like an asshole and tries thinking of something else to say to make it better.

"My father died two years ago in Hama," the pregnant girl says.

"Is that your home?"

"The soldiers came. Nobody lives there now."

Kemal knows of at least a dozen such places. "Was your father a rebel?"

"He was an auto mechanic," she says.

It could have been a heart attack or cancer or anything, but Kemal doesn't push it. The media boasts about coalition forces and Kurdish separatists closing in on ISIL's capital city. It's all confusing to Kemal. The PKK are Kurdish terrorists, and they've been bombing and shooting up eastern Turkey since the seventies. The YPG are their Syrian counterparts, but the United States and other allies support YPG forces against ISIL. Kemal thinks this alphabet soup is ridiculous. He'd bet everything he owned that the Kurdish fighters of the YPG are the exact same Kurdish fighters in the PKK. It's not like they wear soccer kits and take rosters, after all.

"Is it your relative we are meeting?" Kemal asks. A man named Aksander, who gave him the job, didn't mention any details outside of a location. Aksander and Kemal drink together and bet on the races, and Kemal gets jobs from him, but Aksander is only sometimes his friend, and sometimes he is like a stranger.

"My aunt lives in Turkey."

"And she believes you?"

The girl nods. "She thinks it is a sign from God."

Kemal laughs at that. "And you think this is divine? You think you are the Virgin Mary?"

"I woke up like this. That's all I know."

And it was that way. The girl woke one unremarkable morning, not sick or late or anxious, but well-rested and with a clear head, and knew at once that she was pregnant. Perhaps she didn't know it as intimately and as expressibly as that; rather it was a thought tucked under her other thoughts, a bit of knowledge from the socket, so that as it became more coherent to her, she remained calm as if under a strange and peaceful dream. After all, she is a good and pious girl who loves and trusts God more than anyone.

But should she keep this to herself? Early one morning, when she was still in the bed she shared with her two younger siblings, her mother came and shook her gently to start the day. "My, my, how have you gained so much weight?" she said to her daughter. The girl started to say that it was a miracle baby here in her belly, but, though she did not fear being pregnant so inexplicably, she quickly became terrified by how others would react. They wouldn't believe her—she wouldn't have believed it herself if that had ever been a choice for her. She would be called a whore, a sinner, an evil girl. If she had a father still, he would beat her until she gave him the name of the boy who did this. But there was no name but God, and this would only make others boil over with rage. They would call her a blasphemer and a deceiver, and her father and her brother, or a friend of theirs, would get a gun and take her out to the groves around the city, and they would shoot her by the roadside, leaving her there, whether out of shame, or hatred, or fear of what other families in other households would do. But there was only her mother and her brother and her little siblings, and her brother is not so obstinate as her father was. And she thinks that if she explains it was God's will, then God should make them believe her. He will whisper into their souls and convince them. She trusts God and loves him.

The road breaks from the border and follows the Euphrates, but not far enough to be out of sight from the guards. Kemal can see hundreds of Syrians walking along the fence, their heads looking like small poppies bobbing in the wind. A seemingly unending line of people walking in one direction, yet here is this girl in his car paying to be taken across just like them. Kemal thinks this girl's family is foolish to waste thousands of lira for what all these other people in line are doing for free.

"It's a lot of money your aunt is willing to pay, just to hop the border," Kemal says. "Especially when the military brings wounded over for treatment every day."

"A Syrian coming into Turkey is different than a Kurd."

"You're Kurdish?" he asks.

Without missing a step, the girl says: "Does that change things for you?"

Aksander is sometimes Kemal's friend but he's also Kurdish. They talk about it now and again. Every time they talk about what it's like being Kurdish, it starts off with Kemal saying something about how crafty Aksander is when he smuggles, and how it must be because it is so natural for Aksander to commit a crime. Aksander points out that Kemal is a criminal too. Here is where their responses vary. Some nights, Kemal laughs and agrees and says there is nothing different between them. Other nights Kemal insists he is not a criminal, and he believes this. Still other nights, Kemal, feeling vulnerable about this truth, turns on the news or reads a headline about a PKK bombing. One soldier dead, two injured. And he says to Aksander: "What do you think, friend? What do you think of your people? Though you can't help it, I suppose."

"Can you help being Turkish?" Aksander says.

"Is Turkey such a bad country? No, İskender," Kemal says, using the Turkish form of his name. "A country must be strong in unity. The PKK must stop their murders."

But what can Aksander say to this? It is true there are bombings and shootings all the time, but are they committed by him? Are they, if not justifiable, at least in response to something? Yet because of a few killers and bigots like Kemal, he and thousands of others are left to apologize for their ethnicity in the wake of terrorism.

"When have Kurds ever liked Turks?" Kemal asks the girl.

"I've seen Turkish soldiers give extremists guns and tell them to shoot up a school. I've seen them give terrorists bombs and tell them to blow up a market. I have seen a group of Turkish militia come across a farmer on his tractor, and rip him down from it into the dirt, and threaten him until he'd pissed himself, and then, laughing, they shot him and kept shooting his body."

Kemal doesn't bother arguing. She's Kurdish, so she's been indoctrinated her whole life. He has this set of beliefs, Kemal, and he knows that they are truths, and he knows that the only people who dispute these truths are Kurdish, or else Western imperialists, both of whom have been brainwashed, and he thinks he shouldn't have taken this job, no one else did—but then, he didn't really have a choice.

"It's a lot of money is all I'm saying." Too much, really. It makes him suspicious. Even if she was telling the truth, even if she was some miracle, this is a lot of money to pay just to get a girl across a border, even a Kurdish girl in the middle of a war.

What if the baby's father was looking for her? It must be that. She is doing this to hide from him. But Kemal can't shake the notion that there had never been a father. The way this girl speaks, the way she sits with her back filling the car seat, her shoulders rigid, the coolness of her voice rattling down his spine, striking him as some indelible fact—Kemal thinks for a moment that she is telling the truth, there is no father.

"Is that why you agreed to help? For the money?"

Kemal laughs. "Why else would I do this?"

The girl shrugs, turning away from the window to look at him. "It's the right thing to do, to help people."

"I needed the work," says Kemal. One night, playing cards, he and Aksander hatched a plan to clean up at the races. Aksander worked it out so that the only real competitor for Kemal was gone running cigarettes that night. Then he bet a fortune on Kemal to win. But Kemal lost. Aksander didn't threaten Kemal, they were sometimes friends after all, but he didn't hear from him for a few weeks, until Aksander called him up about a job none of the other smugglers wanted, a job worth thousands of lira, a job that Kemal was going to do without question.

"So you don't believe me?" she asks.

"About . . . ?" Kemal says, motioning sheepishly in her general direction.

She nods.

"I don't think it matters. The outcome is the same. You're pregnant."

Their familiar silence returns as they pass a checkpoint for refugee intake. Tents crop up along the road, then a few slapdash shacks and hovels. In the distance, they can see the border town of Jarabulus.

"It mattered to my brother," she says.

Two nights ago, a group of ISIL militants drove into Kobani unhindered, rounded up as many Kurdish families as they could, and shot them in the wide streets and open squares. Just before the massacre, her brother dragged her into her room and locked the door behind them. Their mother begged and cried against the bedroom door. Her brother drew the knife he'd taken off a dead body outside town. He demanded to know the name of the father. Someone far away screamed. The girl wouldn't speak; she couldn't breathe. Her brother, like fire, suffocated the room in his rage. He swore if she did not give up the father, he would have no choice before God but to slit her throat. His voice creaked and he too was crying, and the girl could see he was going to kill her. He raised his knife.

A loud crash beyond the door startled the two of them. Within seconds, ISIL militants flooded the house. They grabbed up the girl's mother and her little siblings, and threw them, screaming, into the street, where up and down the fire of machine guns cut through everything. Panicked, the girl shoved her brother backward, and in the confusion, she wrested the knife from him and stabbed him in the chest, hard as she could, but the knife struck bone and stuck. He made a strange, breathless sound. Startled by what she'd done, she bent over him and touched his torso near the wound, her face, the handle of the knife. The immediate and swallowing crack of machine guns tore open the house and ripped her from the trance of shock. Scared to the quick by her brother grasping for her, by the deafening shooting outside, she jumped out the window and behind the house, clambering down the street in search of anyone who could help.

A CONVOY OF jeeps and trucks climb onto the road ahead and turn toward them. Ten or twelve vehicles, each of them armored and hulking and eating up the road as they speed toward Kemal and the girl. He slows the car and pulls off the gravel road. There isn't enough space for them to pass by. They are coming to eat up Kemal, swallow him into the back of a truck and take him to prison. He stops the car and looks around, wondering if he could clear the ditch on the other side of the road. At last, the convoy passes by them, and he lets go of his breath and is embarrassed at himself for being so silly as to think the convoy was coming to arrest him, for thinking anyone knew who he was or what he was doing. He doesn't usually behave like this. Sure, the first two or three times running the border, it was nothing but worries and tense muscles, but he's been doing it for more than a year now and all the jitters have gone. It's the girl, he thinks, there's something not right about all of this.

Kemal knows Aksander is a dangerous man because he is ruthless even if he's not cruel. Sometimes it's easy to think people are only dangerous if they kill for fun, or are consumed by revenge, or have so much wealth and power, but Kemal knows better. He has this idea nagging away at him: Aksander is setting him up. Why keep so many details guarded? Why a pregnant girl without a father? Panic seeps quickly over Kemal's thoughts. Women without husbands are volatile creatures in this world. Desperate mothers all the more so. But Kemal does not know for sure this girl is a mother; when he picked her up it was still dark out, and he caught barely a glimpse of her. He looks over. There's a little bump under her robes, but he did not check to see if it was her belly; who would? Terrified, he tells her to show him her belly.

"What?"

Her whole story was shit, and now Kemal will surely die aiding a widow-bomber like those Chechen widows, who, after their separatist husbands die fighting Russians, strap themselves with explosives and martyr themselves in a movie theater. Kemal skids to a stop on the dirt road.

"Lift up your jilbab," he says. "Right now."

"I won't—"

Kemal slaps her across the face. "Listen, Kurd. What have you got under there? I'm not helping you blow up a post office or whatever you're doing." Kemal slaps her again and tries to grab her robe. The girl screams and pounds her fist into Kemal's chest to stop him. He makes another move and has her clothes tight in his hands, but she catches his jaw, stopping him before she has to hit him again.

Kemal quits wrestling, each of them with their hands up ready to deflect the other again, but they have stopped their struggle; Kemal puts his hands in his lap and watches the girl cry. The robes have been stretched taut and her belly is round as a dome. She keeps crying. Kemal starts the car up again and drives slowly down the narrow path. He's still sucking in breaths and holding them. He's still gripping the wheel tightly with his hands. All of his nerves have, instead of dissipating, leapt into the caravans of other paranoias. Who would pay so much to have a little girl brought across the border? To whom is Aksander really having the girl delivered?

The girl has stopped crying. The dust will stick to her damp face when she gets out. She sits on her hands to keep them from trembling. Kemal thinks of cigarettes to calm the tremors in his own hands. Stick to cigarettes and beer. They don't kill anyone. They don't kill Kemal anyway. He promises to God if he's listening that this will be the only person he'll bring into Turkey.

"I didn't mean anything. It's this part of the world, you know?"

She's careful and says she understands, because that is what you say to men who have hit you.

They follow the road into Jarabulus, and Kemal turns up the radio. "Whatever they ask, you're my wife."

"There isn't a father," the girl insists.

"I'm not talking about that," Kemal says. "It's just how we're getting you through." He doesn't know the penalty for human trafficking. The judges could play it as sex slavery in court.

Kemal follows the signs directing him to the border crossing. He has driven this dozens of times, but today the route feels new and unfamiliar; he can feel his nerves climbing up the stairs of his spine. He's never smuggled a person across before. The road curves north, and there is this strange sense creeping down Kemal's throat. It's the same town but there are more bullet holes, more bomb craters, more troops, less business. One dead. Two injured. How fast this has happened—only a week. Kemal turns down side streets because there are trucks, artillery batteries, tanks, personnel carriers, soldiers, all barreling down the main road. Despite this, there are people out on their errands, merchants at the market trying to sell olives, kids kicking a soccer ball back and forth, like the whole town has forgotten they are in earshot of a war. Perhaps not forgotten, but grown accustomed to it, keeping it tucked into the wrinkles of their drooping faces.

Kemal turns at this corner, but there's a mess of troops blocking the street. One of them puts his hands up, angry, and gestures to turn the car around. In the road, a bomb squad fools around with a backpack. Kemal turns and turns again and they are back on the main road. Everywhere, small mortars and machine gun nests peek out of the sand like half-covered porcupines. Somewhere to the south of town, a number of artillery batteries opens fire.

They slow near the checkpoint house, a dark building compared to the rest of the white and tan huts around. They join the queue of cars formed at the checkpoint. The line is longer than usual. Kemal stops the car and takes a deep breath. He's practiced this, it's his ritual when he crosses the border. The artillery batteries fire again, rattling the windows and small, loose bits of metal in the car. Kemal takes a long inhale and then releases it all slowly. He tells the girl she should think about her breathing too. He counts for her, inhale and exhale, and the two of them try to relax. Again, the artillery fires. The car ahead of them moves forward and they follow.

"Don't you have a tunnel to use?" the girl asks.

Kemal looks at her and sees she means it.

"We don't need that. Everything will be okay," he says. "I have your papers right here, see? You're my wife." Kemal shows her the passport that had been arranged for her. The car in front pulls forward again and they follow. They're next in line now. The artillery fire another salvo. Kemal's skeleton rattles this time, he can feel it shuddering between the fibers of his muscles.

A soldier by the checkpoint house raises his hand, and Kemal pulls his car forward and turns off the engine. Two soldiers walk down the passenger side, one with a dog, and the other with an inspection mirror. The girl closes her eyes and prays. The corporal on Kemal's side leans down to his open window. Kemal knows this man. They've even shared rakı once when Kemal was detained trying to sneak a hundred *Captain America* DVDs across the border.

"How fast have you got this thing going now?" the corporal asks him.

With ease, Kemal says, "It's still legal, though I haven't seen a speed limit posted in a long time."

"There's a war going on."

"Oh yeah? Where'd you hear that?" Kemal asks. He always finds that the banter makes it easier.

The soldier with the dog taps on the trunk. Kemal looks at the man he knows, then pops his trunk. The corporal is smiling wide. He takes bribes, this soldier, and he's always happy to see Kemal because it means he will get paid.

"Nothing to declare?"

"There never is," Kemal says.

The corporal laughs. Kemal likes this man compared to the other guards. He likes their games as much as a rat can enjoy games with serpents. The other soldiers continue checking the car for a false fuel tank or a pull-away hatch or a phony tire, but there is nothing.

"Where have you got them this time?" the corporal asks so only Kemal can hear.

Kemal looks at the girl and then turns, embarrassed by himself for acting like such an amateur. Whispering back, he says: "It wouldn't be any fun for you if I didn't at least try."

The corporal tells the others to hurry it up, that they've looked long enough, and they'd better start checking a car that doesn't belong to a Turk.

Then another soldier appears at the passenger side, tapping on the window. Kemal rolls it down. "Come on, come on, where are your papers?" the soldier asks.

Kemal shoots a brief look at the corporal, but the man shrugs. Kemal hands over his passport.

"And who's she? Where's her passport?" the other soldier asks.

"I'm his wife," she butts in.

The corporal looks at Kemal. Kemal laughs to put everyone at ease. It feels good to laugh. "I've got it, but I didn't know you needed them both. Hers is newer. Had to get it to come out here. Our first trip together, you see?" Kemal gives hers to the corporal. He feels a heat pushing through the collar of his shirt up his jaw and into his cheeks. He sees it click in the corporal's head. There are no cigarettes in the frame of the car. There's no half-barrel of beer in a bladder in the fuel tank for them to find. The corporal gives a cursory look over the fake passport before signaling to the guardhouse to move the barricade. He winks at Kemal. "Congratulations," he says, eyeing her round belly.

Kemal drives through the checkpoint, down the dirt path through the minefield and into Karkamış, and he doesn't take a breath until they're through the town and back on the road that is tied to the Euphrates. They go over the river at a small dam. He stops the car in the middle and lifts up a drainage cover. Inside is a resealable plastic bag. He stuffs two thousand lira in it and replaces it. Tonight, the corporal will come and take the money.

The road diverts from the border and behind a shallow bluff, and then they are out of sight from the tanks and the fence and the guards and the land mines and the refugees, and they ride slowly into a flat land with green fields irrigated by the river, between shaded groves of olive, lemon, orange, and peach trees that shiver in a slow and warm breeze. They are close now. Grass grows right up to the dirt road. White rocks here and there catch the sun high, high overhead. A tractor sits waiting behind a squat home, and nestled at the edge of this flatland is the village of Göktepe.

"Does your aunt live here? In Göktepe?" Kemal asks.

"I don't know. I don't know where she lives."

"Did she say she would meet you in Göktepe?" he insists.

The girl doesn't answer, she's keeping her head bowed a little, her hands in her lap.

Kemal and the girl curve through groves of olive trees and creep into the edge of the village. It's small, with maybe thirty buildings and work sheds. Kemal follows the path as it narrows between tightly packed hovels. He parks near a tall acacia tree as Aksander had instructed him, and he turns off the engine. Two old men come out of their homes to look at the car, but it is hot and they quickly return inside.

"I believe you," says Kemal.

"You don't have to," says the girl.

And maybe he doesn't. He isn't sure. He felt he should say it as a way of showing he is sorry, but he knows it doesn't matter what he thinks. The girl looks out the window at last, looking for her aunt under the awnings of houses and in the seats of the few parked cars, but the two of them are alone in the village.

"Do you want me to keep driving?"

"Where?" asks the girl.

North, farther into Anatolia. It isn't a long drive to Adana. Now that they are across the border, it isn't a long drive west along the sea, to cities like Mersin or Konya. He stops himself from saying this, he thinks he is acting quite unlike himself. Why would he take her away from here? What is there in those cities for her? Why would he leave a little girl on her own in some faraway city? He is scared of what he is leaving her to. How many girls are brought across borders, and how many of them disappear?

A dust cloud passes by them and they see a car coming from the road. It's Aksander's car. It slows at the turn and bounces down the path into the village. Kemal can't see who is inside, it's still too far away. He is drowned by all these questions: who is in the car, where are they taking the girl, why is the village now empty, why is all of this happening at all, why isn't she just another shambling body in a long and skulking line of bodies marching to pass from one land into the next, why is his heart working so tirelessly to collapse itself in his chest, why are his hands and feet curling up as if starved of air, why is the top of his throat cinching closed, why can't he swallow. He's spiraling. He's having an attack. He holds on to the steering wheel and tries staring at the speedometer to count all the little lines.

Aksander's car parks near the same acacia tree. Slowly, Aksander climbs out of the driver's seat. The girl says something Kemal doesn't hear. Another man gets out of the car, looking at all the houses hunched in their stones and plaster. Kemal holds on to the steering wheel in case he begins to drown. The girl says something again, but Kemal's ears are stuffed with cotton—his nose, his throat, his lungs, his insides are all stuffed with cotton and each part of him feels incredibly far away from itself. The car doors pop closed, one right after the other, and they pierce this muting distance.

Kemal sees the girl crane her neck, checking the car, hoping yet another door will open.

"Do you know that man?" he asks.

The girl is smiling but she shakes her head. She holds on to her abdomen. She leans forward in her seat and puts her hand on the door, but she doesn't open it.

"Don't you know him?" asks Kemal.

The girl is still smiling. There's someone else in the car. In the back seat, there's another person, small, hunched or old. The girl is leaning on her armrest, trying to see who it is. It will be the girl's aunt, Kemal thinks. She will come out of the car, and the girl will run out to her. Aksander will tell Kemal his debt is clear. Kemal will tell them he will keep them in his prayers. The girl will hold him tight for delivering her, and she and her aunt could go anywhere from here, but this thought is evaporating in his hands.

The girl has stopped smiling; she's grabbed the handle but something has stopped her from pulling it, releasing the door. It will be the girl's aunt in the back seat, Kemal says. And he will feel at last like this noose called Euphrates is unwound from his neck.

The Muezzin

WE HAD ALL loved the baker for her pastries. It is a small village, and she was generous with scraps. But I'd only met her daughter, Pembe, at the baker's funeral a year ago. The funeral was a rather traditional affair. I called out to our village from atop the minaret. Here in the country, where the villages are small and ancient, there are no loud-speakers, so muezzins like myself still sing our callings from the bal-conies. The womenfolk of the village came to perform the communal washing. The imam helped shroud the body in rough linen, and, as I was informed later by the imam, Pembe dusted flour over the wrap-pings before they set her mother in the casket.

I called again from the minaret and watched as the faithful came through the narrow streets to the mosque to perform the prayer. There was a reception afterward. The whole village was packed into a room for the sponge cakes, plum cakes, marble cakes, cherried tarts, chocolate cream, nougat, muffins, brownies, split buns, shredded wheat with walnuts and syrup, bulbous sweet rings thinly covered in fine sugar, and sprinkle-dusted blobs of cream with crystallized cher-ries and strawberries.

Everyone ate well, devouring guiltily all of Pembe's treats, for she was just as good a baker as her mother. I myself had three helpings of revani. Pembe came over to me at the table full of condolence cards and bouquets. She thanked me for my help (I carried the casket up the hill with Pembe's husband, Hayrettin; his uncle; and the imam). It was a shallow grave, as all are here; the hills are too steep, and the rains cause flash floods. I asked her about her mother, to give her a chance to take solace in the memories. Pembe told me her mother used to take Pembe's small hands, no wider than a crocus flower, and stick them in dough, saying: "I will bake your fingers into the bread." Little Pembe would leak a sharp giggle-shriek, and her mother would pinch her cheeks, cooing and singing, telling her that she was the sweetness in a cake, the rosy blush of a cherry, the heart of the bakery.

Then Pembe's husband, Hayrettin, came by. He took her glass of tea and my empty plate and then her empty plate into his hands that were already full of other paper plates. He kissed her cheek as delicately as a bird landing on a branch and left to gather more people's trash. I realized then he had been darting around all afternoon, tending to things and taking a break from it only to kiss his wife's cheek or place his hand, cupped gently, right above the small of her back any time he sensed something no one else could have.

I asked Pembe if she would keep the bakery open—the village couldn't survive without it.

"Of course," she told me. "I couldn't either."

SO, HOW CAN it be that I know the story of Pembe the baker as if it were my own? The mosque and my minaret are on the main street, across from the bakery that abuts the river. I speak from the top of the minaret to you, but my voice is a whisper; it is not yet the time for prayer, after all. I am the clock tower, I am the minute hand, I am the muezzin of this small village in Rize province where the pine trees stretch tall and dark between the mountains, and the clouds hang low enough for me to catch their mists in my palm.

They say over the radio that heavy rains are moving in from the Black Sea. I see Pembe locking the door to her mother's shop, closing the refrigerated case with the cakes by the slice, turning off the lights. On the stove, a kettle gurgles. She pours a cup of tea and drinks slowly in the dim. Before her mother's cancer, before her marriage to Hayrettin, she and her mother would relish these moments after closing, drinking their tea with two lumps of sugar, licking their forearms clean of the cake dust like cats, chatting about this or that to delay their return home where Pembe's four older brothers were roughhousing, or drinking, or masturbating the afternoon away.

She pulls the tray of revani out of the oven and wraps up a few slices. She will take it home for Hayrettin to eat as he unwinds from his day at work. Pembe misses the tickle of his mustache on her neck as a welcome home. He works extra shifts now, though they don't need the money. She brought it up once. "I'm surprised you noticed," he said. "All the time you're out of the house anyway."

So she spends a few long days in the shop. Should she not miss her mother? "What else do I have, besides the bakery?" she likes to say to her customers as she hands them their bags and plates. Hayrettin has heard her say this too. Hayrettin has heard her reduce herself to a postmortem existence, and he can't help but notice there is no room for him.

The sun is silver through the forming clouds. The earth is gray with the anticipation of rain. Pembe pours out the rest of the kettle and leaves through the back door.

She walks along the main street of the village that runs parallel to the river, the veiled sun following her in the hollow glints of shop fronts. Rize is a countryside carved into sharp valleys by thin rivers. Each river is crossed by narrow village bridges, the humpbacked Ottoman sort, with a circle arch depressed in the center. On every hillside, tumbledown houses sprout from the slopes like stairs.

A large buzzard then drops from the sky with half-open wings and sulks close behind Pembe as she passes the tailor and the tobacconist, the bus stop, the small fruit bazaar, and the teahouse where men slap clay disks on backgammon boards between sips of tea. The large buzzard keeps with her through the village; the word in its beak is a slow *wait, wait.* She turns the corner with the post office and sees the small carcass of a cat in the gutter, stringy from being ripped and ribboned by a wake of buzzards so recently descended that there are still stragglers in languid dashes across the sky, drooping from lampposts, scratching their talons across the pavement. Their heads shine blackly in the blood and cloudlight. Pembe's stalker cries another *wait, wait!* as it runs with spread wings to a space above the carcass, and this is the only black on the gray street.

Pembe creeps around the birds. A few drops of rain prickle her shoulder. The pines begin to rattle in the breeze. Pembe climbs the steps of the terrace to her house on the slopes of the village. I retreat down the spine of my delicate minaret.

Inside her house, darkness spills like smoke down the hall. Pembe turns on the lamp and sees Hayrettin walking from room to room like he's taking inventory of their lives. Pembe becomes very cold when he passes her for the living room.

She shows him the slices of cake she's brought from the shop.

"Is that where you've been?" he asks, an accusation of something.

She sighs. It wasn't like this right away, Hayrettin's petulance. He went with Pembe and her mother an hour to the city for each of her visits with the doctors. Even when Pembe's mother was hospitalized for her last month, and Pembe had to stay in the village to keep the bakery open, he had others cover his postal route so he could stay by his mother-in-law's bedside and keep her company until Pembe arrived each evening. Then he arranged the funeral and managed the legal affairs and scheduled deliveries to the bakery and kept the house. But she's been detached for a year now, and Hayrettin had to go back to work. I don't blame her; she's entitled to her grief. It's her mother that's died. It's her heart that needs comforting, she tells herself, and then Hayrettin will say something to her like: "You have given up living for yourself."

Mourning is addictive sometimes. Grief is such an encompassing and difficult enterprise, we forget ourselves outside of it, until we have, without realizing, cast out what makes up our lives and become eclipsed in this new identity.

"What a miserable day," she says.

"Hmm," says Hayrettin. He pours two cups of tea from the kettle and sets them on the table in the kitchen.

Like the ones between all these hills around us, there is a rift growing deeper between the two of them. Only a moment together and they have already retreated to these separate silences. Each of them irritable for no reason other than disappointment (with themselves, the other, life itself?), scared they might say something and be scraped by the other, scared they might whisper a honeyed note of love only to be met with a bitter refutation. You are familiar with this pantomime and have played it out in your own homes, I imagine:

"I have cooked your favorite meal!" "And made a ruinous mess of the kitchen I just cleaned!" And then the first sulks so the second says: "I'm sorry, the dinner is delicious and I love you." But it is hardly meant and there is no forgiveness, so they are hurt and angry and regretting everything and nothing, feeling both justified and overcruel.

Pembe and Hayrettin have formed a habit of this awkward domesticity, both of them scared by the other's fragility. Well, what they need is a shout, a start, a jump to shake them out of it. If they could just put all the history of their learned depression aside for one moment, with the swipe of a hand erase the slate anew, then say: how about some ice cream, and then a walk through town, and then a pot of tea, and a fire, and a blanket, and a book each, and holding hands . . . well anyway, what I assume spouses must do when they are happy and in love! I yearn for Hayrettin to wake his wife from her trance of grief, to break her from the hold of the dead so strong over her, to tell her: *Wait, wait, what about me? I am here.* It is the easiest thing in the world, and somehow it is no less impossible. Alas, should we not abandon our loved ones as they abandon us? Perhaps that is the most human thing of all.

They have tea quietly. Pembe is struck by two thoughts: she should have stayed at the bakery because she feels estranged from her husband; she should stop going to the bakery because she feels estranged from her husband.

IT DOESN'T STOP raining, and within a week the river has overgrown its bank. Some of the villagers are digging moats around their houses with sluiceways leading from these to the lowest crevices of the countryside. Why the rain hasn't stopped is anyone's guess.

I keep picturing an enormous faucet over us; it has swung out to cover up the sun and the moon and it is pouring water endlessly, water not even from the seas and clouds but from beyond the atmosphere. More and more water, more than can fit on the earth. I keep thinking, why doesn't someone shut off the faucet? But I have a nervous disposition and an overactive imagination.

Pembe sleeps through the early morning. She should be rolling out pastries in her shop; a line has awaited her every morning despite the weather. She should be preparing for a flood. The water is rising, reaching its teeth for the foundations of our street. But she has decided to empty out her mother's house. She asks Hayrettin for help, but he's confused, he wasn't listening. "Why are we moving into your mother's house?" he asks.

She gets a few large storage bins from the garden shed and has Hayrettin to drive her. The house sits at the base of a hill just outside of town. The river has washed out the garden. The corner of the house is in the water, like it's hiked up its skirt and dipped its toes in to test the temperature. The hill is very steep behind the house with another terraced garden and two gravestones. This is where her parents are buried. Here the hills are too steep and wet for large cemeteries. We live close to our dead.

Inside, on the ground floor, the water is already at your ankles. Here and there, little trinkets of the house go floating by from room to room. She picks them up thinking she will save them—a candle box, a bottle of wine, a few file folders, a DVD case, a raft of hand towels—but everything is soaked through, and she only has a few bins. She'd been meaning to clean out the house before, but she hadn't gotten around to it.

From the corner of the ceiling comes a drip, drip. The window glass is full of water. She picks up the debris of the house. She feels like she is weirding in her movements, like she is watching them in a delay of acting them.

"Is the bakery okay?" Hayrettin asks.

Pembe stops, her voice now a creak of a floorboard: "What's wrong with the bakery?"

"I thought you must've been worried about it. I was only going to tell you it's not worth worrying about." He's grabbed up the detritus in the front room and takes it outside to throw away. When he returns, Pembe hasn't budged.

"It's just . . . it's raining a lot. Will it stop?" she asks him, looking insecure in her own presence, like she might disappear into the air with hardly a fizzle to mark her. She feels uncoupled from gravity and is rising out of her body with only a few things keeping her tethered—her memories of her mother, her husband, this house, the bakery—but they are coming undone.

"What are we going to do?" she asks, thinking about the bakery.

"About what?" he says.

———

PEMBE SHAKES OFF her umbrella in the entryway of the teahouse and wrings her hair like she has just finished a swim. She's come in to warm her bones by the old brazier and sip a strong glass of tea. She hangs her jacket up on the rack and sees Hayrettin's jacket there among the other few articles. He should be out on his route now, unless he's taking a late lunch break. A nice turn of fortune, she'll bump into him and they'll enjoy a pastry and tea, though there is a small part of her annoyed to be running into him.

Someone leaves, passing Pembe, and in the sliver of the opening, she can see Hayrettin walking from the bar to a table with a young woman Pembe doesn't recognize. Hayrettin has a strip of paper in his hand, and he is tenderly pulling stamps from its waxy surface, then pressing them to the woman's forearm, unworried about the pale little hairs on her arm, as if they both enjoy the prospect of peeling them off later with little winces that flash teeth. The woman has about a dozen stamps over her wrist already, and Hayrettin has more in his pockets. The two of them are oblivious to the teahouse around them, the rain on the roof, and Pembe knows this is the scene of a rendezvous.

This is when we are expected to become something. When we are greeted by death, my friends, we become actors—actors of grief, of resolve, of denial. What is this discovery if not a small death? What is this affair if not an end? Pembe stands in the doorway for only a moment in which the brief account of her world is condensed into one thought: all the years together, wasted now and what a setback— she is embarrassed, and she goes out the door into the rain, swallowed as if drowned.

I was not surprised to hear of Hayrettin's affair. Though he was getting on in age (yet still very much my junior), Hayrettin took more of an interest in himself since his mother-in-law's death, so that when the muhtar's boy told me about Hayrettin and a young woman in a teahouse, I imagined he'd laid out his ego in her lap for her to stroke while he purred as satisfied as a housecat.

I admit I had seen Hayrettin and the girl together a few times. Sibel is her name, and it rings warmly on the tongue like happiness. Sibel is one of those people who enjoy staring at maps of places they will never see. Maps of transport are her favorite, with trade routes and railway lines dissecting the gossamer sheet or the veined, yellow page. At home, she prints out maps with the printer her father gave her for graduating from college. She chooses maps with thick lines. As they come out of the printer, she takes the warm pages and stamps them over her belly, her arms, her thighs, until the lines are manifest across her skin, the routes of cargo ships cut around her own topography.

They had met in the teashop in the village on her way to the fruit market. He was gambling with the other mailmen: who had the remotest return address in their bags. That day he carried a letter from Chile. Sibel went to the table after Hayrettin's friends left. "Have you really got a letter from Chile?" she asked.

Hayrettin asked if she would join him for some tea. They talked about all the places Hayrettin had come to know through the return addresses of envelopes. She said he had a nice smile, and that he knew how to laugh. He thanked her, he was unsure of himself these days. "My hair is going gray," he said, pointing a finger to his temple.

"It looks thick, rich."

She asked him to drop her off at her house outside the village; he walked her to her door even. And after she undid the lock, she kissed him; he kissed her back. They smashed her bag of strawberries beneath their bodies as they stumbled onto the floor, bleeding sticky red stains into their clothes. He drifted off to sleep in her bed afterward, and she went to the doorway where his shoes and mailbag were. Inside the mailbag she found another faraway origin: Yemen. And another: Wales. She tucked them back into his bag and went to bed where he lay. He stirred and she asked, "Is there someone important that lives around here? A diplomat maybe?"

"What do you mean?"

"Your letter from Chile."

He took her hand and licked her fingers, but they tasted metallic and inky.

"There's a botanist up the way," he said. "He orders seeds from all over the world."

Whenever Hayrettin the mailman visited, Sibel would sneak into his mailbag and rifle through the envelopes, looking for the farthest-traveled letters. She would smell them to know what these places smelled like, she would listen to the rattle inside the envelopes, guess the size and weight and number of seeds in the packets for the botanist. She would then wake Hayrettin from his postcoital nap with the slap of the printer cartridge as she printed maps of the origin countries. She taped them to the walls of her bedroom.

If you stand in just the right place on the minaret and use your hand like a brim to shield your eyes from the rain, you can see Sibel and Hayrettin now driving round the winding roads into the hills for her house. They are pulling off each other's jackets before they are even through the door. They embrace in the narrow hallway where everything is liquid like a dream, and Hayrettin asks her to tell him she's in love. She does; she doesn't mind. It's not that Hayrettin wants to be fooled. She likes that about him, that he has a need that isn't physical and he is quick to say it.

Hayrettin is sleeping, and Sibel is now looking at the map on her wall, at all the voids left by countries she has yet to find tucked into his mailbag. Sibel runs her finger over the edges of the paper. Thick black lines mark the countries, empty landscapes heavy with the white of the paper. She groups them by continent—South America is by her nightstand, North America above it by the window, Europe to the right, Africa reaching all the way to the floor, Asia and Australia running the length of the doorframe. The square voids indicate the countries the villagers haven't yet received mail from. These are the rules. Sibel can't print them out, not until Hayrettin has delivered envelopes from the countries left unfilled. The gaps bother her, the incompleteness.

HERE COMES HAYRETTIN, driving home through the downpour in his mail van when, at a curve in the highway just outside of the village, he swerves to avoid what looks like a boulder fallen down from the hillside. His van goes off the narrow road and scrapes the retaining wall. The van stops in a big, sudden quiet—the rain is the only sound. Hayrettin makes small movements in the aftermath, checking his body tenderly for injuries by wiggling a finger at a time, then his toes, then making a fist and stretching his legs. He lets go of the wheel. I see him with his heart beating in his eardrums. Hayrettin climbs out of the truck and walks back to push the boulder off the road. In the rain, the stone appears soft, fleshy, and gray. Closer I can see him realize it is not a stone. Maybe it is a dead fox or a wolf pup in a ball. But when he is standing over it, when he can now see better through the wet, he realizes it is a head, not a boulder, looking up at him with hollow sockets. The skin is gone, mostly decomposed. Muscle cords glint in the rain, torn at the hinge of the jaw. The mandible is missing. Patches of skull press through the soggy, rotted meat melting from the bone. Hayrettin stands next to the head on the road, thinking God have mercy—he is sorry—but, God, please have mercy.

He dials the gendarmerie. He leaves the head where it is and sits on the guardrail, waiting for the gendarmes to show up, four in a jeep, all as lanky as beanpoles with their sleeves barely covering their forearms and their trouser hems tight around their calves.

The gendarmes collect the head in a plastic bag. You can imagine the stench from here. The one with the mustache offers Hayrettin a cigarette. He sits in the jeep with the driver, letting his cigarette burn out, answering questions: *Do you recognize the head? Were you the one driving? Was there no one else in the car? Was there no one else who saw the wreck? Did you hit somebody to cause this?* The man with the bag looks scared as he tucks it into a container in the trunk.

"What do you suppose has happened?" Hayrettin asks.

"I wouldn't worry too much," they tell him. It's easy for them to say; they're not from around here. Who wouldn't worry about a head? All this rain and now a head. Hayrettin asks for another cigarette, and the gendarmes leave in their jeep.

He drives home slowly, tired from the gendarmes' questions. The rain pecks the windshield; the bends in the road are slick. His heart jumps for a moment like he's eaten too much candy. He thinks about his wife, and a small grain of dread lodges in his throat. He swallows and swallows trying to get it, but it is stuck like a hair.

When he gets home, he looks like he's seen a ghost, and Pembe thinks it is because he knows he's been found out. Hayrettin washes his hands at the kitchen sink. Hunched over like that, with a small tremble running through his body like electricity, Pembe thinks he might cry, and for the first time she becomes aware of Hayrettin as something very brittle.

He is trying to say something, she can see it. And she gets up off the couch to go to the bedroom. She doesn't want to hear whatever he has to say. She doesn't want to face facts, not because she is ashamed, or because she is shocked or in disbelief, but because she doesn't have room for it right now. She has her own worries. The bakery has started leaking and she's run out of bread pans to catch it.

"There was a severed head along the highway," he says.

She stops near to him, near enough she could reach out her hand and place it on his shoulder. "Just like that?" she asks.

The phone rings. It's the gendarme officer with the mustache on the other end: "Well, I was just calling to let you know about the incident earlier. It appears to be an animal that's done this. I hope that's some consolation. I told you it wasn't anything to worry about. No psycho out there. You see, we could tell from the markings. The head was over six months old, anyway. Its grave might have been washed out from all this rain. Just be sure to take care walking around until we look into this some more. We'll be calling the muhtar and his village council as well. There's a village meeting for the rain in a day or two anyway. We'll bring it up there if you want to come."

A sigh of relief from me that there is no dark murderer stalking our streets.

Hayrettin hangs up and turns to Pembe, watching her.

"What is it?" she asks.

"A meeting tomorrow, about the rain."

Pembe would rather be at the bakery. She doesn't know what to say so she says: "There was a buzzard out this week that I thought was watching me. I had that sensation, of a fly crawling down your back, and sure enough there it was watching me. Do you ever feel this: being watched?"

But Hayrettin doesn't hear her. He shrinks away to the bedroom. He spreads out over the sheets still wet in his work clothes and falls asleep.

IF THESE RAINS keep up like they say, there won't be any land left on which to stand. And what are we supposed to do about that, anyway? Our faith is in God. The industrious collect the rain into bottles destined for Syrian relief missions. The clever give swim lessons for fifty lira an hour. Most of us go about our days as usual. It is hard for me to call the prayer without the sun for reference, but I make do, it is like muscle memory.

Hayrettin wakes to sounds of the television coming from the living room. He steps out of bed and jumps when his feet slosh on the floor. The carpet has soaked through in the night and there are thick threads of water leaking from the ceiling, thin cataracts dribbling down the walls. He finds Pembe snoring on the couch. He leaves carefully, without waking her, and drives to Sibel's house.

Hayrettin parks hastily in the swamp that is Sibel's garden. He bangs on the front door, shouting her name, but the clink of the bolt in the baseplate is the only reply. Her house is dark. He runs around the back of her house, sloshing his boots through the water until his feet and ankles and calves are slick with mud. Sibel is in there, he knows it. He peeks through one of the back windows into the empty kitchen. He walks back to the front door but before he can resume hammering away, she opens it.

"Hello, Mr. Mailman."

Hayrettin pushes past her. "We have to talk."

"I'm not much good at talking. Say, where's your mailbag?"

"What?"

"Where's the mail?"

"Just listen for a minute. Who cares about the mail, what about this rain? Huh? Don't you notice it?"

"It rains," she says.

"Not like this, this is a flood," says Hayrettin. A strange wave of anger washes over him. It is vibrating under his skin so close to the surface he thinks of all the ways he could expel it. Then a small prick pinches him—a nugget of regret like a watermelon seed in his stomach.

"It's a sign," says Hayrettin. He's walked into her kitchen and he's gripping the counter with both of his hands. "And now there is a head."

"A head?" she asks, stifling a giggle because she is uncomfortable, because it is hard to believe, and, embarrassed by her manners, I almost giggle too, nervous as a child caught in a lie.

"A body. Well, no body, they couldn't find it. I was driving home from here earlier and on the road was a severed head."

Sibel pulls two coffee cups from the cabinet and sets a cezve on the stove. "I'm not sure I understand you," she says.

Hayrettin pulls her away from the stove, grabs her shoulders in his hands, and looks her in the eyes. He tells her he is here to end things. He's here to break off their affair. These are signs from God, he says, the rain, now a head. This is God telling him that he is a sinner and must stop. Sibel thinks what I'm thinking: it's an awful lot of fuss to send this much rain for one person. But she doesn't say it. He's still talking about how she's a lovely woman, and something else she doesn't hear because now she's thinking about the mail and her game. It's over, and so sudden. Her wall is left unfilled. No more stealing envelopes and peeking at their origins. This feels not like the end of an affair but rather like the botanist up in the hills has died. No, it feels like Hayrettin has killed him.

Hayrettin has stopped finally, he's said all he's come to say, and he feels relieved. He feels as though he's escaped from a nightmare of falling. Well, so much for him, but Sibel now stands here feeling empty as a pitted cherry, feeling cruelty come over her. While she puts one coffee cup back in the cupboard, she says as plainly as she can manage: "My heart was not a charm you ever had, Mr. Mailman."

He leaves her house for the rainstorm and tears off in his van.

Her map is ruined, frozen fast into this deficient constellation. Sibel shoves her fingernail under the tape and pushes. She tears off small flecks of paint from the wall. She tears down every country, stripping Europe from the plane, then the Americas. She stuffs the paper into a trash bag. She does away with a few of her own things as well, taking the opportunity to clean out her house. I can see she is tricking herself to make this easier, spring cleaning is all.

Sibel takes the bag out back of her house, to the river that has spilled and is eating up her yard in small nibbles by the minute. The river is smooth as syrup. On the opposite bank, the bushes shiver. At the edge of her terrace, Sibel hurls the bag but it splits, pouring a mess of pages out as its flies into the river. She watches it sink quickly, invisibly, then grabs up the errant pages around her, throwing them at the river, throwing them deep into the air like a celebration. They plop onto the river before dissolving. A few of them tangle around tree branches, stick to mossy rocks along the shore. A few are caught in an eddy across the river. It spirals slowly, waving at Sibel from its place. For the first time since her childhood, Sibel cries, broken-hearted over her closed world.

There through the curtain of rain, Sibel spies movement on the opposite bank. Gleaming and slick is the matted-fur face of a bear gazing at her. Trapped in its maw is an arm without skin. Red cords like power cables drip from a bone. The bear drags the dug-up body of my poor friend, the carpenter (buried only yesterday), into the forest and up the hill until Sibel can no longer see it. She vomits and calls the gendarmes as I say a prayer and look up into the cloudy ceiling for a leak, a hole, a sliver of sunlight.

PEMBE IS FRYING an egg, but she isn't paying attention and burns it, so she scrapes the burnt egg out of the pan and into the garbage, and starts frying another one. She keeps burning the eggs one by one and scraping them into the garbage bin, and it's midafternoon by the time she remembers the town meeting.

I climb to my minaret's balcony and call out to the town. I am saying to everyone: *Please come! Please come! There are important things to discuss—haven't you noticed the water?* But most of the villagers are gossiping about the head.

Half the town is in the small mosque. Most everyone is standing. In the front, there are a few chairs before a couple of risers the gendarmes have brought as a stage for the speakers. Bare chandeliers ring the open area, full of electric lights made to look like candles. The muhtar is over by the imam, and next to them are a few gendarmes from the barracks. "A lot of you have already heard about the incident on the highway north of here," starts the muhtar. He goes on to congratulate the gendarmes for their prompt handling of the situation. The gendarmes smile. "They have informed me that we are all quite safe—"

"God bless us," says the imam.

"—but our graves are in danger, the graves of our loved ones."

"God bless the dead," says the imam.

Bodies have been found in nearby villages as well. Bodies long since buried and now dug up. They say there are bears coming down from their mountain peaks and forest dens. They say they are slinking into the farther-flung family graveyards and exhuming the dead. Pembe thinks of her mother's grave, but she isn't worried about a bear, she is worried the water will wash it out. Her parents' house has all but disappeared—the doors and windows collapsed, the contents ripped out into the river, the roof pried off and slid away. She has only the bakery left of her mother, but not much of that is left either.

"What drives these creatures to such cruelty?" someone shouts from the crowd.

"They are hungry," says another.

"It's that hydroelectric dam up north," shouts a third. "It's driving the bears from their feeding grounds, driving them right into our backyards."

"God forbid," says the imam.

"We don't know that," says the muhtar.

"Bah! You don't know anything," says one.

"Yes, what makes the gendarmes think we are safe?" says another.

The people in the prayer hall begin shoving one another, shouting once more about the head, and the bears, and saying very little at all about the rain.

"What are we going to do about the rain?" Pembe shouts.

"What about our graves? Our own necks?" someone shouts.

"Who cares about a little rain with bears roaming about?" says another.

"It's the dam, not the rain. It rains every spring," shouts a third.

The crowd now boils with shouts about the dam, the danger of bears, the desecration of graves. Some people stay on topic, say it is only natural that a hungry bear driven from his home will search for whatever food he can find. Others say to exhume a grave is not natural for an animal, it is a sign from God. Then the soothsayers divide into two camps, one calling out that the bears are an omen that Turkey is on the wrong track and we have been duped by our politicians into idolatry; meanwhile the opposing camp contends we have not heeded our politicians' warnings and have given our lives over to sin. Then there is the third camp solely of my friend the imam, who is shouting that it is indeed a sign from God, but to try and divine its meaning is to consider oneself an equal of God.

"We ought to shoot the bears if they come to our graves," says someone.

The gendarme officer with the mustache cuts in: "It is an eighteen-thousand-lira fine to shoot a bear."

"What will you fine the bears for digging up my uncle?" asks one.

Perhaps the bears will come and dig them up, perhaps they won't, but the rains are continuing. Pembe knows the floods will wash out graves and pour their contents into the rivers and streams and even down the main roads. The caskets will break apart from rot, and the bodies will catch along the errant shores. Here and there it is already happening. You can't help but wonder if they mean to rise and walk again, if they mean to mingle once more among the rest of us left behind. There are villagers now leaving boulders over the graves of their loved ones, like paperweights for the afterlife. *Sit still,* we say, *sit still in the earth.*

The crowd is jostling now. The muhtar is jumping on the stage, stamping his feet, asking everyone to remain calm. The imam has his hands up in prayer, asking God for guidance, asking if this is some curse sent to the village, but if it is not to tell him. The gendarmes are offering up suggestions on how to deal with hungry bears: cover the graves with cement, light bonfires, keep loud vigils.

Pembe can feel the rush of the clouds over the mosque. She can feel the movement of the river the way one can feel the turn of the earth when they lie very still in a small hole in the dirt. No one talks about the water, how to stop it. The crowd spirals into a brawl, and even the muhtar joins in on the fistfight.

She is about to leave when the door collapses from a surge in water. It pours in while the villagers continue their brawl, throwing punches even while they are picked up by the water and deposited here and there, out a window, atop the prayer niche, over the railing of the staircase, and at last the fight is washed out into the street, and the water, pent up for a moment, breaks somewhere and drains, but it will rise again.

OUTSIDE THERE IS a group of children splashing in small pools like sparrows in a bath. Their mothers are nearby watching the river wrap around now a wood shack, now a smokehouse. Their fathers tote shotguns in protective circles, searching with hysterical eyes for the bears. Over the next half hour, the parents watch the water take the small structures, brick and board at a time, downstream, until even the stones of their foundations are washed away. Every once in a while, you can hear the faraway pop of a shotgun going off.

This is the way we pass our time now: guessing which buildings will drift away under the sweep of flooding waters. Some of the old food vendors take their carts to the overlooks and make small fortunes off the onlookers. It is surprising, everyone says so, it is surprising how fast a flood can grow, how little there is to do.

The road through the lower village is flooded. At the top of the street, you can still see Pembe's bakery; the water's up to your waist there. Now coming from the south, from the top of the highest point in the road is Hayrettin's van. Behind him the pass between hills is washing out on his heels. His van loses traction in the rising water and begins to lift away. He crawls out the window and swims to a point where there's no current, between a squat building and a lamppost. He holds on to the lamppost as he watches his van slide off. He hurries along the bank of shop fronts, like a child hugging the edge of a pool. I'm watching him from inside the cap of my minaret. *Hurry, hurry,* I think, *hurry, little Hayrettin.* He breaks out of the river's grip. The water's back down to his knees. He trudges to the bakery. The door is wide open and the lights are off. The place is rising up out of its frame: the stove, the ovens, the refrigerator, the pastry cases; they are all floating in a slow swirl about the bakery, but no Pembe. He splashes to the back to find this door open too. No sign of her outside either. He climbs the ladder to the roof, slipping twice on the rungs, but when he gets to the top there is no Pembe waiting for him.

IN A FEW languid strokes through the water, Pembe is by the side of the shop and takes the ladder out of the water to the top of her bakery. Hayrettin is there, sprawled out by the edge. He is breathing heavily and watching the sky. Pembe realizes there hasn't been a single flash of lightning, there has been no low rumble of thunder. There is only the rain, popping in the ear.

Splash, splash, splash, Pembe walks to Hayrettin. He sits up quickly, startled by her presence.

"I figured you went back to the house," he says. Then, thinking about it: "We both should have gone to the house. It is higher up."

"What's left there, anyway?" she asks.

And I can see him understand he has been found out. He doesn't know how exactly, but it doesn't matter, does it? His affair with Sibel has been found out.

"I'm surprised you haven't gone," he says.

"How we will stop this rain?" Pembe asks him. His face is surprise, the color of a popped balloon, because he hasn't thought about stopping it.

He doesn't know what to say. He knows he wants Pembe to ask him about his affair so that he can say he ended it, so that he can say he did the right thing, but instead she's asking about the weather. Instead of hiding in their house up in the hills, they are at the bakery, the only thing left she cares about. But that's not true, there is no bakery anymore.

"Isn't there anything you want to ask me?"

Pembe doesn't bother answering him because he doesn't understand. She sits down on the gravel of the roof. The water grows louder, the torrent is an explosion she can feel through the roof into her skin and sinking straight into her bones. Beside her, Hayrettin shouts and bandies about the roof, kicking the puddles and throwing a tantrum, a very narrow tantrum. She lies down with her back on the roof, staring up at the sky. Hayrettin has gone very quiet, though he thinks there is a world of things left to say. But that's not what there is time for. That's not what there's space for.

Hayrettin lies down beside her. She asks a question very quietly. She reaches her hand out for Hayrettin's, searches for his knuckles with her fingertips as the water below starts to push against the roof, she can feel the weight of it. He has found her hand in his and takes it. She pulls his hand to her mouth, kneads it and kisses it. She squeezes tightly but suddenly she can't feel it. She squeezes again to feel his grip in response, but she can't feel anything.

Around them comes the soft cradle of water swelling up against their backs. He grabs her hand as tight as he can, he holds it so as not to let it slip away. He is thinking all these things at once: *I am sorry, I want to be forgiven, I will love you and you will love me, just in time.* She is thinking all these things at once: *I miss my mother, I want to save her bakery, I miss my husband, he will love me again and I will love him again, just in time.*

If you thought this was the sort of story where two people can reconcile their love for each other and turn off the deluge, I have misled you, and I am sorry. I don't know how else to tell you that the vastness of humanity is still only a human drama, which, as undeniable as rain, is of the lowest order and smallest scale employed to measure the universe. I don't know how else to tell you there is no satisfying end when there is no end but the end. Still, have I not chiseled this story in the walls of my spire? Perhaps one day someone will find it.

There are a few shouts from the bivouacs high in the hills: "The grocer's is gone!" "The tea is ready and getting cold!" The world is washing away, yet people are concerned with their affairs, their sins, their petty trespasses and desires. Even as the water rises into our throats, we have in our thoughts only the next moment of humanity, as if it is a great and unyielding absolute, as if there is nothing more natural and inevitable than another day dawning over humankind, and yet, and yet, and yet . . .

We are all waiting for the clouds to break, for the sun to beat down and boil steam into the sky. I haven't heard anything from outside the village for weeks now. Some of us are climbing up higher and higher on the few trees left at the tips of hilltops; others of us are learning to swim. I run up my minaret as the water creeps over short trees. I use the hawk's perch as a diving board for my afternoon plunge, until my life is sucked across the wide and flat scrape of water, until there is no longer a minaret, just the conical cap pregnant with the scrawl of these words—and then, not even that.

The Birdkeeper's Moral

IF YOU ASKED Sami how it came to be that he could talk to the birds he would have laughed and said it was not the sort of thing to question. In truth, it happened in the sudden manner of a summer rain, taking even Sami by surprise.

It was the beginning of September 1955, and Istanbul, that ebullient city, was a powder keg. Everyone was nervous about what was happening in Cyprus—separatists were fighting to unite the island with Greece, but a good portion of the island was Turkish. There had even been a referendum about kicking out the British and joining Greece, but they hadn't let the Turks of Cyprus vote. Then all the Turks worried that things would unfold as they had on Crete not long before, and they would be massacred or exiled. Still vivid in many memories was the carving up of the Ottoman Empire, the occupation of the city, the plundering of the countryside, the hard-won war of independence. Yet easily forgotten were their own crimes, their own rapes and pillages and murders in the name of the Father-land. You know how it goes, the way paranoia festers. Things fell apart quickly—militias were formed in Cyprus earlier that year. In Istanbul each week it seemed there was a story in the sensationalist papers about a Greek or a Kurd or an Armenian being arrested for selling heroin, or stabbing someone, or robbing a jewelry store.

But Sami, being ever since his youth such an insular person, had not paid any mind to the papers or noticed the roiling of the city, and perhaps it was this precise myopia that had, on this fine warm day, made such wonderous things possible.

Like any other day, Sami went out early that morning to sell the birdcages he made. Sami spent his whole life catching birds and making cages, first as a boy with his father for the merchants and petty nobility of his family's village, then as a young man in Istanbul between the wars, and now as an old man he made his pittance selling them to the petite bourgeoisie of Şişli and Beyoğlu.

On his way to Galata Square, as always, he stopped first at the little ablution fountain to wash up. The fountain sat tucked in the corner of a little green square at the head of Sami's street, lined on one side by a bit of grass, a few trees and shrubs, tulips, and a rosebush. Halfway through washing his feet, a man in a linen suit arrived at the fountain and swatted his hat about, scaring off the finches that were resting in the shade of the fountain, scaring them off because they were shitting all over the place.

Sami told the man to stop, that all of God's creatures had a right to the water. He told the man all the beauty in the world can be found trapped inside a little bird and that surely their songs were enough to overlook the occasional mess, but the grouch wasn't listening and continued swatting at the birds as they sang their morning welcomes. So Sami promised a solution to the man who had not asked for one, and he ran back to his apartment in a flash, leaving wet footprints in his wake. Sami gathered up a few dishes and a bit of what little food he had in his kitchen and ran back to the fountain, but the man in the linen suit had left, and the birds returned to the spigots and basins of the fountain, shaking their bodies under the water, dribbling it between their wings and taking it into their beaks. With the food in one dish, Sami filled the others with water from the fountain and took them to the shade of the tree and nestled them in a pad of grass. He stepped back gingerly from his buffet and shouted into the sky (the home of the birds, after all) that this was their place now and to stop shitting on the marble. No sooner had Sami rested on a bench than a dozen birds climbed down from the tree and began eating, shouting: Shelled pistachios! Cherries, goodness! Still with their pits! Pumpkin seeds, a delicacy!

One of the birds—a tiny finch like a golden ball, not even a year old—began trilling a song and dipping its beak in the water, giving thanks over and over in a voice like honey: Teşekkür ederim, efendim, teşekkür ederim. But its mother soon fluttered down and, with a wing reached over its back, said shoo along quickly, and the two were off. Soon the first bowl was empty and Sami refilled it with water.

From a hidden place across the square, an owl had been watching Sami, swiveling its head as he went back and forth across the square to refill the water bowls. It jumped from its invisible perch and glided to the corner of the fountain where, silhouetted against the bright marble and with golden eyes upon him, it hooted at Sami. He could just make out the frame of the small owl. It stepped forward on the eave and he could see that its feathers were marbled, its legs white like gaiters, and its tiny beak made its eyes larger. Sami thought it looked soft.

—Why are you laying traps? asked the owl.

—My God, I really can hear you!

—Of course, said the owl. Of course you can hear us, so hear this: leave the birds be, huh?

—Isn't it nice to leave a little food for delicate creatures?

—They have warned me of you, said the owl from its perch.

—Why don't you eat some of the meal I've brought? Sami asked, pointing to the seeds.

—I don't eat seeds.

And the owl hooted, and leapt into the bright morning.

Sami would have liked to stay, to abandon his chores to listen to the birds as he gathered up more seeds and nuts and fruits for them, but he needed to make a living, so off he went with his wheelbarrow full of cages and wood to the square around Galata Tower because there was a café owner there who liked Sami's birds. Sami brought his own bird with him, a white-eared bulbul with indigo, gold, black, and white feathers that Sami could smell in his dreams. He'd had the bulbul for years, and always brought it along to attract other birds (it was an old trick used by the birdkeepers of the hills). Sami would sing to his bulbul and it would sing back, and all the birds would come to listen, but only if Sami brought his bulbul.

He could imitate calls only so well—never as well as his father. Sami's father, Celahattin, had such a gift of mimicry that he used to practically become a bird. When he ran out of greenfinches to sell, he'd go into the forest with a cage and whistle just like one, so greenfinches and greenfinches alone would come down from their nests and sing with him and he'd sing something back and they would hop into his cage content as housecats. All his life, Sami wished he could imitate a bird half as well as Celahattin, but for all his practicing it was no use, and besides, there were other ways to coax a bird into a cage.

Sami would whistle and his bulbul would sing back, and all the birds would see he was no threat because the bulbul was there, happy. Today, however, his bulbul trilled a song too melancholic, and Sami worried that if it didn't change, the free birds might be put off; he worried they would mistake him for a jailer.

The day passed slowly by as Sami tinkered with his birdcages, filling them with seed and hanging them from the branches of the horse chestnut that was in bloom, leaving open their doors as an invitation, but no birds came to fill them and soon the tree was stuffed to the brim with silent cages.

Evening bloomed up from the cobblestones. The café owner brought Sami a lamb sandwich out of pity and asked him where all the birds were, the way someone comments on the weather. The best birds are in the hills, Sami said, but he was too old now to be clambering up after them. Sami ate his sandwich and whistled to his bulbul, who managed only a listless tweet in response. For the past week it had been like this, his bulbul sending out weaker and weaker songs through the bars of its cage. It made Sami nervous about its health, but he was the sort of man to ignore things in hopes they might improve.

Then, from around the great base of Galata Tower, a woman stepped into the square, a basket in her arm ready to be filled with fruits from the stand down the alley, a soft scarf slung loose on the top of her head that left open her face, a face that Sami knew instantly: eyes curved down like they were pouring coffee from her dark irises, eyebrows like buttresses, lips that pouted at all times as though they were blowing steam from strong tea. Sami knew her from decades ago, before the fall of the empire, before the mess of the world, as the little girl in Dedeağaç whom he had adored. Suddenly, he became overly aware of his existence—miserable and squalored on a small crate picking crumbs from his mustache. She took in the noise and the lights of the café, then glanced into the windows of the restaurant, and soon she noticed the multitude of cages hanging in the square. She took a step back and turned to leave, when suddenly Sami's bulbul began tweeting its melancholy tune. The woman looked around for the bird but it was impossible to find with so many empty cages in the air. Instead she found only Sami next to a pile of his creations.

"Have you done this?" she asked him.

"I make these every day," Sami said, sweeping his hand across the cart of birdcages.

"I meant the song."

"Oh," said Sami. "That was my little bulbul." And he turned toward the lowest cage in the tree and pointed at the crossbar where the bird was perched. Sami grew anxious that she had not yet recognized him, or if she did, she hid it well. Surely she remembered his bulbul!

"Such a wonderful bird, such a cutting song. I don't know how to tell you what I mean. It sounds silly and you will laugh at me thinking: 'Poor old woman!' but I was drawn to this square today."

"The breeze," said Sami. "A sweet breeze can carry a soul anywhere."

"No, no. This bird, these birdcages, they must've drawn me here. I knew a man," she said. "A good man and his boy, who sold these capricious things. That was some time ago."

Sami understands what she is trying to say. "And I knew you, Fatima hanim."

"I'm sorry," Fatima said with feeling. "I haven't seen you before, but my memory . . ." For a moment the weight of time flashed across her face, illuminating wrinkles, sallowness, and hardened eyes, but quickly her features shed her age and she was muliebral once more, illusive of erosion as the djinn are. Sami saw the slightest of smiles escape from her, one of those coy little tricks to make respectable men blush.

"These are beautiful cages, could I have one? I mean I would pay, of course." Fatima giggled at herself. "With a bird in it, too?"

"With as many birds as you like."

She pressed a fingertip to her pouting lips. "Better have two so they don't despair."

Sami thought this intelligent foresight on her part. He told her

188 I Am My Country

not to worry about paying, but she insisted, so he said they would take care of it upon delivery. The bulbul started up again, its body shuddering with each chirp. And then she was gone—in her stead a breeze that knocked the petals from the tree and swayed the cages into a waltz about gravity.

⁂

HE HAD MET Fatima in Dedeağaç all those years ago, in an orange grove outside the village. Back when he was still a young boy, maybe eight or nine, the rest of the boys from the village would parade down to Sami's house singing songs they made up on the spot. He hid from them upstairs, especially on days while his father was out in the hills catching birds. They would call up to the balcony, sometimes throwing stones as well, demanding Sami come out to the river or to the fields freshly plowed or to the lemon, orange, and olive groves. Sami would stay quiet and still in the corner of his room while his father only whispered to him that it was unnatural for a boy like him to pen himself up behind the shutters. But Sami's father had forgotten the tortures young boys could inflict upon each other. Sami would have begged his father to hide him, to lift up the floorboards and bury him there, if he could speak, but he was trembling. These boys, you see, wanted Sami handed over to them for their tricks and pranks. He was that type, quiet and a bit simple, and young boys are merciless.

The boys of the village started climbing the walnut tree just outside Sami's window, some of them hanging upside down by their legs, others straddling the large branches, others still dangling by their arms and making sounds like monkeys.

"There's an orange grove I know of with oranges the size of your head," the chieftain of the child-rabble called. "Honest, Sami, I have tasted the fruit myself."

Sami's father, yelling over the songs of his finches, urged Sami to
go and run over dirt paths with the other boys, to take flight through
the hills until his skin was dark with the dust of raucous adventuring.

Sami went to the window to count the faces of the boys ruddy
with sun. He recognized some of the older boys and thought it better
to stay home, tales of their abusive games having circulated among
the village children, but Sami's father, now desperate to silence the
racket competing with his birds, took Sami by the shoulders, dragged
him downstairs, and flung him out the front door, locking it behind
him. Sami looked around the street for a place to hide, but through
the walls he heard his father tell the children to come round and get
him, and it wasn't long before all of them were moving through the
cramped streets into the hills, a pack of bare limbs, mangy and hungry, throwing rocks at the squirrels or stray dogs.

The mob of boys poured down the cart path. They climbed a
whiskered knoll littered with rocks that sliced their palms and feet.
At the crest they lay, belly down, across the dry and prickly grass,
their gazes fixed beyond, into the sea of glossy green leaves of citrus
trees, speckled with globes of orange enamel in the sun. The earth
beneath the canopy was shaded, dark. The sky above was a layer of
blue paint so close you could scrape chips of it with your fingertips.
In the breeze, the trees shimmered like salmon scales. On the wind:
the bite of citrus.

"Go on," said one of the boys.

"Why me?"

"Because you spend so much time with the birds you must know
something of flight."

"Because your mother was Greek."

"Because you smell like vinegar."

They told Sami that because he was the shortest and lightest, he
would have to go first and spot for the watchmen. In those days,
the lords hired watchmen for their groves and orchards—there were

the issues of brigands and thievery en masse that precede war. Sami protested but the other boys grabbed him by his limbs, hoisted him off the ground, and carried him down into the grove, shouting that they'd ram him into a tree if he didn't climb up at once. "They're too tall," he shouted. They were only ten meters each, but a meter is great when you are an ant. The children at his legs held firm despite his writhing. The four captors started running for the trunk of the nearest tree, aiming to cleave Sami in two with dull force. "All right," he cried. "All right, all right. I will climb. Put me down."

So they stuck him up into the tree and urged him through the bundle of branch and fruit and leaf and sap—half with cheers, half with threats—until the offshoots creaked from his weight and the limbs were thinner than his own frame, and he swayed to and fro with the squirrels. Some of the boys had climbed up after him, already at work plucking oranges and releasing them into the waiting nets of outstretched shirts below.

"What do you see up there?"

Sami didn't know any words that meant something so encompassing as all of an orange grove, all of a hillside, all of an empire, the complete bond with the earth but also with the sky. "Nothing," he said.

The boys made him stay posted while they gorged, their tan bellies growing bulbous until they looked like roasted meats on spits. Some of the boys napped in the shade. The oldest boy, the self-appointed bey of daytime orphans, followed yellow and black butterflies in weaves between the trunks. Around him lay orange rinds splayed open, sticky shells of a feast picked clean. Sami watched the boy as he waited for the butterflies to land. He would catch them and stick their slender legs in sap to watch them struggle. When he tired of listening for the noises they made, he pinched their gossamer wings between his fingers and tore them off. Some other boys took interest and joined him in catching the butterflies by their velvety bodies and dewinging them, perhaps all of them using the wings to make wishes by.

Over the crown of trees, Sami saw a dust cloud fast approaching, too near to tell the boys to run off, too near to climb down himself and escape. "Guards," he shouted to the boys. "They're riding this way."

"There's no time."

"What do we do?"

"We'll kill you for this, Sami."

"What do we do?"

"Hide!"

And in the frenzy of tawny bodies scrambling for cover, no one could hear Sami ask, "What about me? Help me down, I can't make it."

No one noticed except of course the oldest, who, from his hiding place in a patch of tall grass, shouted at Sami to keep still.

"I can't. Let me down. I can't move," Sami said, petrified.

"Please," said Sami.

The cloud of dust billowed closer, and the sound of clopping hooves rushed toward them. The oldest lay flat in the grass and pulled leaves over himself. Some climbed up into the branches. Others stood like idiots behind the thick trunks. None thought to hide the orange peels.

The tree trembled with Sami, as he watched for the procession of guards in brilliant white turbans and crimson fezzes, as he thought of calling down to them upon their arrival to help him out of the tree, but what would befall him then?

Yet there were no guards on the horizon, no flowing green robes or banners of the local bey. Instead, down the path that cut through the grove rode a figure like porcelain atop a horse as black as the hopes of lepers. From the heavy hooves rose a plumage of dust, white to match the robes and salwar worn by the rider. Sami froze in his perch, eyes losing sight of all things but this rider as she neared, her face like oleander behind a sheer veil, her hair dark and long, falling to the horse's mane and mingling indistinguishably. She looked small on the horse, but not frail. Her head was only partially covered; she looked a few years older than any of the boys but she was still young, and you could see that she would stay that way. The horse stopped a few trees from Sami's and pushed its nose across the dry grass and orange peels. The girl, without huff, gracefully drew her own blade. "Who's been stealing from me?" she shouted. "Who's been eating what is mine?"

"We're terribly sorry," said Sami, almost choking with regret for making a sound. But all the other boys—unworried by a girl, fascinated by the blade, curious about the horse—had already begun emerging from their hiding places, shaking off dirt and leaves and grit.

"Stay back," said the girl. "I'll spill your blood with this."

"And who are you to give commands?" the oldest boy asked.

The horse grunted as if to answer for its master, but she needed no tongue other than her own. "I am Fatima," she pronounced. "Daughter of Metin Efendi who owns this grove and the land around it you dogs dare trespass." She sounded like the men, twice her height and thrice her age, that Sami's father haggled with at the bazaars.

"Be careful not to hurt yourself," called Sami, eyes on her blade and wanting to say something.

"Who's talking?" asked Fatima.

"That's no one," said the oldest.

"Just the son of a bird peddler stuck in a tree," said another.

"And so he behaves like a bird?" asked Fatima.

And all the boys began claiming Sami thought he could fly, thought that his father's birds had taught him, that he had water in his brains and spent too much time with the finches and larks. In truth, heights made Sami dizzy.

"If he cannot fly, then how did he get so high?" asked Fatima.

"That's no great distance," said a scrawny boy. "I could throw a stone up there. I could hit him with a rock from here."

"Maybe you couldn't," said the oldest. "But I could."

And erupted the competition of hitting Sami with rocks in order to impress the girl on horseback. The branches were dense with foliage; fewer rocks snuck through than Sami expected. He was bruised only in a few places, and anyway, he didn't blame the boys, he would have done the same and more to impress Fatima.

"Stop at once," said Fatima, swatting at the tops of heads with the flat of her blade. "Get him down from there."

"Get him yourself," said the oldest, and though Sami thought she might, hoped she would climb up to him and ask him about birds, she instead turned her horse around and told the rabble to leave, told them if they wanted to live they should go now before her father's servants arrived to lop their heads off. Reluctantly, the band of village boys broke rank and retreated down the hills for their homes. Fatima looked up into the tree and smiled her first smile. It was clumsy and filled up Sami's throat with a giggle.

"Is your father truly the bird peddler?"

"Oh yes. If you come to him, I will make sure he gives you anything you desire for nothing in return."

"Can you make it down?"

Sami nodded.

"Hurry down," she said impatiently. "The servants are looking for me and will surely check here." For though it was her father's groves and her steed, she was out without permission, skipping another of her dozens of lessons and teachings arranged by Metin Efendi to prepare her for courtly life. Sure enough, in the distance came the faint call of a few of her father's servants, shouting her name genially, glad to be walking the groves on such a beautiful day instead of teaching her etiquette and manners.

She rode off, the dust dissolving her image. The insides of Sami's chest fluttered with butterflies, and he wondered, if the boys could reach through his ribs, would they tear off these wings of his heart as well?

⁂

NOW SAMI WENT to work on this new cage for Fatima. Unlike the simple cylinders and boxes he normally built, this one would be fashioned as a miniature palace, taking as its inspiration the bright and verdant palaces that dot the shores of the Bosporus. It would be built two, maybe three stories high (that is, in scale to a bird), with a carved façade, perhaps even inlaid with mother-of-pearl. But what of the roof? He could make a surmounted dome, or a bell dome, or a traditional shallow-pitched square, or an octagonal crown. It would depend on how wide he built out the little palace, how many apartments he would give it, and he laughed at this idea, little rooms for the birds. It would be the most resplendent cage he had ever made. A testament, he thought, to Fatima's beauty.

But why had she played that game, pretending not to recognize him? Sami wondered if she had really forgotten him. No matter, this cage would remind her, would bring him back to her mind just as seeing her again today brought back so many rose-sweet memories for him.

He organized piles of wood along his floor; one of primary pieces, another of secondary wood for the interior of the cage, and lastly a miscellany pile. He sawed and planed and pared and hammered away at his workbench, whistling as he went and taking time to make and remake prototypes of the different elevations. He ransacked cages he'd already made for their parts, dismantling a board here, a rod there as they were needed.

He finished a cage and put it aside, disappointed with how it'd turned out. He worked like this for hours in the corner of his apartment until his eyes stung, until his spine cried, until he missed with his saw and sliced open his hand on the umpteenth cage. Around him sat saggy, half-dismembered cages like Greek ruins. "What's the use in having a hundred cages if I haven't any birds?" Sami asked. And the bulbul warbled pitifully, its white feathers looking even paler in the sunlight caught in the window. "I'll need help coaxing the finches into these things," Sami said to it as a way of asking: Are you still unwell, my friend? The bulbul looked at him as if asking its own question. It lifted one wing and touched its beak to its flank, then, crawling slowly across its perch, it went to the cage door and sighed. "Don't look so glum, little friend. You simply need your health," Sami said. "Rest up. I will find another bird to help me."

Sami hoped the bulbul would say some little words of encouragement, but it didn't even peep. He had for years now kept only his bulbul as company, but there was that curious owl at the fountain. Perhaps it wouldn't mind helping him. He could appeal to its tender heartstrings, for surely such beautiful creatures held love in high regard. And if not, then perhaps he could bribe it with food.

Quickly he packed a bit of birdseed and some other things into his rucksack and set off for the square at the head of his street. Once there he set about remaking an inviting little oasis in the grass, but it was already very late in the day, and the birds were all gone to sleep or not yet up for the night. Evening fell like a light going out, and Sami was alone at the fountain, thinking how peaceful the square was, how sweet the air tasted: warm, baked with nuts. He searched about the fountain, hoping that owl would turn up again, but soon enough the sun had fully set and there was still no sign of the owl. Thinking she must be out hunting and about to call it a night since he didn't know where else to look for her, he climbed down from the tree and headed home, but before he left the square, the owl hooted phantasmally from some unseen perch. Delighted,

Sami spun around and called out to the bird in a whisper so as not to disturb the peaceful night: I have brought you more than seed, little owl.

The owl hooted again.

—What have you brought? she asked.

Taking off his rucksack, Sami turned it upside down and out splattered the mushy corpse of a rat from his building's basement, fat with cheese because the traps didn't work. From the darkness, the owl materialized, swooping down onto the rat.

—Would you mind looking away while I eat? the owl asked.

Sami said sure, that he didn't mind one bit. He turned his back to the owl and could hear the snapping of muscle cords, the rip of furred flesh.

—Do you have a name? asked Sami, his back still turned.

—Of course I do. Why do you ask?

—I'm curious what sort of name a bird would have, said Sami.

And the owl said her name was Mermer, and she had been given this name by a Spaniard who fought at Granada and stole Mermer from a dead Berber.

—What kind of bird is so sarcastic? asked Sami.

—It is the truth, said Mermer, shaking her head into a tornado. I have been here for five hundred years, and before that I was in Spain because they know how to take care of birds.

—You look very good for your age.

The owl Mermer fluttered into the air, made a long circle, and then glided back down to the cobblestones, and Sami loved the way Mermer slipped from here to there so effortlessly.

—I've never seen a prettier owl than you, Sami said.

Mermer turned her head all the way around and then back, smiling, or so it seemed, before she reached out her wings and spread her feathers all about.

—You must be very wise, too, Sami said.

—Oh no, even though I am myself an owl, I admit to you we owls are not very wise. It is a funny thing to us that people think so.

Mermer picked at a few tufts on her belly, then took long strides toward a puddle.

—But you must be, having lived for centuries, I mean, said Sami.

—I suppose I know more than your average bird.

—Can you tell me then why I can talk with you but not my bulbul? Sami asked.

And the owl Mermer, dipping her beak into the water, said with a voice like seltzer: You can talk to your bulbul, but they are impatient and have little regard for the cacophonous sounds man makes. Haven't you heard their beautiful language?

Sami thought the owl was being unfair, disregarding the poetry of the human tongue, the vast lyricism of lip and tooth.

—Could you talk to my bulbul, then?

Mermer made a very strange sound for an owl that Sami assumed was laughter.

—Of course I could.

—I want to know why it's sad. It's not singing like it used to. If something's changed, I mean, or if it's sick . . .

—Where are your cages? asked Mermer, as if remembering she'd left the stove on.

—I've quit selling them.

—Why?

—There's no time. I am in love, said Sami.

—What's love have anything to do with cages?

Sami thought the two had plenty in common, but he just told the owl: I'm building an enormous cage to hold a dozen birds for my dearest.

—So often people say such things that mean very little to a bird, said Mermer. My this, my that, as if everything must be in relation to possession. We birds use names.

—Her name is Fatima, Sami said.

The owl hooted and fluttered her wings a moment.

—Who is Fatima?

—I knew her long ago, from my childhood, said Sami. Though I don't think she recognized me.

—Is she as beautiful as me? asked Mermer, and Sami laughed at such a jealous bird.

—She hasn't changed in all these years, and I feel as though I'm back in Dedeağaç.

—Is that where you met her? asked Mermer. Sami nodded and the owl said: It must have been a long time ago if she has forgotten you.

Sami agreed it was three, almost four decades ago. How had that much time passed? Had he spent each day with her in his thoughts? Perhaps at first, but after a while less and less so, and now not anymore.

For a time in Sami's life there was the chase, the search for Fatima. His move to Istanbul from Dedeağaç, his morning wanders through Bebek, Nişantaşı, Şişli. In his heart there hid a compass of longing, decaying over time, breaking down, pointing in strange directions until he could no longer remember her nose, her ears, the grit of the dust from the roads through her land, the scent of orange peels, her eyes wrinkling just before a laugh. She was gone to him before long, hidden beyond the thicket of his history made of wooden bars and hollow bones. And in a moment, in the flash of their encounter, he drowned again in the remembrance of her.

—And you think that maybe she will fall in love with you again just because you gift her a wooden prison with terrible creatures trapped inside? asked the owl. She had narrowed her eyes and now seemed exacting.

Sami laughed at this owl with her sharp tongue. Perhaps it

sounded a little strange spoken aloud, but what else do you do when you are in love besides construct tokens of adoration. And Sami admitted to Mermer that it was a gift of meaning between them. It was a way to remind her of their past, and then perhaps for her, too, the memories would come flooding back and they would find each other in Galata Square as if all the time that had passed had been only the blink of an eye.

—It is no good to try to win this Fatima's heart with your cages, said Mermer.

Mermer clipped her talon swiftly into the leftovers of the rat. She hooted and then apologized as though it were a belch.

—Why is it no good? Sami asked.

—People are only impressed by pirates and soldiers.

—What?

—That's right, only the pillaging of pirates and the valor of soldiers is enough to impress the heart of a woman, and you are neither conqueror nor pillager.

—That's ridiculous, said Sami.

Mermer began to count with her talons all the instances she could recall of Barbary pirates or valiant Ottoman sailors or brave janissary captains winning the hearts of their sweet things back home through their tales of conquest.

—Men don't construct symbols of love. Destruction is their evidence; their spoils are what win them the hearts of others.

—What about Shah Jahan's Taj Mahal? Sami asked.

—Think of all the countries conquered to provide the slaves, Mermer said.

And the bird was right, of course. Many slaves were needed for the Taj Mahal.

—Your cages are in their own way very similar, as they stand as evidence of your oppression over the finch.

—Bah! Sami said, and waving his hands, he left, but walking back to his home, a thought coiled around the stem of his mind and took hold: one cage would not be enough to enchant Fatima.

OUTSIDE SAMI'S APARTMENT building stood a few men in ragged suits, one holding a pail of paint, two holding pickaxes, one holding his tongue between his teeth, his lips curled back, his arms folded. They huddled around Sami's neighbor and superintendent of the building, Tarik.

"What's all the trouble?" Sami asked.

"Nothing's the matter, nothing's the matter."

"We're just here to do a little painting," said the man with the paint can.

"Yes, but as I've told them, there are only good Muslims living here," said Tarik. He looked very anxious.

"Muslims like paint," Sami said.

"This is blue paint, it's really only to the liking of Greeks," said the man with his tongue clamped between his teeth. And that's how he talked, squeezing the words through the cracks of his incisors.

"There are some Greeks I know of in the next building," said Tarik. "But none here. Sami bey, do go inside. The fumes, you know, aren't good for the senses."

"You all ought to invest in coveralls," said Sami with a laugh. "It'd be a shame to ruin those suits."

The men agreed with Sami and bid him good night before returning to their hushed discussion. They told Tarik they knew there were a few Greeks in the building and if he didn't want trouble he'd show them which were their apartments. Things like this had been happening all over Istanbul the last couple days, even if Sami didn't notice them.

In his apartment Sami set to tinkering a bit with the cage he was making for Fatima, but he couldn't focus and felt all his inertia deflated by Mermer's words. He kept looking to his bulbul for a cheery tone but none came forth. Compared to just yesterday the bird looked worse, having lost some of its color at the roots of its feathers. Sami asked it if it was feeling all right, but it didn't speak back. It tucked its head into the pit of its wing, and Sami felt cut open watching this. "Have I not given you a comfortable life and loving home?" he asked. "Have I been callous and unkind?"

THE VILLAGE BOYS came along and found him at his window, moping like an idiot, and they told him they had an idea to make him forget about his worries. They told him the sweet taste of fresh honey was the cure for anything. They took him to a field where buzzed a hive of bees, and they told him to wait while they lit a fire underneath the hive to smoke the bees. Then they dragged him to the tree and threw him up on the branch with the hive.

But Fatima so enjoyed disobeying her father that there wasn't a field unvisited by her as she went for long rides, leading her father's servants in searches all over the countryside. As before, she found Sami stuck up in a tree, with a grin light as a feather on his face. She convinced the boys the honey was bad, would taste like onion because of all the onions growing nearby. And just as before, she ran off, leaving Sami hanging by his small hands from a branch that rubbed red across his soft palms.

Every week they had these little rendezvous. She harassed the village boys away during their games of cruelty that Sami enjoyed submitting to in order to be rescued by Fatima atop her steed, and in each of her displays she was strong and her demeanor assertive, but

Sami could see that her beauty betrayed her mortality, and for all her bravado, her heart seemed just one small touch by the breeze from coming undone.

It was not long before Fatima cast off the pretense of rescuing Sami to pay him a little visit. Sometimes, at Fatima's request, they would play with the birds in the aviary downstairs, or if Sami's father, Celahattin, was home, they would have him introduce each bird to them and marvel at its beauty. And Sami would ask his father to mimic the bird, and Fatima would ask Celahattin things like: How far does this bird travel? How high up into the sky can this bird fly? How difficult is it to catch? How clever is it? Clever enough to escape?

Other times when Fatima visited, she and Sami would leave for the forest, telling Sami's father they were out to practice bird calls, and they'd walk the dirt path into the hills, one on either side of her horse so that the horse was like a curtain between them. Along the way Fatima would open up to Sami in a way that is difficult to do under the scrutiny of eye contact. With that equine border between them, Fatima felt she could say anything.

They walked into the meadows around the village and tied the horse to one of the widely spaced shade trees and watched the clouds and listened to the birds in the prickly grass cropped up between them. She felt she could admit to Sami the silliest fantasy and the hardest fears in equal measure, and in response Sami offered only gentle hums and giggles.

Sami was tickled at how often she would bring up birds. It made him feel, in a way, that she meant to talk about him without that awful and bashful business of having to talk about oneself.

"If you could be any bird, which would you be?" Sami asked her, their eyes on that blue heaven above.

"Is there such a difference between birds?" she asked in earnest.

Sami smiled. "Oh, there is all the difference in the world between just a goose and magpie. You could be a beautiful bird, or a crafty bird, or a cunning bird, or a songbird, or an ugly and mean bird, though you wouldn't be."

"Does it matter, though? I mean, if they can all fly, who cares what they look like or sound like or how smart they are. It would be enough just to fly." Fatima saw that this was not the way Sami wanted her to answer. "And what bird would you be?" she asked.

Sami pretended to think for a long time, pretended he didn't have his own answer ready when he asked her the question. "I wish I could be a falcon. My father says they are strong and fast and smart and brave. If you were a bird, I think you would be a falcon." Sami smiled at this assessment.

"Do people keep them in their aviaries?"

"Yes, yes. They make great hunters. Falconers train them for it, too. Oh, the skill it takes—all the time too, to get the bird to hunt and bring it back to you."

Fatima nodded. "Perhaps that is like me, then. But I don't want that."

Sami was upset to hear she wouldn't want to be a falcon with him.

"My father owns me," she said. "With his obsession of legacy, he shall always own me, as his father owned him. All that matters to him are the lines on a map, the accumulation of titles and land, a return to the time of timars and sipahis and feudal contracts, though it is long, long over."

Even though he didn't understand some of the words she said, at least not the way she said them, Sami felt sorry for Fatima as she went on comparing her life to that of a falcon or hawk or even a little finch kept in its cage. She made living in an aviary sound cruel and abysmal, and Sami wanted to tell her that he didn't keep an aviary like that. He wanted to tell her that his birds and his father's birds lived in a paradise. She was wrong to say it was a prison, but he didn't know how to convince her. He didn't have enough of an understanding to explain it, though he was certain of this.

"Isn't there a bird that's never kept in a cage, a bird no one wants to have?"

Sami thought a duck at first and laughed at the image of it in a little aviary, laughed at the thought of someone asking the duck to sing a beautiful song only for it to quack back. But people keep them in pens like chickens. Sami thought very hard and realized every bird in his mind had been kept or trained or eaten. "I suppose a vulture. No one wants a vulture."

"And they fly about?"

"Yes. They can fly incredible distances."

"I want to be a vulture," said Fatima.

"Because you are scared of cages?"

"Yes," she said. "Why else would you want to become a bird?"

Sami thought it was strange that if someone were afraid of cages, they would wish to be a bird. For him it sounded like someone scared of water wishing to be a fish.

"But a bird . . . it is natural for birds to be wary of cages," said Fatima. "It is natural for birds to escape them. With people it is tricky—we are not always so aware of our cages."

"If you are scared of something you shouldn't become it," said Sami, not understanding.

"If I were scared of something, I should wish to become its opposite," said Fatima. "The opposite of a cage is a vulture, as you say."

Sami found himself confused; he was too young. He had heard these words before, but differently. The way Fatima talked, there were meanings piled on top of meanings and he couldn't keep track of what she was saying. All of it, though, reminded him of his father, how he would often say to Sami that to love something is to become it. Sami didn't really know what this meant, he was too young, but this line had been repeated to him enough times that it took on a meaning for him detached from the definitions of the words. He thought it meant when we love something with enough intensity, we take on its aspects. He loved his father, and saw how he could become the birds. He loved the birds and wanted to become them, too.

Eventually, Fatima's acts of heroism became infrequent; her father had enforced stricter boundaries and hired more austere tutors. There had been talk of arranging her marriage to a landed notable in a nearby village. Metin Efendi refused to see, however, that he was raising his daughter for a time fast coming to an end. In the village things seemed to change as well. The children's games with Sami shed their blithe façades, evolving quickly into anxious rituals with a clear goal of harm, their tongues sharp with curses for Sami, the half-Greek son of a whore. In the same season, the brigands in the hills too shed their halfhearted nature and organized into militias, each with their own faction called: Serbian, Bulgarian, Albanian, Greek.

A COMMOTION SPURRED Sami out of his slumber. Outside, Istanbul was buzzing. It was the sort of commotion that comes from heat and frustration and newspaper headlines, and waits for a simple leak in the valve to burst forth—here a traffic accident, there a stolen bicycle; it is enough to bring simmering blood to a roaring boil. In the street below two men were at each other's throats. To Sami it was yet another foolish fight that happens dozens of times in the city.

He rolled to the edge of his bed and rubbed the sleep out of the folds of his face. Sami had spent all last night worried and restless, his thoughts vacillating between the few miserable gurgles his bulbul managed to sing, and Fatima's reentry into his life but coy dismissal of him. By the time he fell asleep and woke up again, these thoughts submerged and became a pit in his stomach. He couldn't say exactly what was troubling him, but it felt like with Fatima's return, other parts of his life were coming back to him. He whistled good morning to his bulbul, but it buried its head against its breast and slumped to the floor of its cage. Feeling anxious and with no one else to talk to, Sami went to the basement to empty the rat trap and left his apartment to seek out the owl Mermer.

Sami crept up his street ceilinged by webs of clotheslines strung across the sky, their white sheets like clouds in the early morning. From upper floors children dropped baskets by lines to be filled by the man who came around with yogurt and cheese.

When he arrived at the square, he saw in the shade of the tree that his little seed and water station was busy, busy with birds; even the owl Mermer, having just finished taking a drink, was now relaxing on the branch of the tree. He approached it quietly, not wanting to alarm any of the birds, but Mermer with her oscillating gaze caught him.

—My, the generous man has come with his gift bag again! Mermer hooted, and then to a little finch nearby she said: Remember this handsome man as the most generous soul you ever saw.

Sami shrugged to the bird.

—I felt bad for storming off yesterday.

—I have known sparrows to leave midsentence, Mermer said.

—One ought to be more suspicious of a man bringing so many gifts, said the finch, and it flew off to preoccupy itself with the concerns of finches.

Sami plucked a rat from his bag and dropped it on the cobblestone. Mermer leapt from the branch—her wings thrumming in their great beats—scooped up the rat with her narrow talons, and severed its spine by the base of the tree where the shade spilled between blades of grass. She ate quickly, out of Sami's sight; he could only hear the little snaps, splashes, chips, tears.

—Do you know many sparrows?

As Sami spoke to her, she'd caper out into the sun of the square to reply before hurrying back to her meal in the grass.

—Sure. I know all the birds in the Greek quarter, and I know most in the Jewish quarter. I even know a sad old falcon in the ruins of Rumeli Fortress.

—And you can speak to all of them? I mean, you don't have different languages?

—No, no, the language of birds is one, said Mermer between gulps of rat.

—My bulbul worries me. He doesn't speak a peep. He is losing color and I don't know what to do.

—Have you thought of letting him out? Taking him to the hills around the city and releasing him?

The little owl slurped up the rattail and bellowed a long hoot from the cavities of its bones.

—Are you full already? I have more if you want, Sami said.

—The finch was right, I ought to be suspicious.

—Perhaps I could help you catch rats if you help me with something, Sami said.

—That fool's errand you're so ruffled up about?

—My gift for Fatima.

—I am not a slaver, said Mermer.

—I'm not either. I give the birds beautiful homes, and they are fed and groomed and protected. Such lives they live, men kill for it.

—I believe you, said Mermer.

—Well, what if you helped me hire some birds. Just for a little while. I will pay them. Surely you can't object to honest work and honest wages?

Mermer made a motion like waving her wing dismissively.

—Even if you say you will set them free, once they are in your cages how quickly you will change your mind. It is your greatest quality to forget the exploitation your endeavors cost.

—That's true, said a little magpie from a place unseen.

—Are all birds such eavesdroppers? Sami asked.

—Humans are all the same, said Mermer. There has always been a need for people to turn the beauty of one thing to rubble, then from the rubble erect their own ideas of beauty. Save yourselves the time and appreciate the beauty already there. Take your Fatima to fields on the slopes around the city, show her the songs of cicadas and free birds. Don't steal the field and cram it into her apartment.

—I am humbler than that, said Sami.

—Even when you think you are virtuous and acting goodly, destruction is your by-product. Haven't you heard of the man who tried shooting his beloved to the moon?

—I haven't, said Sami.

As Mermer cleared her throat, a fat nightjar with stippled feathers and whiskers like the eyelashes of a princess waddled out of the sky and alighted in the tree. It was in the middle of its migration and sighed the way you sigh after a long journey in a tightly packed bus. It had in its claws the nub of a discarded cigarette. The nightjar ruffled its wings and said: Say, have any of you got a light?

—Birds don't smoke, said Sami.

—And just who are you, anyway? asked the nightjar.

—I am Sami from Dedeağaç, I build homes for birds from the wood of linden trees, and by the fountain I wash my feet and thank God for my life.

—You mean you are the cage builder.

—What is your name? Sami asked.

—I am called Kabuk, said the nightjar.

Mermer hooted like a shot at Kabuk.

—I was just about to tell this man a story, said Mermer.

Kabuk bowed his head and apologized and the owl started her tale:

A long time ago, maybe five or six hundred years, while the Black Death was ravaging the country, there was a man from Frankia who found himself in love. He was the sort of man who always bragged about the purity and boundlessness of his love and sought to praise the great immeasurable beauty of his beloved. But you know this type of man—instead of speaking his adoration, for he doesn't trust words (that's always how he says it too: "there are no words to describe . . ."), instead of telling his beloved how he feels, he plucks up the finest tulips right in bloom, or has metals bent into shackles for glittering adornments, or has quarries and mines depleted for palaces, or worst of all hears of the natural beauty of a foreign land and sets out to conquer and loot it all as gifts meant to praise his beloved's beauty. It is always the same and this man was no different, but with the Black Death coursing through Frankia, there was hardly anything beautiful to be plucked and given to his beloved. It would be a miserable gesture to offer up a wild, dilapidated estate, or rabid animal, or bloated, poxy corpse as a gift to woo her.

He spent day after tortured day trying to come up with something when, late at night, woken by the flagellants crying under their whips, he was struck by the idea to pluck the moon (the last unmarred thing in existence) right out of the sky and give it to his beloved as a talisman. What second-rate poet hasn't thought of that? Impossible as this feat was, however, the man was a creative architect of sorts, a clever engineer of machines, and had built as his profession many catapults and trebuchets for his lords, and he hatched upon the idea not to bring down the moon, but to deliver his beloved and himself to the moon instead.

Confident in his abilities, the man set about his preparations at once. He had his peasants clear a stretch of forest to supply the lumber for his machine, and tirelessly he worked them all through the day and late into each night until they had completed the largest trebuchet the man had ever made. He had his peasants roll it up the hill over the estate, and that night he prepared to test it. Having selected a boulder roughly the weight of two people, they loaded it, readied the counterweight, wound the ropes, aimed for the moon, and fired! The man said a prayer for the boulder to make it to the moon, and though it soared higher than any he had seen before, soon enough it peaked and began its course back where, well into the distance, it crashed to earth.

The man was not deterred. He constructed a larger machine, larger than any in the kingdom of Frankia. And though it managed to launch the next boulder a bit higher, it too failed. On and on this man went designing and constructing, as news and rumors of his exploits spread, and his peasants, having exhausted his forest of lumber, began plundering other forests. Well, the boulders kept climbing a little higher than the previous, but in the end, they all came back down long before they reached the moon. He would have kept doing this, making larger and larger machines in the hopes of finally reaching the moon, but the boulders, being fired so far away, had in fact been crashing down into the next kingdom, smashing up first the inn, then a number of wheat fields, and the stables, and part of the castle wall, and then even whole villages, their inhabitants sleeping as the boulders crashed. The people of the next kingdom had thought it was divine punishment, and so resigned themselves to prayer and digging caves for their new homes until the rumors and news of the man making enormous engines reached the kingdom. Without a word spoken between them, the peasants and squires and knights and barons and even the king himself grabbed up their weapons and marched for the architect on his hill. They caught him and his peasants just as they were loading another engine. In an instant, the rabble grabbed the man up and hacked him to bits, each of them taking a turn with their weapon before chasing down the man's peasants and killing them, too.

But Sami had stopped listening. Slowly he turned his head left then right then left, dispelling the fable-web from around his face. Throughout the story he could see where the birds were going, and now as they shrugged their wings and opened and closed their beaks, their story was soundless to him. They were trying to ruin him with this tale, to dissuade him from his project, but he wouldn't hear it, or rather, he started hearing something else.

The birds did not realize right away that while their story had gotten through to Sami, it was not in any sort of manner they would have liked. A fear was running up the steps of Sami's spine as Mermer's tale came to a close. Sami became convinced at once that he and Fatima were in danger, and plans began hatching in his mind, incomplete and impossible plans, each of them sharing images with Mermer's tale, images of contraptions and woodworks and flight and the moon. Instead of being discouraged from his project, Sami was now envisaging an undertaking so encompassing and complete that no matter how wonderfully he described it to them, the birds would only find it monstrous. Swiftly and anxious to avoid hearing the end of the silly bird's obvious tale, Sami left the fountain.

Back in his apartment, he paced about as horrid ideas zoomed by in the slipstream of his thoughts. He ransacked the room of all his tools and offcuts of wood, thinking up uses for them and abandoning them in turn.

Then Sami thought he heard a knock at his door—and yes! there it was again. He left his work for the door, thinking it might be Fatima. Perhaps she had remembered him after all and asked after him as a surprise. Perhaps she gave him the wrong address and was coming to correct it. But in the hallway stood just the shabby thing that passed for a neighbor in Sami's building: the fat, bearded, balding Tarik.

"What's wrong with you, making a racket so late?" Tarik asked. It was past midnight.

"I'm sorry, I hadn't realized—"

"Never mind, I'm not really here about that. You're Greek, aren't you?"

"No," Sami said, and as he had spent all his life praying at the mosque and fasting during Ramadan, no one would call him Greek.

"Don't go out tomorrow night."

"What do you mean? Why not?"

"Sami bey, there are people out in the city who . . . There are bad men in the city. Think of it like your birds. Some men want an aviary full of every kind, and some men want neat cages occupied only by finches."

Tarik closed the door behind him, and with the snap of the catch, Sami became aware that his cage-making would not return Fatima to him. Without being fully conscious of it, indeed without even understanding why, Sami became aware of an insurmountable problem, though he could not name it. Such was the fear and excitement bounding about his insides, that in a moment of ridiculous clarity, Sami came upon the solution of an escape.

※

BOUNCING OUT OF his apartment after a long night of planning and thinking, Sami packed up all the rats from his basement in a hurry, hoping to still catch Mermer and Kabuk at the fountain.

Sami carried the rats he'd gathered by their tails, five in each hand. What owl could eat more? He worried people would look strangely at him, but on his way through his street, there was no one out. He could hear a noise like a riot building overhead but thought it must just be the thunderclouds forming.

At the fountain, the fat nightjar and the little owl were talking about the prices of meats, others' plans for migration. They stopped when Sami sat on the bench. No little birds were splashing in his bath.

—Look who it is, said Kabuk. The builder of the grotesque—why don't you just go away from here, we're both enjoying our morning.

—That's no way to talk to a friend, Mermer said, eyes on the rats. But I must say, Sami, I am surprised you are still in Istanbul.

—I need your help, he said to Mermer, for surely the birds trust you more than me.

—I thought you had given up this plan of yours, said Kabuk.

—Are all those rats for me? asked Mermer, hopping closer to Sami along the eave of the fountain.

—They are if you agree to help me.

—You want slaves, said Kabuk.

—Is it so bad to keep a bird as a pet?

—You mean keep them as a prisoner? said Kabuk, and Mermer flapped a wing at him to shush him up.

Sami made a face at the nightjar. Kabuk was being unfair. He thought of his bulbul, of how much he cared for it. He thought of all the birds he kept, all birds his father kept, and knew them all to be happy, to have loved him and his father back. And then suddenly he didn't know this anymore.

—They say the forester loves trees the most, said Sami.

—And do the trees love the forester? Kabuk asked. Take a walk along the Bosporus, and in every beauteous palace there is a story behind its existence, a way in which these mansions came to be the thousand pearls of Istanbul. Each of those grand houses hold—stitched into the framework or buried in the foundations—the woes of slaves who built them, captains who killed for them, pirates who stole from them, sultans who conquered to keep them; in the massive grandeur of human achievement, in the greatest evidences of construction, there is a shadow licking at the fringes, the shadow of ruin.

Sami sat on the stone bench of the fountain, put his face in his hands, and exhaled to make room for thinking. He could talk to the finches but they would not agree. He could explain that he wanted to rent their services, hire them as a performance, but what bird would believe that?

Mermer was flapping her wings now, very excited by all the rats

Sami had brought. She could eat just her favorite parts and still be full for three days. She thought about agreeing to help Sami, even without knowing what he wanted. She thought if she said yes, he would cheer up and stop constructing these bizarre tears into the corners of his eyes. Then he would feel indebted to Mermer and he would go and fetch her more and more rats. More than she could eat in her whole life, or better yet a large, large rabbit. Mermer fluttered over to him, hooting lightly, sitting beside him and nuzzling his elbow with her beak.

—We can at least hear Sami out, said Mermer.

Sami stood straighter and looked down his nose a little at Kabuk. He explained to the two birds his plan to make a series of harness and cages and the like, and fasten them to Fatima's home. Then with Mermer and Kabuk's help, he would have all the birds of Istanbul come and help lift her house right out of its rootings, and into the sky over the city, and then beyond even that. Kabuk croaked a loud laugh as Sami said this, but Mermer only cooed and listened and watched the rats dangling in Sami's hand.

—I would need the help of at least five thousand birds, I suspect.

—Oh, we could gather up that many birds easily, said Mermer.

—Are you serious? asked Kabuk.

Mermer couldn't control herself; she was an animal, after all, trapped by the constant concern of food. She nodded and said she thought it would be very easy to put Sami's plan into action, though she hardly heard it with her mind going crazy about the idea of rabbit or maybe even a bit of veal.

—Oh, I am convinced, Kabuk. Sami is not a bad man. He loves the birds. Of course we will help. All the songbirds of the city would be delighted to help Sami.

Kabuk couldn't believe it—never mind the insanity of lifting a house into the air, but how little it took to bribe Mermer cast serious doubts against his belief in the nobility of his fellow birds.

Sami and Mermer reached an agreement. She told him to leave out his cages in the square here and she would spread the word that the man who feeds and protects the birds needed help. He gave Mermer her rats as promised and ran home to set out all his cages before getting to work making more of all sorts, some small, some large—all of them fastened to a rope that could be tied to Fatima's house and pulled.

When he made his cages, he didn't think of them the way others do: as traps, as constraints, as heavy things that drowned their contents with restriction—he thought of the hollowness of birds and how one day he might make a cage so hollow, so spacious, it would float without strings, it would float with the birds inside, directed by their beating wings, by the wind, so light that you would need strings to anchor them lest they, like balloons with wishes tied to them, lift their birds beyond the atmosphere.

⁂

IT WAS VERY soon after Fatima's last visit to Sami's house that war broke out across the Balkans. All through the winter months the sultan's derelict soldiers marched along the roads from Istanbul toward Thrace, just on the heels of the news of war. Their boots sloshed through the mud, their faces saturated with rain and exhaustion. More wars came, Sami still too young to be drafted, his father too old, and the ranks of the village boys thinned as they killed and were killed by the tribes of boys from other villages.

Sami and his father, like every other villager around Dedeağaç, cloistered themselves up into their house, boarding the windows and barring the door, waiting for the war to pass. But through the seasons the war raged on, each faction exacting blood from the village in their turn. The Greeks were the first to sack the city, a month of horrors. Just behind their house, Sami and Celahattin could hear the cries of their neighbor Belma hanim. She screamed into the dark with her desperate breaths, filling up the air until no one else could breathe, no one else could strip oxygen from the night full of shrieks.

At daybreak, two men with rifles stole the imam from his bed. They didn't take him far. It was behind the potter's workshop that they shot him through the forehead while he counted prayer beads on his tespih. Soldiers came and separated people into groups. Fires in the houses of Turks signaled the retreat, and before the din of marching footsteps was lost in the hills, the people, starved, cut any remaining meat they could from the rotting corpses of their beloved horses.

The next month the Ottoman soldiers came and exacted revenge in equal measure, rounding up non-Turks, ransacking what was left by the Serbs or Greeks. Then they retreated or ran after the Serbs, making way for Bulgars to come and take what little there was left.

A camp was set up outside the village. Sami could hear them throughout the night from his bedroom windows loading the guns and firing and reloading. Sometimes Sami and his father heard jovial commotion from the camp, sometimes screams from the field hospital, but above it all they heard the salvos of artillery fire stretching long fingers into the sky. For the first few months, Sami's father kept at his bird-catching, trying his hardest to grab as many of the prettiest creatures out of the forest before they could be decimated by artillery shells and firebombs and gas. He ran out of space in the aviary, and so he packed them into cupboards, shelves, and windowsills. The shelling didn't stop—in their chests they felt the boom of the black guns competing with the beat of their hearts until finally Celahattin had captured so many birds and packed them onto every wall and rafter in their squat house that Sami could hear nothing but the clamor of wings and tweeting, and at last he wasn't scared.

The next spring, the Turks, on one of their marches through Dedeağaç, arrested Sami's father for his previous marriage to a Greek.

They would have arrested Sami too had he not been thrown out the upstairs window by his father at the last moment before the soldiers broke down the door. Sami followed them as they took his father to a makeshift prison in the town hall. Celahattin gestured at his boy to get away, and so Sami did, hiding at first in the neighbor's outhouse, then in the loft of a barn up the road, sometimes sneaking out to steal food and other times going to the houses of his father's friends to beg for bread.

But before the Turkish soldiers could finish their arrests, once more they were called away to some other front, and when they left, the Greeks returned. They freed Celahattin and the others held in the cellar, and Sami thought he would have his father back, but the Greek soldiers marched the free prisoners out of Dedeağaç to a work camp back in Thrace in a long line, hundreds of men long.

Halfway into Macedonia, Celahattin woke along the roadside to the faint clapping of many, many boots far away. He woke up the men next to him. Their Greek escort had disappeared and everyone was asking what to do, when a long procession of men in khaki shirts and black caps and black boots up to their knees came down the road singing a song. They smiled at all the people hiding in the ditches. They grabbed them by their scalps and dragged them to different areas along the road, still smiling. They hauled Sami's father down the road to a service ditch where a number of other Turkish men were huddled, all mumbling into their clasped hands.

"We are Greeks! We are Greeks!" cried some of the men.

A tall officer in a red cap came to them without a smile. He said something to his aide, who then said in Turkish to the men that they must dig. The soldiers threw them shovels and the men started digging. Men came down the road in pairs with the bodies of Greek soldiers in their arms. They brought the bodies to the trench Sami's father and the other Turks were digging. Their arms grew limp, their backs cried shivers up their nerves. The sun climbed high and began its dip before Sami's father and the others had dug a wide enough trench. The captain in the red hat said something to his aide, and the aide said in Turkish: "Make it wider still." And the men kept digging until sunset, soggy to the bone, their hands bleeding from blisters. Then the captain in the red hat said something to his aide again, and the aide told the men in Turkish that now they must strip. Sami's father and the others took off their overclothes. The man shouted, "Everything. Everything, dogs." Each man who had been circumcised they shot with a single bullet and left them with the bodies of the Greek soldiers.

Sami shut himself up in his father's house for the rest of that year until he too was finally arrested for having a Greek mother. He was taken across the Sea of Marmara and into Anatolia and stuffed into a prison with a hundred other men, where they stayed, growing desiccated and crippled and forced to work, for the remainder of the war, and even after the peace treaties were signed, and the men of other countries redrew new boundaries for nations, Sami and the others stayed imprisoned, even after the empire was dissolved and the caliphate abolished and the national party embroiled in a bitter war of independence, until the formation of the new Republic of Turkey and the orchestration of population exchanges when they were finally released. Sami was returned to his father's small house in the village outside Dedeağaç. The place was hollow and crumbling, the insides stripped of their possessions. The aviary was empty.

Most people began building back their lives, but Sami spent his first month trying to collect up any news there was to be had of Fatima. He heard bits and scraps about her from other villagers. Her family had started the war moving into the hills for safety, Metin Efendi forcing his servants to drag along as many of his treasures as they could manage. After the war, they returned to their mansion, now plundered and half-razed, but their troubles did not end there.

With the dissolution of the empire, many of the sultan's staunch loyalists were either arrested or dispossessed of their estates. For Metin it was no different. He watched as Republican soldiers finished cleaning out his villa, taking even things as small as copper coffee kettles and candy dishes. They seized and nationalized his land for their war effort. They burned down the husk of his mansion. And now there was a rumor they would be back to arrest and execute Metin Efendi for his crimes against the republic (though no one had heard which crimes those might be). But there had been no word of Fatima; no one knew what had happened to her during the war.

Sami went to Metin Efendi's estate straight away. There he discovered that everything had been reduced to rubble as he'd heard, save for the south wing. Slowly, people crawled about in the rubble, moving and lifting and clearing things away in preparation for rebuilding. Sami asked them where to find Metin Efendi, and one of the men led him around to the back of the estate and into the remaining wing of the mansion, bringing Sami to a room lit by the holes in its walls and roof, with a large, makeshift table in its center. Metin Efendi sat at the table with a couple of books and a broken gramophone before him. He sat alone in the shambles, beneath a vaulted ceiling dripping yesterday's rain.

Metin Efendi gestured for Sami to sit down, and then he asked who Sami was and what he wanted. Sami explained he knew Fatima before the wars—as little children they sometimes played when she snuck away from him. He didn't know how to explain what he was here to do. He wanted to know that Fatima had made it through the wars just fine. Instead he asked how Metin Efendi had managed, and Metin Efendi, always being one to delight in taking his time, told Sami an entire account of the wars. Sami was polite, pretending to listen, save for the few mentions of Fatima. A servant brought in what he called a stew but was hardly more than warm water with a few bones and an onion in it. When at last Metin Efendi finished his story, Sami then said: "And what of your daughter, Fatima hanim. Is she here? I didn't see her when I arrived."

Metin Efendi leaned back in his chair and patted the air with his hand. "Oh no, she hasn't been here in years. I sent her away soon after the war with England and France, to Istanbul to live with my sister. It's not safe here. I suspect there are very few places safe in this country, but Istanbul must be one of them."

Metin Efendi would follow his daughter to the city when his health declined, he would follow, when he could no longer bear the walks past the crumbled rooms laden only with debris and memories.

Sami left for Istanbul the next morning, but the chaos of the country only multiplied there. Everything was changing, remaking itself into the shape of a new country. Refugees from all corners of the former empire flooded the city. Each day he tried to find Metin Efendi's sister and Fatima with her. He walked the streets asking people coming out of their buildings or delivery boys or merchants, but no one had heard of either of them. For months he looked for her to no avail. Still, he did not give up entirely. Maybe once a week he went about the old city, looking for any sign of Fatima, then another day he might go north into the Greek and Jewish and Albanian quarters.

For years he did this. He was young and lost and desperate and then suddenly, just like that, he had become a birdkeeper and then an old man, and had been living in Istanbul for many years, and he had given up looking for Fatima, until one day she bumped into him in Galata Square as he was selling his cages, and she said, "There was a man I knew, a man and his son who sold these capricious things."

"And I knew you, Fatima hanim."

She smiled at him then, and the two of them embraced immediately and started babbling to each other like a broken tap all the tales they had missed out on, recounting to each other the whole of their lives and as if this were some sort of spell each thing they told the other made them younger, undid it from their lives, and just as quickly as time had flown, it was all now reversed and they were very young and back in Dedeağaç. All through the night and into the next day they stayed arm in arm, walking the city and asking each other all the questions they had saved up.

In the morning now dawning, the two of them found themselves at the top of a wide road. Down the wide road came a procession of open trucks passing under telephone cables with the clatter of diesel machinery. In the backs of the trucks were unsmiling men, men who did not look to be from the neighborhood. Quickly the line of trucks continued for the hills in the Greek quarter. And Sami and Fatima knew at once they were in danger. But Sami told her of his plan to escape Istanbul, to lift Fatima's house with all the birds of the city and deliver them away from here. Fatima was delighted and said to Sami he should pack his things and she would go and pack her things and he and all the birds would meet her at her house and they'd set off from there. With a quick kiss on his cheek, Fatima ran home, and Sami did the same. There he found Mermer and Kabuk waiting to give the orders. He packed up his wheelbarrow full of cages and equipment and told the birds to bring what they could to Fatima's house. She was gone, out getting provisions no doubt. So Sami and the birds set about their preparations.

They worked tirelessly tying up all the cages and harnesses and sometimes even just the birds themselves to the beams of the house. When that was no longer possible, Sami instructed the birds to pack into the house itself, pack up as tight as they could and they would help by pushing up against the ceiling and the floors from the inside. They went on packing the birds like this into her house until from every corner of each room, on ropes strung back and forth across the ceiling, in stacks and piles, tacked to walls, under tables, on divans, between cupboards, beside books on their shelves, between the legs of chairs, by the stove, and even in the sink, there were a thousand finches, their songs visible as vibrations in the few slender blocks of air not totally filled with feather and beak and tweet and tail. Their bright shades like a watercolor Sami was swimming through, taking sips of it to fill his lungs with all the pastels of the universe. Sami could feel the air around him on his skin because he was barren compared to all the other fleshy, boisterous, and jockeying creatures with heartbeats pumping out whistles. Sami could taste the motes of feather dust with quick licks into the air. He could hear the grip of perching claws, the whirring of many small wings. And if you had asked Sami if this was the meaning of life, he would have said you didn't get it, he would have said only the village fool asks a question like that in the presence of something grander than meaning, only the fool is smart enough to know how to diminish something encompassing with questions, and he would tell you to climb an orange tree on a clear day and look out across the empire of time if you wanted something else to ruin.

The way a peasant looks at their budding crops, Sami looked at his labor and said to Kabuk: Well, what do you think?

—It is rather simple, said Kabuk, comparing this in his mind to the feats of obelisks and pyramids and domes and arches and even the aqueduct.

—That is part of its beauty.

—Is it beautiful or crude? Kabuk asked, shrugging his wings and tilting his head as if to say he had seen many things in his lifetime.

Sami had a few of his own things to pack still, and Mermer and Kabuk seemed to have a handle on their task, so Sami went back home to fill his suitcase with a few of his tools, a bit of cash, some underclothes, and his other pair of pants. He was all flustered and out of breath and terrified and then he looked to his bulbul, still in its cage, to calm himself down, but it was no longer moving and all its color was gone and it seemed like a porcelain statue. He went over to it and reached a hooked finger through the bars and when still it did not move, he opened up the little hatch and pulled his bulbul out of its cage. He asked if it wanted a little something to eat though he no longer had any food to give it, but the bulbul had given up even its little forlorn tweets. Sami cupped it in both his hands and watched it blink very slowly and then turn its head up to him just a little bit. He thought he should ask it something, but the words swelled and grew heavy as they came up his throat, so he swallowed his voice like marbles and put his bulbul back into its cage and said it would be safe here. He left its hatch open but he asked it to promise it would stay here and not go away.

Kabuk the nightjar then tapped on the glass and Sami threw open the window.

—Is she back home yet? Sami asked.

—I did not see, said Kabuk, his gaze on the bulbul now curling into a ball in the open cage, but everything is set as you wanted it.

Sami grabbed up his suitcase and closed the door behind him. Sami turned to the nightjar waddling along the floorboard and could see it had something to say but wasn't speaking.

—You still don't believe in me, do you? Sami asked the bird.

Kabuk shrugged his wings.

What did Kabuk know about the ways of human hearts? What did Kabuk know of the world so far beneath the sky, so weighted compared to his world of light?

A streetcar shambled by as Sami stepped out into the evening painted many different colors by the crowded sky. Sami plodded up his street past the little square now completely empty of birds. He took a turn here at a narrow alley, then a larger avenue, until he was in the delta of city boulevards along the Bosporus and up into the

Greek quarter. He could hear people chanting, "Onward to Salonik! Onward to Athens!" The people all clustered around one another, their limbs inseparable, their hands clutching pickaxes and shovels. Then all of a sudden, from side streets and narrow avenues poured forth even more people now armed with hatchets, revolvers, drums of gasoline, lighters, matches, torches. Their feet drummed along in rhythm with their chants as soon they marched all through the city quarter with faces of rage, hate on the tips of sharpened teeth, sweat dripping down temples.

Soon they started smashing in windows and hacking down doors, broken glass peppering their hair. Up and down the street they broke into stores and homes and threw the insides of each into the road: chairs, divans, wardrobes, copperware, chandeliers, coffee, tea, spices, jackets, trousers, skirts, shoes, bags. They had enveloped Sami and the nightjar but did not block them or even seem to notice them. Kabuk started crowing and flapping his wings as more and more things were brought out into the street for smashing. Sami and Kabuk, desperate not to draw attention, crept off İstiklal Avenue and hid away in a niche just outside a jewelry store while the riot continued. Sami heard a crash from inside the jewelry store and, turning to look, he spied a man in the dark taking out strings of pearls, diamond rings, necklaces of gold. Very carefully he laid out all the jewelry on the countertop. With a hammer, the man smashed pearls one by one in the dark, pop, pop, the white explosions, pop, pop, pop, pearl smithereens falling to the floor.

The crowd grew around Sami and Kabuk and they became trapped in this niche. On the avenue everyone was calling for revenge. They said they must murder each and every Greek in the city. They must clear away and purge Istanbul. They had heard the Greeks had blown up an embassy, they had blown up the childhood home of Atatürk, founder of the republic. The people called for the blood of Greeks, the blood of Jews, the blood of Armenians. They hacked with their axes at the shops and homes with blue paint on their doors. They set fire to buildings and cars. Sami and Kabuk cowered lower and lower to the ground, desperate not to be seen, but then a set of hands grabbed Sami, another set took hold of his legs and they dragged him out from his niche to be broken open in the street. Kabuk squawked and Sami cried out as the vandals raised their fists, their pipes, their clubs, but then in a great and furious rush there descended a black sweep over the street. As if dripping from the night sky, from their unseen roosts in the trees and on the eaves and in little crevices of the city, an endless flock of swifts swelled through the neighborhood immediately dowsing the light of every lamp and torch in the street. It was deafening, the slapping of so many pairs of wings. They came from awnings and silent alleys. They came from the clouds and the mosques. Thousands of them in one fell shadow rushed down İstiklal Avenue. The rioters screamed and were stunned, and in the chaos, Sami ran blindly toward the end of the street, feathers falling over him like snow. He heard another scream and then the quick fire of three rounds from a revolver to disperse the flock, but it did nothing. There was hardly any space between the bodies of all the swifts, there was hardly a morsel of light to pull from between their black breadths. Sami slipped the clutches of the riot and ran, ran toward the water, to the edge of Beyoğlu.

Kabuk fluttered his wings and squawked something to Sami, but the sound of raging fires drowned the words of the nightjar, the crack and boom of flames large enough to eat neighborhoods swirled down the drain of Sami's ears and, like cotton, stuffed them until he and Kabuk were far from the pogrom, moving west along the Golden Horn.

—Sami, you shouldn't have stayed in Istanbul.

—Hurry up, we must get to Fatima.

—Sami, she is gone already.

Sami ignored this. She couldn't be gone. They walked and walked all night long, but the fires were only growing, the crash of the pogrom spreading out into that infinite mantle of night. They hurried and felt that soon they would get to Fatima's house where all the birds were waiting for the command to alight and deliver Fatima and Sami into the sky and away from this crumbling earth. But at the next turn, Sami had a clear view ahead and could see that in the distance, the whole Greek quarter was burning, Fatima's house right in the middle of it, all those birds, those thousands of birds in their harnesses and cages trapped inside her building in the middle of a deafening fire.

Kabuk cried out, terrified. The two of them were paralyzed now by all the noise, all that terrible noise of fire and shooting and killing and breaking, my God the sound was so great Istanbul was rent open under the night. The fire continued to grow, threatening to eat the whole city.

—We should keep going, said Kabuk, not knowing in which direction.

But Sami was frozen to his spot. Kabuk pecked at Sami's leg to get him to move, but he just sat down there in the street along the water with Istanbul coming undone around him. Kabuk pecked again, trying to tell Sami to move, trying to tell him they had to get out. He wished he and Sami could fly away, but Sami would not move.

—What hope do I have? Sami asked.

—For a bird, it is easy. Ours is this blue to leap into while yours is the earth to suffocate under.

Over the long, very long night, the two of them stayed sitting on the street watching as the riots continued well into the early hours, well into the pale mist of morning. They sat side by side until the fires at last subsided and revealed in their wake the kingdoms of man: capriciousness, vapidity, and strife.

In the sky were flocks intermittently, larks and storks like arrows, sparrows like schools of fish, finches here and there flying up from the fires, escaping the soot and smoke as black dashes in the illuminating twilight. How easy it looked, how smooth, as if gravity were an afterthought, the breeze was the only truth for those with wings. Sami asked the nightjar: Sing me a birdsong—the sky over the sea, hydrogen bombs and make-believe, the greatness of humanity.

ACKNOWLEDGMENTS

I am forever grateful to my agent, Martha Wydysh, and my editor, Noa Shapiro, both clever, generous, and patient.

An incalculable amount of gratitude goes to Aneesa, Brad, Christina, Jeremy, Kit, Matt, Rachel, Shaun, and Tessa, who were the first readers and proponents of these stories.

A heartfelt thanks to Katy Karlin and Steve Yarbrough—insightful teachers and incredible champions of my work.

Thanks also to Robin Desser, Andy Ward, Avideh Bashirrad, and Erica Gonzalez, Benjamin Dreyer and Rebecca Berlant, and Nancy Delia, Amy Schneider, Maria Braeckel, and Barbara Fillon, as well as the many editors and readers who selected and polished some of these stories for appearances in various publications, but particularly Emily Wojcik, Emily Nemens, Laura Furman, and Heidi Pitlor.

Last and most important I am thankful for the love and support of my large family, especially my parents, Mo and Inci; my brothers, Erek, Devran, and Taylan; and my partner, Ashton.